CRIMES
OF CYMRU

CRIMES
OF CYMRU

CLASSIC MYSTERY
TALES OF WALES

Edited and Introduced by
Martin Edwards

Poisoned Pen
PRESS

CONTENTS

INTRODUCTION

Wales is a country with a distinctive and fascinating character. A land of mist and mountains, of myths, magic—and mystery.

The close geographical and historical association between Wales and England, coupled with the bilingual nature of Welsh literature, contribute to the unique flavour of Welsh writing. Today, Welsh literary culture flourishes, with a celebrated annual festival held at that wonderful book town Hay-on-Wye. Its history is equally impressive, dating back to the sixth century and encompassing the *Mabinogion*—wonderful medieval folk tales—as well as the work of poets such as Dylan Thomas and R. S. Thomas, and writers as notable as Roald Dahl, who was born in Cardiff and achieved success in two very different fields: children's fiction and macabre "tales of the unexpected."

Macabre fiction has been a particular strength of Welsh writers over the years, perhaps in part inspired by the alluring yet sometimes eerie quality of the landscape. Arthur Machen was a master of this form of writing, while another of the authors featured in this collection, Cledwyn Hughes, wrote a good many interesting weird stories which deserve to be rediscovered. Emlyn Williams, the playwright and actor most famous for the psychological thriller *Night Must Fall*, often worked on the boundaries of crime writing. Until relatively recent times, however, Welsh authors of conventional detective fiction have been few and far between—so, perhaps surprisingly, have crime stories set in the country, whether or not written by Welsh authors.

The "Golden Age of Murder" between the two world wars, for instance, can scarcely be claimed as a Golden Age for detective fiction set in Wales. *The Great Orme Terror* by Garnett Radcliffe (an Irishman) has a promising title which refers to a rocky promontory close to Llandudno on the north coast of Wales. The story is, however, pulpy and lurid. On his arrival in the area, Dr. Constandos brings news for the lovely young tennis player Mona and her admirer, the monocled Lord Basil Curlew, about golden treasure in a Spanish galleon sunk just off the Great Orme. Mona believes, for no obviously compelling reason, that she has a moral right to the gold, and she and Lord Basil determine to find it. Unfortunately, various villains are also searching for the loot—and they include characters such as a nasty fellow with green fingers known as The Lizard and the mysterious and bestial Gravenant. Superintendent Fibkin is helpless when faced with such devilish adversaries, who have at their command an army of weird death-robots, and will stop at nothing—certainly not torture and murder—to get their wicked way.

More impressive, if still outlandish, are the "impossible crime" mysteries written by Virgil Markham, an American. In *Death in the Dusk* (1929), Victor Bannerlee is an antiquary travelling in Radnorshire. After a couple of bizarre encounters, he finds himself lost in the fog, and stumbles on an ancient mansion, which just happens to belong to an acquaintance. The house party gathered there for a wedding, is a motley crew, and the sense of impending doom intensifies with the appearance of a bizarre apparition rejoicing in the name Parson Lolly. A non-stop sequence of weird occurrences helps to disguise a pleasing plot twist.

Another Markham mystery, *Shock!* (aka *The Black Door*, 1930), boasts a remarkable subtitle: "The Mystery of the Fate of Sir Anthony Veryan's Heirs in Kestrel's Eyrie Castle near the Coast of Wales." A sub-subtitle adds: "Now set down from information supplied by the principal surviving actors, and witnesses." The first edition contains an elaborate pull-out folded family tree of the descendants of Horace Veryan. Some addenda to the tree, although printed, appear to be handwritten, bringing the toll of fatalities in the family up to date. For good measure, a map of the local area, featuring St David's and Ramsey Island, is included, and there are plans of the ground and first floors of Kestrel's Eyrie. The viewpoint character is Tom Stapleton, an American who comes to Wales hoping to see Sir Anthony Veryan, recently incapacitated following a murderous attack, only to find himself embroiled in a complicated mystery.

Richard Hull, one of the most innovative exponents of the "inverted mystery" during the Golden Age, had strong Welsh connections, and *The Murder of My Aunt* (which, like *Excellent Intentions*, has been published as a British Library Crime Classic) is set in a house modelled on his family home, and the events take place close to a fictional version of Welshpool.

The Welsh archaeologist Glyn Daniel adopted the pen name Dilwyn Rees when publishing his debut mystery *The Cambridge Murders* in 1945. The novel later appeared under his own name, as did his second novel, *Welcome Death* (1954).

Daniel wrote no more crime novels, concentrating on his academic career at Cambridge, where his pupils included the future crime novelist and critic Jessica Mann.

Dylan Thomas enjoyed (and reviewed) detective fiction, although his novel *The Death of the King's Canary*, co-written with John Davenport during the Second World War, is a spoof of the genre brimming with in-jokes which fell rather flat when it was posthumously published in 1976.

A good many English-born writers have an affinity with Wales. This is especially true of those who come from the Welsh Marches (a vaguely defined area which arguably includes counties such as Cheshire and Gloucestershire as well as Shropshire and Herefordshire). A notable example was Edith Pargeter, who wrote many books under her own name before becoming famous under the pen name Ellis Peters.

Dorothy Bowers was born in Leominster but grew up across the border in Monmouthshire. Her five novels showed ability and the promise of future achievement before TB cut her life tragically short. L. P. Davies, who was born in Crewe and who also wrote under the name Leslie Vardre, penned a number of interesting macabre stories set in Wales, while the climber Frank Showell Styles, born in Birmingham, enjoyed success with a series of mysteries written under the name Glyn Carr and featuring Sir Abercrombie Lewker; his titles include *Death Under Snowdon* (1954).

Perhaps the most successful mystery novel set in Wales during the early post-war period was *Cat and Mouse* (1950) by Christianna Brand, a contributor to this volume, several of whose books have been reprinted as British Library Crime Classics to widespread acclaim.

Nine years later, *Strike for a Kingdom*, the first novel of Menna Gallie, was set in Cilhendre, a fictional version of Ystradgynlais, a mining village in the Swansea Valley where she grew up. The story is set in 1926, at the time of the General Strike, and combines a whodunit plot with a picture of tensions within a small mining community. The book was a runner-up (to Eric Ambler's *Passage of Arms*) for the CWA Gold Dagger, but Gallie was more interested in politics than plots or puzzles and she did not return to the genre.

Published in 1970, *Die Like a Man* is an enjoyable bibliomystery from Michael Delving (the pseudonym of American writer Jay Williams), which benefits from a very well-realised setting in south Wales. Book dealer Dave Cannon finds himself stranded there and soon gets mixed up in an exciting, albeit improbable, series of escapades involving an ancient bowl which is claimed to be the Holy Grail.

Welsh-based crime fiction remained relatively uncommon until the latter part of the twentieth century, although some of the mysteries published by the prolific Rhondda Valley-born Roy Lewis were set in the country. In modern times, however, Welsh crime writing has experienced a boom, and bilingual TV series such as *Hinterland* and Hidden (aka *Y Gwyll* and *Craith,* respectively) have also enjoyed considerable popularity.

Against that background, this anthology, like its sister volume *The Edinburgh Mystery and Other Tales of Scottish Crime* offers a wide range of criminous fiction from an eclectic group of contributors. Some of the stories are written by Welsh-born authors; some are set in Wales; some meet both criteria.

In putting this book together, I have been given a great

deal of help by Jamie Sturgeon and others, notably Nigel Moss and John Cooper. Cledwyn Hughes's two daughters, Rebecca Hughes and Janet Laugharne, supplied me with invaluable material as well as a range of their father's stories to choose from. Siân Griffiths also kindly discussed the life and career of her father, Jack Edwards Griffiths, with me. I'm also grateful to the members of the publishing team at the British Library for their work in making this book a reality. And finally, a word of thanks to those who read these anthologies and who often get in touch with interesting comments and suggestions; your support and continuing enthusiasm for this series is much appreciated.

Martin Edwards
www.martinedwardsbooks.com

A NOTE FROM THE PUBLISHER

The original novels and short stories reprinted in the British Library Crime Classics series were written and published in a period ranging, for the most part, from the 1890s to the 1960s. There are many elements of these stories which continue to entertain modern readers; however, in some cases there are also uses of language, instances of stereotyping, and some attitudes expressed by narrators or characters which may not be endorsed by the publishing standards of today. We acknowledge that some elements in the works selected for reprinting may continue to make uncomfortable reading for some of our audience. With this series British Library Publishing and Poisoned Pen Press aim to offer a new readership a chance to read some of the rare books of the British Library's collections in an affordable paperback format, to enjoy their merits, and to look back into the world of the twentieth century as portrayed by its writers. It is not possible to separate these stories from the history of their writing, and as such, the following stories are presented as they were originally published with the inclusion of minor edits made for consistency of style and sense, and with pejorative terms of an extremely offensive nature partly obscured. We welcome feedback from our readers.

The Murder in Judd Lane
Frank Howel Evans

True originality is much-prized, not least in the field of detective fiction. The unfortunate reality is that it is extremely difficult to achieve. Many authors have had the experience of coming up with an idea that they thought was brand new, only to discover subsequently that, in one way or another, they had been beaten to it. This isn't a matter of plagiarism, conscious or unconscious; it's just something that happens regularly. When Agatha Christie introduced the Belgian refugee Hercule Poirot in 1920, there is little doubt she was sure she was doing something fresh. However, her fellow author Marie Belloc Lowndes, who had previously created a detective called Hercules Popeau, was (mistakenly, in my opinion) less than impressed and believed that Christie had borrowed from her.

Strangely, though, a Welsh writer anticipated both women. Francis (aka Frank) Howel Evans (1867–1931) created Monsieur Jules Poiret, "late of the French Secret Service," but now based in Britain, more than a decade earlier. Evans was a prolific writer of stories for the magazine market and his output included half a dozen contributions to the Sexton Blake franchise. A film made in 1914, *The Shadow of Big Ben*, was based on one of his stories. However, Poiret had long been forgotten until Bob Adey gathered together the five stories about him in *Old Pawray*, published by a small press in 2000. This story, the first in the "Old Pawray" series, originally appeared in *The New Magazine* in October 1909.

——

I

"HEAVENS! HE'S DEAD!"

With the involuntary fear that comes to everyone when suddenly and unexpectedly faced with a lifeless body, Police Constable J. 413 drew back, and then pulling himself together, again flashed his lantern on the figure of a man supported against the side railings of a house to let, in Judd Lane, just off Adelphi Terrace.

At first the constable had taken the figure for a drunken man, as one arm was grotesquely stretched over the railings, the head lolling to one side, and the legs in a bent, limp attitude. The constable, with the policeman's usual good nature and unwillingness to be bothered with a tipsy man on his beat at half past one in the morning, had shaken the figure by the shoulder once or twice, and suggested that it would be a good thing for the reveller to take himself home. But there had been no response, and it was then that he had flashed his lantern to see a dead, white face, with dropped jaw and staring eyes, with an indescribable look of fear imprinted on the features.

There was no mistake about it. The man was dead.

Police Constable J. 413 in the course of his duties had become well acquainted with death in many forms, and here undoubtedly the King of Terrors had been at work.

He just touched the arm, which slid off the railings, and the figure collapsed, as it were bonelessly, into a huddled heap in the corner of the doorway.

Police Constable J. 413 raised his whistle to his lips and blew. In a few minutes policemen from the Strand and neighbouring streets, including a sergeant, were on the scene. They all had a look at the heap near the railings, and then the sergeant made everyone stand back.

"The inspector'll be round directly," he said. "Don't touch the body, anyone."

The inspector, a smart, alert man in his neat, unobtrusive uniform, soon arrived at the spot in the course of his rounds and made a quick and experienced examination.

"Dead!" he said. "Rigor'll be setting in directly, so he must have been gone some time. When did you find him, Saunders?"

J. 413, otherwise Police Constable Saunders, an excellent specimen of the intelligent policeman, told his story briefly and clearly. Judd Lane was not a thoroughfare; in fact the title of Lane had only remained because it had once led through into the Strand; there were only three houses in it, the end of the lane being formed by a blank wall which was the back of the Regency Theatre, and opposite to the three houses stood another high wall, the back of the building where the Regency scenery was stored. A narrow pathway ran between this wall and the railings of the three houses, and as there was a large gas lamp just at the top of the lane, it was not likely to be frequented by those unfortunate homeless wanderers of London who may so often be found crouched up trying to snatch a brief sleep, undisturbed by the policeman, wherever there are dark corners.

"I walked down to the end of the lane, sir," explained Saunders, "saw that the back of the Regency Theatre was safe, and the scene dock as well, and I'll swear that there was no one outside these houses then."

"Well," interrupted the inspector sharply, "how did you come across him, then?"

"Well, I don't suppose I'd gone fifty yards down the street, sir, when I found that I'd lost my matches; I'd been seeing to my lantern in Judd Lane, and I thought perhaps I might have dropped them there, so I turned back to look, and there I found the body. I thought perhaps he'd been visiting at one of the houses, and had had a drop too much, though it didn't seem to me very friendly like to leave him outside in that state, so I shook him once or twice and then found that he was dead."

"Yes, that's it, dead!" said the inspector. "Here you two, Jarvis and Melcombe, you go for the ambulance. And you, sergeant, inquire at No. 1, and I'll inquire at No. 5."

The inspector and the sergeant each knocked and hammered at the respective houses until they roused all the occupants. The houses were let out in tenements, being old-fashioned, roomy dwellings, of which there are plenty to be found in London in parts that are now almost slums. But each of the families disclaimed all knowledge of a guest or friend having been with them that evening, and the third house, in the doorway of which the body had been found, was empty, and had been empty for a considerable number of months.

"Very well, then," said the inspector as the two policemen returned with the ambulance, "put the body on there, and I'll go back to the station and report to the Yard; they'd better send a detective down to take charge of the case."

The ambulance, with its grim burden, was rolled off to the mortuary, and then once more the inspector went into details with Constable Saunders.

"You're sure he wasn't there when you went down to see that the theatre and the scene dock were all right, Saunders?" he asked.

"I'll swear it, sir! You see the gas lamp at the end here throws a brilliant light, and it would have been impossible for me to have missed seeing him. And I'd only got fifty yards down the street when I turned back, so it would have been impossible for him to have passed me or have been carried by me without my noticing it."

"Perhaps he came out of one of the houses in this street, behind your back, Saunders, and being possibly tipsy, took the wrong turning into Judd Lane, instead of walking straight down into the Strand?"

"I don't think he could have done that, sir!" answered Saunders, respectfully. "All on this side down to where we're standing are shops, small lock-up shops where no one sleeps, and the opposite side, as you see, is all blocked up with hoardings."

"He might have been in one of the shops," said the inspector.

"Couldn't have been, sir! They're all locked, barred, and shuttered from the outside. So, if I may say so, sir, he must have been in one of those three houses."

"Well, we'll soon find that out in the morning. Not a soul leaves this lane until we've cross-examined every one of them thoroughly, and then we'll soon find out whether there's anyone who knows anything about it."

But the well-known Detective-Inspector Drayton and the local superintendent and other crime experts were obliged to confess themselves baffled in the morning. The families occupying the two houses in Judd Lane, who were questioned most closely, were all respectable, working people, in whose voices and bearing and answers to the searching questions, innocence itself was apparent to those keen investigators of crime, to whom the human face and manner is like a book.

Plain-clothes men were, however, told off to keep each lodger and tenant under detailed observation, and the somewhat terrified inhabitants of Judd Lane were free to go about their business. One man, a respectable and thrifty mechanic, was exceedingly annoyed at the whole affair.

"What do they think we do?" he asked. "Have friends in, and then murder them, and chuck them out on to the doorstep! I shouldn't be surprised if that German waiter in No. 5 had something to do with it; he's a nasty brute!"

Inspector Chalmers, who had taken charge of the case

the night before, expressed an almost similar opinion to Detective-Inspector Drayton.

"That German waiter, Guggenheim, or whatever his name is, I don't like the look of him," he said. "I suppose you've got an eye on him?"

The great detective patted the inspector on the shoulder.

"We've got an eye on all of them, my dear Mr. Chalmers!" he said. "I think it'll be very strange if I can't find out the mystery before long. How long did the doctor think the man had been dead?"

"Three and a half hours at the least. And poison had been put in his whisky."

"Three and a half hours!" mused Detective-Inspector Drayton. "And poison had been put in his whisky! And according to Saunders's evidence, the body was not there when he went down the Lane for the first time, yet three and a half minutes later when he returned, there it was in the doorway. Now it couldn't have been put out through the back wall of the Regency Theatre, because there's no door or window, and the same with the scene dock; they're both absolutely blank walls. And the body could not have been carried up the street under Saunders's eyes, neither could it have come out of one of the lock-up shops or through the hoardings, so that it's evident that somebody in one of those houses is guilty. It's as pretty a little problem as I've ever come across, Mr. Chalmers!"

And so it was. But at the end of six weeks Detective-Inspector Drayton ceased to think of it as pretty, and began to stigmatise it as something very different, for not a single clue could he or his men obtain. From the mechanic in the top floor of No. 1 to the little seamstress who lived by herself in the bottom floor of No. 5, all the inhabitants of those two houses were watched and spied on, and their whole lives examined with a minuteness which is only possible to the trained police force. And yet the murder, for murder it undoubtedly was, must have been committed in one of those houses, unless, as Mr. Chalmers grimly suggested, an airship had come and dropped the body down on the door-step. But not a single scrap of evidence, not a thread was there on which any possible excuse for an arrest could be hung. The man was found dead, and at the inquest by delicate suggestion Detective-Inspector Drayton managed to hint to the jury that a verdict of "Suicide while of Unsound Mind" would meet the case, as it was evident that the man had been drinking to buoy himself up with the necessary courage, and then had found his way into Judd Lane to take the poison and die.

And so was the verdict returned, and when the foreman, an enormously stout, elderly man, with grey hair, pink face, overlapping cheeks, and gold-rimmed glasses, waddled out of the coroner's court, breathing and wheezing heavily, a young policeman looked after him and nudged his companion.

"Old Pawray!" he murmured.

"Old Pawray! Who's he?" was the whispered reply.

"Used to be in the French Secret Service; got too fat for the job, though."

"Well, what's he doing on the jury if he's a Frenchman?"

"Oh, he's a naturalised Englishman now, as they call it, and wherever there's mystery about, he always likes to be in it just for the sake of old times, so the coroner's officer generally manages to land him on a jury when it's possible, and they made him foreman today."

Monsieur Poiret, or, as he was known by the rank and file of the police, with an utter disregard for French pronunciation, "Old Pawray," wheezed and waddled away to the little flat he occupied in Chatterton Buildings, Adelphi.

The flat was so small that it seemed really as if Monsieur Poiret were too large for it, as he sank into a massive armchair and sat with his mouth open, his hands crossed on his big paunch, and his fishy eyes protruding, till he looked almost like the fat man out of a penny show in the Whitechapel Road.

He sat there grunting and wheezing for some time, and then finally struggled to his feet, laughed thickly to himself, and going through his bedroom, went into a little dark-room at the back. Here he took out his tie-pin, which was composed of a large stone like a cameo. It was a lengthy operation this of taking out the pin, for to it was attached a thin india-rubber tube, terminating in a little ball which lay in Monsieur Poiret's waistcoat pocket. But finally the operation was complete, and the fat man, still grunting and wheezing, busied himself with photographic chemicals, and in half an hour he emerged with a complacent smile on his face. Then he turned to a large cage which stood in front of the window, containing half a dozen beautiful canaries, and, opening the door, he whistled melodiously, and one by one the little birds came out and stood on a long stick which he held, and as he whistled, so did they. Then, with a polite bow, he held the stick close to the cage door.

"*Messieurs et Mesdames, c'est fini!*" he said, giving another little chirp. The canaries went back into their cage, Monsieur

Poiret sat himself down in his big armchair, and in three minutes a volume of snores seemed to shake the walls of the little flat.

II

MONSIEUR POIRET HAD BEEN FOR SOME YEARS IN THE employ of the French Government as their Secret Service agent. Now, however, he had retired, and on a small pension lived a life of slippered and obese middle age, in his small flat at Chatterton Buildings. His hobby was the breeding of canaries, and this fat, elderly man, with the huge girth (he weighed more than eighteen stone), was quite a well-known figure at all the bird shows in England. His one accomplishment, as he himself expressed it, was whistling, and the melodious, trilling notes that came from his thick, pursed-up lips were sufficient to induce the most morose of birds to rivalry of song.

Monsieur Poiret had had a most distinguished career according to the accounts of those who knew him best. He was not the detective of fiction who went about with a microscope, and an insatiable thirst for out-of-the-way clues. He simply sat in his office in his big armchair, and put his almost superhuman intelligence to work, for in that gross body and behind that fat, florid face there was a brain which cultivated trifles and made them bloom into accepted facts. The line of the least resistance was his policy. He would not, perhaps, have expressed it in this classical way, but he would have said:—"Always, my dear friends, attend to the obvious. Never mind so much about the clue, the slight smear of wet paint, the finger mark, the man missing from his home! But always take the simple path, that is, the broad road that leads to—the dock!" he would add, with a grim smile.

And so he sat, a huge, bloated spider, thinking, thinking, thinking, weaving the webs into which the criminal flies might enter. As he used to say, he simply thought and let others do the work; thinking was quite exhausting enough. A terror to the anarchist, the spy, the murderer, the forger, Monsieur Poiret had served the French Government for fifteen years before he retired. Gradually, year by year, he grew stouter and stouter, until at last locomotion was with him almost a matter of impossibility. He could walk, he could waddle, but it was at the rate of about a mile an hour, and his huge girth became such that there was not a criminal on the Continent who was not acquainted with him by sight. So reluctantly he accepted not dismissal, but gentle removal from active service by the French Government and became the recipient of a small pension sufficient to keep him in comfort, and at the same time, he was the owner of credentials which enabled him to act for them whenever occasion required.

For some years he had taken up his abode in England, a country for which he had an abiding admiration. His sister had married an Englishman, a worthy clerk in a corn business in Mark Lane, and from his small but comfortable rooms in Chatterton Buildings, Monsieur Poiret kept an eye on the anarchist and the alien, to whom England always affords an hospitable refuge. He was known to all the criminal classes, that is, the members of that higher aristocracy of crime whose speciality is a speedy disposal of crowned heads by means of bombs, forgeries on a large scale, and international espionage, of which the headquarters are in London—London, the capital of England, the home of the free. He was an accomplished linguist, speaking most European languages with fluency, but with the English tongue he always confessed himself fogged. He spoke the language without the slightest trace of an accent, but in a curious, clipped way which proved him at once to be a foreigner.

But still Monsieur Poiret enjoyed himself with his birds and his social following, for, like most stout men, he was lovable, and of a genial disposition, and his experience in the world of crime made him an excellent raconteur and an amusing companion. Often at Charing Cross or Victoria Station, when he was on his way to a bird show, he would meet some of the old hands whom in past days he had been instrumental in sending to punishment. The greeting was always cordial and cheerful, and whether the rascal was French, Italian, German, or Spanish, Monsieur Poiret always had a friendly word for him.

"My children," he would say in his curious accent to a friend, "my children, the children of crime! Ah, yes, they are good fellows, all of them! I have put the—the bracelets, the handcuffs, on many of their wrists, but no matter! It's all in the day's work. They are out to procure the necessaries of life; I am out to procure them, or rather, I used to be. Well, well, we each earn our living, so what does it matter! They succeed perhaps for a time, but after all they come to the arms of old Poiret. Dear, dear, they are good fellows many of them, and I have a great sorrow and a liking for them. I see them at the station; they say, 'Here is the good Poiret! The good Poiret has retired from business; then we will buy him some brandy-soda drink! Voila! Come on, old Poiret, son of my soul, what is it thou wilt drink?' Oh, yes, my children; though it has grieved me to send them to the guillotine, to Devil's Island, and other unfortunate places, still I have a love for them. They are clever, yes, they are clever, and so is Poiret, or, alas, so was Poiret, for with this roundness (here he would clasp his stomach), Poiret is what you call a back number."

The morning after his appearance as foreman of the jury, he went into the dark-room, and by lunch-time he had before him a fully developed plate and print of the face of the murdered man who had been found in Judd Lane.

He examined it carefully for at least ten minutes, during which time his thick lips were emitting a most melodious whistle which was joined in by his pet canaries in the cage. Then he sat down in the spacious armchair, and with his hands, as usual, folded in front of him, he sat for an hour with eyes half closed as if in thought. Then he got up and from a corner of the room produced an easel, and, with the photograph before him, he set to work on the stretched canvas.

For two hours while the light was good, he painted, for Monsieur Poiret was no mean hand with the brush. And each time he painted the same face, the face that was on the photograph, but instead of depicting it as a man with dead-white, clean-shaved face, he preserved the outline of the features, but in each case added a beard. Sometimes it was a close-cropped dark beard, at others a full flowing flaxen one, and at others only side whiskers, with just a suspicion of hair on the chin. At last, at the ninth attempt, he stopped. A little thick chuckle escaped his throat, and he looked at the last sketch, that of a man with the features of the corpse, but with a thin, black moustache, and a pointed black beard just touched with silver. Then he turned to his bookcase, took down a black, leather-bound volume, looked in it for a few seconds and then closed it with a snap, and restored it to its place. And from his lips there poured a melodious whistle as of triumph, in which the canaries joined. Then he went to the telephone which stood in the corner of the room, and spoke into it in his quaint, clipped English, and called for the number of a big West End hotel.

"The manager!" he said. "Yes, I am Poiret, Jules Poiret. Yes, I want you to send me down Jacques Beautemps, the second waiter of the—of the—excuse me, I cannot pronounce it with propriety, the G-r-r-e-e-l Room! Thank you! Yes, I am well. Good-bye."

In three quarters of an hour Jacques Beautemps arrived. He was a typical specimen of the alert, courteous foreign waiter. Without a word Monsieur Poiret took him by the arm and pressed him into a chair.

"Now, you know all the anarchists! You know him?" he said, pointing to the ninth sketch on the board, the sketch of the man with the beard.

"Oh, yes, Monsieur Poiret!" said the other, cringing until he seemed to have shrivelled up. "I did know him, but I have not seen him for two weeks."

"Then tell me what you knew of him up to the last two weeks. And look you here, Monsieur Beautemps, I have you here, is it not?" The fat man pinched his finger and thumb together as if destroying an insect. "You are an anarchist, yes? You are hater of kings, yes? You are hater of everything, yes?

Very good! Well then, you will do what I say to you without any argument on the matter, or *psst!* I have you away back to France, and the widow, she chops you so!" (He made a movement as of chopping his left hand off at the wrist.) "You keep a tongue of quietness, is it not? So come now, Jacques Beautemps, the truth, and as they say in the courts of the police here, all the truth, and nothing whatsoever but what truth is!"

And a fat forefinger prodded the waiter on his chest, while a pair of steel blue eyes looked straight into his. Jacques Beautemps's knees shook beneath him, and in a flood of French he poured out his tale.

The man with the beard was one Jean Garnier, at one time a notorious anarchist, but for the last five years he had ceased to have any active connection with that body, living, as he had confessed to Beautemps in a drunken moment, a life of terror. Jean Garnier had acknowledged to his bosom friend the waiter that he had twelve years ago murdered his wife, and though escaping justice, he was in terror of his life from a former sweetheart of hers, one Pierre Gaudon, a music-hall artist, who specialised in what is known as "the quick-change business"; that is to say, he appeared on the stage for about twenty-five minutes in a one-act play, during which he enacted no fewer than fifteen different characters. For years he had been a success all over the world, and at last, five years ago he had quite given up the business, having made enough money to live upon, and no one knew what had become of him.

"And believe me, Monsieur Poiret," concluded the waiter, "Jean Garnier lived in terror of his life because of him, and said that if ever he came to a sudden end, it would be because of Pierre Gaudon."

"But the beard, my dear Beautemps, the beard? Why the false beard?"

"Ah, Monsieur, it was a disguise. Garnier told me that when he was arrested he had, a week before, shaved off his beard, so that he stood in the dock clean-shaved, and it was in the dock for the first time that Pierre Gaudon, Madame Garnier's old sweetheart, saw Garnier. So, just lately then he had been wearing a false beard."

"But why just lately? Come, come, the whole truth, my dear Beautemps, quick!"

Monsieur Poiret spoke sternly, and the waiter hurried to reply.

"Because he had heard that Pierre Gaudon was in England, and he went in terror of his life. 'He will hunt me down, I know he will, Beautemps!' he said to me. 'I know he will! I shall not forget his look that day in court!' And so he wore a beard. And Monsieur," went on the waiter, looking round fearfully, "I, too, have been in terror of my life, for I knew Pierre Gaudon some years ago on the Continent, and rashly enough, I told him one day what Garnier had confided to me, namely, that he had murdered his wife himself. 'I thank you, Beautemps,' said Gaudon—I remember his look now—'I shall kill Jean Garnier one day, yes, you tell him that I shall kill him!' And so, Monsieur, it was I who gave the warning to Garnier, conveyed in an anonymous letter, that Gaudon was in London, for I had seen him in the Strand. But I never see him again. He never come near the café, and Garnier has disappeared. He is either frightened, and he has run away, or else he is dead, Monsieur. And now, Monsieur Poiret, that is all I know. You will let me go, will you not? I am living an honest life now, and I have no more a desire of any troubles. Say yes, Monsieur, say that you will not pursue me, and I am yours for life."

The terrified man almost grovelled at Monsieur Poiret's feet, who dragged him up by his coat collar, and with that same emphatic finger, once more emphasised his words.

"It is done, Monsieur Jacques Beautemps," he said. "Now you go and hold your tongue, or else *psst*! There is the Devil's Island!"

The waiter cringed out of the room, and Monsieur Poiret two hours later called at the office of the agent who had the letting of No. 3, Judd Lane.

Showing his credentials, the detective had the books examined for the last twelve years, and there, under a date almost twelve years ago to the day of the murder, was an entry proving that the house had been let to one Jean Garnier for a period of one year.

In five minutes Monsieur Poiret had taken a lease himself of No. 3, Judd Lane, for one year also.

III

THE AGENT GAVE HIM THE KEYS, AND HE WENT ALL OVER the house. It was in the usual dusty, dilapidated state consequent on a house not having been let for eighteen months, and Monsieur Poiret only sent in enough furniture for two rooms, a sitting-room and a bedroom, and for the next three or four weeks the figure of the stout, elderly gentleman who had taken the house, as he explained to friendly neighbours, with the view to letting apartments, was a familiar sight up and down Judd Lane.

In the morning he would leave his windows open, and his melodious whistle trilling away to the canaries soon became quite an accepted entertainment in Judd Lane. The children of the families occupying Nos. 1 and 5 on either side simply worshipped the fat old gentleman, who always had his pockets full of sweets for them, and in time he became acquainted with all the occupants of the tenements, including the mechanic, who confided to him his suspicion that the German waiter in No. 5 was the murderer of the man who had been found in the doorway.

Even the little seamstress who lived on the ground floor of No. 5 had a word and a smile for the fat old gentleman who was so fond of his birds. Every morning at eight o'clock she went out to her business as a machinist in the West End, and every evening at eight she returned, always to receive a bow and a smile from the old man who sat in the window of No. 3.

As soon as Monsieur Poiret had taken possession of his rooms he examined the old house carefully from top to bottom, sounding the walls, and using all his trained knowledge to try and ascertain whether the murder had been committed in this house. But after a minute and detailed examination which took the better part of a week, he came to the conclusion that it could not have been so. The dust and dirt lay thick on the stairs, in the passages, and in the rooms; the lock of the front door was heavy and rusted; and he knew that it would have been impossible for anyone to have been in the house without leaving a trace behind them, and he thereupon ruled No. 3, Judd Lane, as being unconnected with the tragedy.

But still he lived on in his new rooms, gradually becoming almost intimately acquainted with all the residents in the two houses on either side of him, and as the evenings drew out, and it began to get lighter, the fat old gentleman with his tasselled smoking cap, sitting on a heavy chair on his door-step, was a familiar sight to them all. Sometimes he would sit there whistling with the sitting-room window open, and then stop for a moment to allow his beloved canaries to raise their voices in tuneful emulation; then he would whistle again, and the little children of the neighbours would stand open-mouthed, gazing almost spellbound at this big man who could make such wonderful music with his lips.

"You like the whistling, eh?" he said one night to the little seamstress as she passed. "Ah, yes, it is perhaps clever, but it is not natural; I teach myself, it is not of nature. It is my birds who can whistle; it is they who are of nature. Come you in and see them! You have not looked at them properly, except from the outside of the house. You come?"

"Oh, certainly! I've often admired them from the window; they're such dear little things!" replied the seamstress, a well-made, well-figured woman, with dark, glossy hair, straight nose, and well-shaped mouth and chin; her hands were well kept, and she walked with the independent firm stride of a woman who knew that she could take care of herself.

"Ah, but wait, wait, attend an instant!" said Monsieur, as politely he conducted her towards the sitting-room where was the bird-cage containing his birds. "Wait but just a second, and I fetch the candle. It is dark on these steps, and you must not break your pretty little ankles. No, no, you do not move until I have secured the light!"

The old man lit the candle which stood on the hall table, and gallantly extended his hand to the seamstress to help her down the two sunk steps that led to the sitting-room. As she was stepping down, Monsieur Poiret half tripped, and inadvertently the lighted candle came in contact with the seamstress's hair. As quick as lightning, however, he blew it out, and there was just a little smell of singed hair, a few scorched ends of the black locks, and no harm was done. Monsieur Poiret apologised most profusely, and insisted on lighting the candle again and holding it closely, but at a safe distance, so as to see that not much harm was done.

"I have pleasure that it is not worse," he said. "I hold the candle against Mademoiselle's hair, and *psst*! the mischief is performed. But it is not a great mischief, I am pleased to see, and Mademoiselle is of a verity too charming to be cross. Now see we the birds!"

The birds having been examined, Monsieur Poiret conducted the seamstress back to her own house, and at about ten o'clock, he carefully locked up, and sauntered slowly back towards his own flat. He telephoned through to Scotland Yard, and in a few minutes was speaking to Detective-Inspector Drayton.

"The affair of Judd Lane, my dear Drayton?" grunted Monsieur Poiret. "Have you found anything? Do you make great discoveries?"

"No," said Drayton. "After exhaustive thought, inquiry, and search, I have come to the conclusion that it was a case of suicide."

"Certainly, certainly, my dear Drayton!" said Monsieur Poiret. "I think your conclusion is of great feasibility. Suicide, yes! A drug that anyone could take, and anyone could buy, was the poison, eh?"

"Oh, yes! It's a fairly harmless drug taken in proper quantities. It's a new drug called 'Norma,' something like laudanum, only not so powerful. It's under the Poisons Act, but by going to half a dozen chemists you can get enough to poison yourself."

"Yes, yes, I see it all!" said Monsieur Poiret. "Now I have a little affair of my own! Could you, with your usual benevolence, ascertain for me—I know your wonderful staff, my dear Drayton—what has become of one Pierre Gaudon, the music-hall artiste, who retired with a small fortune some years gone by? Five years ago, I should say, my dear Drayton!"

"Pierre Gaudon? Oh, yes, I remember him! A smart, clever little fellow! Oh, yes, I can easily trace him through some of his music-hall friends."

"*Ah, oui*, the good Drayton! Always the obliging Drayton! And just one more little favour, dear Drayton! If any of this Monsieur Pierre Gaudon's friends remember any little peculiar—peculiar—how is it you say?—ah, peculiarity or disfigurement, perhaps they will enlighten you, and you will pass the enlightment on to me, yes? I have seen him once, but not sufficient for a long examination."

Drayton promised, and when the detective rang off, Monsieur Poiret sat back in his armchair, clasped his hands over his stomach, and smiled to himself.

"The good Drayton!" he said half aloud. "Suicide, eh, and the suicider crawl up the Lane while the excellent Saunders's back was turned, and place himself dead in the doorway, eh? The good Drayton forgets that the doctor said that *death had arrived three and a half hours before*! My good Drayton, I think the case is too much for you, and you are glad to make the suicide excuse!"

Monsieur Poiret returned to Judd Lane, and within two days he received a note from Drayton which stated that Pierre Gaudon had been living quietly at Brixton ever since he retired; he was said to be very popular with all the members of his profession, and about a month ago he left London on a visit to Paris. The only peculiarity that his friends could remember about him was that the third joint of his little finger of his left hand was turned inwards towards his hand, the result of an accident.

"Ah!" breathed Monsieur Poiret, with a deep-drawn sigh of satisfaction.

The next morning when the children were at school, and the men had all gone to work, and only the women were remaining in the Lane, Monsieur Poiret went out on to the pavement with one of his beloved canaries perched on a little stick; he walked up and down whistling cheerily, and one by one the various women who lived in No. 5 passed by him with their baskets on the way to do their marketing.

"One, two, three!" counted Monsieur Poiret. "Four! That is the last!" he muttered to himself, as the fourth woman tripped down the steps and set off to do her shopping. "Enough then, Napoleon, *mon ami*! Away back to your cage! Come along, my sweet!"

He gave a little peculiar whistle, and a jerk of the stick, and away flew the canary back through the open window to its cage. Monsieur Poiret looked round, and then with a wonderfully swift and light movement for one so huge, he stepped into the open doorway of No. 5, and took from his pocket a long, slender piece of steel which he inserted in the lock of the first room on the ground floor. A little pressure, a turn of the wrist, and the door was open, and Monsieur Poiret stood in the seamstress's room.

It was comfortably furnished as a bed-sitting room, and was such as might have been occupied by any ordinary working girl, such as she was. Locking the door again with the steel instrument, Monsieur Poiret, with incredible swiftness and the trained precision of the detective, began to examine every drawer, every nook and corner in the room. He apparently did not find what he wanted, for an expression of vexation came over his face as, with extraordinarily nimble and delicate fingers, he turned over the contents of every drawer, replacing them exactly as they were, and then he began to search the bed. Here again nothing yielded to his search, until at last he took up the pillow; he shook and felt this, and listened with it to his ear; then he squeezed and pinched it, and poked it, and then, taking a sharp penknife from his pocket, he slit open the end, put his hand in the inside, and pulled out—a false beard and a small bottle. A needle and cotton lay on the table; he seized these, and as deftly as any woman would have done, he sewed up the pillow case, and then let himself out of the room and locked the door behind him, and returned to his own house without having been seen.

For the remainder of that day and part of the next, Monsieur Poiret apparently did nothing except eat and sleep, and sit and attend to his birds. But in his massive brain was being arranged an array of facts and details, which, when put together, formed a wonderful mosaic.

At eight o'clock that evening as the little seamstress returned home, Monsieur Poiret was standing at his open door.

"Good night, Mademoiselle," he cried, gallantly. "Is the beautiful hair grown again, yet?"

"Oh yes, thank you, Mr. Pawray," came back the reply. "I shan't see you again, perhaps, for I'm leaving tomorrow."

"Leaving on the morrow! Dear, dear, it will be like losing the sunshine of the street!"

The seamstress smiled and passed on to her room, and still Monsieur Poiret continued at his door, smoking his cigarette.

In about a quarter of an hour Guggenheim, the German waiter, came down, smoking a long, thin, Italian cigar. He bore the air of a man who was taking an evening's well-earned rest.

"No waiting tonight, Herr Guggenheim?" inquired Monsieur Poiret. "Taking a little holiday, is it not, eh?"

"Oh, yes," answered the waiter, a man with light side-whiskers and a sallow complexion, speaking with a strong German accent. "Oh, yes, I take some holiday. I have been working very hard, and now I make some monies, and I go back for a leetle to Germany. Oh, ja, I leave tomorrow!"

"Leave tomorrow!" said Monsieur Poiret. "Ha, ha, then we must take the glass of parting together. Come you in now, and we will drink some whiskies together."

"It will be much pleasure!" answered the waiter.

He followed Monsieur Poiret into the sitting-room, where the birds were, and as the detective closed the door, the well-oiled key turned with the slightest of clicks, which was, however, unheard by the waiter, who stood with his soft hat in one hand, and his long cigar in the other.

"Oh, your hat, Herr Guggenheim! Allow me!" said Monsieur Poiret.

And stepping forward he took the hat from the waiter, and with a quick, almost imperceptible movement, slipped his own right hand round to his back pocket, and the next second Guggenheim was staring, hypnotised as it were, at the muzzle of a revolver, which this fat man held pointed straight between his eyes.

"Sit down in that chair if you will have the goodness!" came the soft, silky voice. "I wish to have some conversations with the murderer of Jean Garnier!"

"Ze murderer of Jean Garnier!" repeated the waiter incredulously; "Jean Garnier! I have not quite ze understanding, Monsieur!"

Monsieur Poiret chuckled in his throat, and he fumbled with his left hand in his tail coat pocket.

"I find that it tires me to hold the pistol at your head all the whiles, so excuse me with the ornaments, and we will speak in German if you like."

Quickly and almost before the waiter was aware what was happening, he was securely handcuffed, and Monsieur Poiret drew up a chair and sat opposite to his prisoner.

"It is a very good performance, a very grand performance, my friend!" he said. "But dear, dear, why keep it up with Papa Poiret?"

As well as he could the man in the chair shrugged his shoulders.

"You will be sorry when I get out. It will be a case for

damages. Are you mad, or what is it?" he said, speaking in German. "Who is this Jean Garnier that you accuse me of murdering? Will you let me go, or I'll call the police!"

The waiter worked himself up into a passion, and half rose in his chair, but with a prod of his forefinger, Monsieur Poiret sent him sinking back again.

"You will make no call for the police," said the detective, quietly, speaking in German. "Or you will be sorry, very sorry!" he added emphatically. "But as you appear to wish to give me some trouble, I will give you the little story of Jean Garnier, and then perhaps you will not be so eager for the police!"

"You will have to pay me for this!" muttered the German, at which Poiret only smiled and continued in his even voice.

"Jean Garnier was the man who was found a corpse outside this house but a few weeks ago. How do I know that, you will ask, perhaps? I will tell you! I hear of the murder. It is a mystery. I love the mystery, and I see to it that my very good friend the coroner's officer, summons me as a foreman of the jury. In my tie-pin I carry a little photograph instrument; I photograph the dead man in the mortuary; I develop him once, I develop him twice, and I magnify him. What do I see? On the cheeks little, small lines and marks that tell me he had but lately been wearing a false beard."

"This is a foolish tale!" muttered the waiter. "I will go."

"You wait and still listen, my friend. I know, yes, I know everything of disguises, and I see, what perhaps Detective-Inspector Drayton did not know, and what nobody else, perhaps, would know either, that the dead man had been disguised with a large beard. The marks are peculiar, but when the photograph was magnified they were (to me) easy to see. Then I copy the face of the dead man on my easel, and paint a beard one, two, three, four, five times, perhaps more, a different beard each time, until at length it comes to me, *psst*! like that! I have got the right beard at last, and before me there shows the face of one Jean Garnier who had worn a beard some twelve years ago, when I knew him."

"That, of course, is impossible!" said the waiter sneeringly. "But you interest me, old gentleman, with your lies. Go on! But I tell you, you will have to pay me for this afterwards!"

"Nothing is impossible, my friend!" answered Monsieur Poiret, placidly. "I thought I had recognised the nose and the forehead of the man, and when I see that he had worn a beard as a disguise I paint on until I get the right one to fit him, and, behold, there before me is my old acquaintance, Jean Garnier. I refresh my memory of him in the little book that I keep, and I soon see what a scoundrel he was. He was anarchist; he was everything. And so I satisfy myself that I do one thing which the police do not. I find the name of the murdered man. It was Jean Garnier."

"It is a good tale, as I say," said the waiter, wriggling in his chair; "but it has not interest for me, so I will go, if you please. I do not wish to be unpleasant to you, but you are a foolish old man, and I will make you pay!"

"Now, who murdered Jean Garnier?" went on Monsieur Poiret, ignoring the interruption. "He was an anarchist. Perhaps he had enemies? I interrogate one of his bosom friends and brother anarchists—Monsieur Jacques Beautemps, a waiter. He then tells me the tale of Pierre Gaudon—the same Pierre Gaudon who, I remember (for I was present at the Garnier trial), had been ejected from the court for threatening to kill Jean Garnier when he was acquitted of the murder of his wife. From what Beautemps told me then, I say to myself, 'Pierre Gaudon murdered Jean Garnier! Find Pierre Gaudon then, Poiret!' I think perhaps there may be something in this house which may give me ideas, and I rent it myself after I look through the back list of tenants and find some years ago the name of Jean Garnier as tenant. 'Oh, oh,' I say to myself, 'the murdered man was placed outside the very house where he murdered his wife! Sentiment—eh, the beautiful sentiment! The murderer placed at the door of the very house where he murdered his wife! Oh, oh! Yes, yes: Pierre Gaudon, Pierre Gaudon, for certain!' I say to myself. It is what I would do if I had the chance. If I wished for revenge, I should like to do it in a sentimental way; so once more I say to myself, 'Now go, you fat old man, go quick! Hurry! Find one Pierre Gaudon, and hear what he has to say.' I find this Pierre Gaudon, then, and I say to him, 'You murdered Jean Garnier. Tell me how and why?'"

"My goodness!" said the waiter angrily. "If you talk much more like this, I shout for the police. You say you want Pierre Gaudon for the murder of Jean Garnier. You find him, and yet you keep me in this chair. My good old man, you are mad!"

Monsieur Poiret leant forward, and once more he prodded the waiter in the chest.

"I keep you, my dear Herr Guggenheim, because you are Pierre Gaudon. See you here, it is a good disguise, but it does not deceive Papa Poiret!"

The old man stretched forward a hand, and with a quick twitch two fair eyebrows came off, disclosing dark ones underneath. A fair wig followed suit, showing a head of shortly-cropped black hair.

"I have my own purpose for wearing a wig," expostulated the waiter; "but that does not make me Pierre Gaudon."

"Oh, oh!" chuckled Monsieur Poiret. "Then what you say when I show you the false beard worn by Jean Garnier and the little bottle which contained the poison that was put in his whisky, eh? What you say when I tell you I find them in the little seamstress's room, in the pillow of her bed? How do you like it now, Monsieur Pierre Gaudon?"

"My God, but here is madness indeed!" choked the waiter. "You find some things in another room, and you say to me that proves I am Pierre Gaudon! Good gracious! I shall go mad myself as well as you in a minute!"

"Yes; and you go madder when I say to you quietly that Herr Guggenheim, the German waiter, Pierre Gaudon, and the little seamstress are all three one and the same! Now how do you like it, Monsieur Pierre Gaudon? I am not quite mad, perhaps, yet! Papa Poiret still keeps his senses—oh, yes!"

The man in the chair wriggled uneasily. His features worked, then he broke into a half laugh, and in the purest French he said:

"Very well, I may as well give it up now. I am Pierre Gaudon, *alias* Guggenheim, *alias* the little seamstress. But how in the name of goodness did you find me out, Monsieur Poiret?"

"Then you own up you murdered Jean Garnier?" said Monsieur Poiret, also speaking in French.

"According to your lights, I murdered him," was the reply. "According to mine, I was his executioner."

"Yes, yes, poor fellow," murmured Monsieur Poiret, "so

you were. I quite understand—at least, I think I do. Will you tell me everything? Perhaps I may have something to say to you which will not be unpleasant."

"Oh, certainly," said Pierre Gaudon, shrugging his shoulders. "I may as well tell you everything. I shall go to my death with a gay heart, for I sent to his death the man who killed Julie, the dear, sweet little Julie whom I loved as a child, but who married this scum instead of me, and he killed her! Yes, he boasted in his cups that he killed her! He grew sick and tired of her, and so he killed her by putting poison in her whisky—she, my poor Julie who never drank! He said afterwards that she drank to excess and took drugs. On the night that she died the poor little one had been suffering from toothache, and had taken some of the whisky to rub on her tooth—so it was said in the evidence given at the inquiry. And it was then that he forced her to drink some of the whisky, saying that it would do her good. Oh, yes, he told it all to an acquaintance of mine, and the acquaintance told me, but long after the trial, and when we met on the Continent in a music hall."

"The acquaintance was Jacques Beautemps, I suppose?"

"It was," went on Pierre Gaudon; "and I expect he's been living in terror of Garnier ever since, lest he should find out that he had told his secret. Then Garnier found out that I was on his track, for ever since I gave up my work as a performer, I have been searching for him night and day, for I had sworn to kill him as he killed my poor Julie. I heard he frequented a certain café in Soho, and there I went and soon obtained employment as a waiter, and I recognised him through the beard, good as the disguise was, which he wore out of terror for me. But *he* did not recognise *me*—oh, no, I am too good a performer for that!"

Monsieur Poiret smiled slightly.

"We became acquainted at the café," continued Pierre Gaudon, "as I make out that I am anarchist and general scoundrel. We become friends. When I am off duty, we go out together. He calls to see me several times; everyone knew the bearded man who called to see Guggenheim. At last he came on that night, the anniversary of the day many years ago when poor Julie was poisoned. We talk of anarchism, we talk of many things; and then I produce the whisky. Into it I pour the Norma, the poison which I have so easily procured, and as he drinks it, I pull off my disguise, I look into his face, and I say to him, 'Good health to you, Jean Garnier, the murderer of Julie Garnier! Good health to you, for I am Pierre Gaudon!' And I had hardly finished speaking when he dropped down dead!"

Monsieur Poiret made a note on his cuff.

"And you got him out of the house—how?" he asked.

"Oh, very simply!" continued Pierre Gaudon. "First of all, I stripped off his beard so that no one should recognise him as the man who used to call on me. I knew all the times of the policemen and their beats. I kept him in my rooms three and a half hours, and when I knew that the policeman had been down the passage and back, it was for me with my muscle a matter of no trouble to lift up Jean Garnier and prop him up against the door of the very house in which he had murdered poor Julie. Then I hasten back to my room and am asleep when aroused by the policemen. I have covered all traces, and I am perfectly happy and content, for I have done justice, and there is no chance of my being found out."

"As you will have seen, Monsieur," said Monsieur Poiret, "I am a detective. I was lately of the French Secret Service, and though I am not officially engaged on this case, I consider it my duty to inform you that you are under arrest for the murder of Jean Garnier."

"As you will, Monsieur. But I thought I was clever. Perhaps you will tell me how it was that you were more clever?"

"Certainly! It was settled in my mind that Pierre Gaudon must have murdered Jean Garnier. Someone in one of these houses, then, must be Pierre Gaudon, for common sense told me that it was impossible that Garnier could have been murdered anywhere else. I kept careful watch, Monsieur, and it seemed strange to me that whenever the little seamstress went out to work during the day, Herr Guggenheim was never at home either, and when the waiter went out to wait in the evening, the little seamstress was never at home, though she might have returned from her hard work in the West End only half an hour before.

"And, further, Monsieur, I soon ascertained that the little seamstress did not work at a shop at all, but went regularly to a flat in the West End situated in a building devoted otherwise to business offices, where she generally spent the day until it was time for her to return to Judd Lane. It was easy to ascertain that the flat was rented by one Pierre Gaudon. Pierre Gaudon had the little finger of his left hand turned in, so had Herr Guggenheim, and so had the little seamstress. The little seamstress wore a wig—a fact which I ascertained by the simple process of applying a lighted candle to the side locks. Artificial hair burns very differently from real hair, owing, of course, to all the natural sap having been dried up. After discovering all this, it was plain to me that Herr Guggenheim and the little seamstress were one and the same person, otherwise Pierre Gaudon."

"Very clever, very clever, Monsieur!" said Gaudon appreciatively. "I certainly spent my days at my own flat, sometimes in disguise, sometimes not. But tell me, how did you find Garnier's false beard and the bottle which I hid in the seamstress's pillow?"

"I let myself into her room with a false key of my own invention, examined the room thoroughly, and found, first of all,—what I had been suspecting for some time—quick-change dresses made of the thinnest possible material, so that they could be thrown on and off at a second's notice, as you talented gentlemen do on the music-hall stage. You had left some of Herr Guggenheim's quick-change clothes down in the seamstress's room, Monsieur Gaudon! That was a mistake. And the false beard and the bottle of course completed the clue."

"My thousand compliments, Monsieur," said Gaudon. "And now there but remains for me the guillotine, or I suppose, in England here, the hangman's rope. Yes, I murdered Jean Garnier. I carried him out of the house with the greatest of ease, and then I went back to bed. It was easy enough to be in turn the waiter and the seamstress, and when the police had examined the seamstress, standing in my dressing-gown with dark, long hair flowing over my shoulders, it was very simple for me to get out of my back window, climb up the drain-pipe, and through the window into my other room, to be ready as Guggenheim to be cross-examined. I was always prepared for emergencies, Monsieur, for I was determined to

kill Jean Garnier. And as regards the tenants of the house—
pouf! They are good, easy-going, hard-working people. Why
should they bother, then, thinking about the seamstress or
the waiter?"

"But why, Monsieur Pierre Gaudon," interrupted Monsieur
Poiret, "why was it necessary for two disguises—the seamstress and the waiter? Surely as the waiter you were capable
of dealing with Jean Garnier, without troubling with any
other disguise?"

"Capable?" answered Pierre Gaudon. "Oh, yes, I was capable, for I am a strong man, Monsieur Poiret, or else I should
not have been able to carry that body down the stairs. But
supposing—supposing, Monsieur Poiret, there had been a
hue and a cry after Guggenheim? Supposing he had been
suspected? Very well, then, with my quick-change clothes, I
should at once have become the little seamstress; then, ho la!
Guggenheim has disappeared, and no one suspects the little
quiet woman in black, and after a while she disappears too.
And now, Monsieur, I am ready to go with you."

He rose and stretched out his handcuffed wrists, and at
that moment a form passed the half-open window. With a
quick movement Poiret opened the communicating door
which led to the next room and thrust Gaudon, handcuffed
as he was, inside.

"Whatever you do, keep quiet, and do not try to escape,
for I have something to say to you," he whispered hurriedly.

A knock was heard at the door, and Monsieur Poiret admitted Detective-Inspector Drayton.

"What on earth's made you take rooms here, Monsieur
Poiret?" said the detective. "I was quite staggered when I got

your note saying that you had moved here! Been trying to find the murderer as a bit of relaxation?"

Monsieur Poiret laughed in an embarrassed manner.

"I am afraid the man who was responsible for that dead body that looked so ugly will never be brought to the gallows, Monsieur Drayton," he said slowly; "and as for me, for Papa Poiret—well, it suits my purse to reside myself here for a while. You will not pry, Monsieur Drayton, but chambers in the Adelphi have great expenses, you know, and—well, I am no longer on the active service, as you say in England."

"That's just what I've come to see you about, Monsieur Poiret. Unofficially, I believe there's a matter which you might attend to which hardly comes within our line. In fact, we couldn't touch it, because official reports have to be made of everything we handle, and this is a sort of thing that mustn't be reported on. Can I see you next week about it?"

"Yes, yes," answered Monsieur Poiret. "I think I should like some work once again now."

For a brief space the two chatted, then Drayton left with a promise to see Monsieur Poiret next week.

As soon as the well-known Scotland Yard man had left, Monsieur Poiret once more opened the bedroom door, to find Gaudon seated on a chair, with his handcuffed wrists in front of him.

"Now then, my friend," said Monsieur Poiret in French, "we speak together, you and I, as man to man. I should have done the same as you did, regardless of consequences. You loved the girl. She married another; but all through you kept the same good, pure love for her, though she never knew it. A bad man killed her, you killed him. I am a Frenchman: I should have done the same. Yes; but I am a policeman also, and it would be my duty to my Government, which still pays me a salary, though I am no longer in active employ—it would be my duty to the country of my adoption to hand you over to justice—but for *the fact that you did not kill Jean Garnier!*"

"I did not kill Jean Garnier!"

"No. See, listen here! What time did Garnier call on you?"

"At about nine o'clock."

"And when did you give him the poisoned whisky?"

"At about half-past nine—the very hour at which poor Julie was found dead."

"At what time did he die?"

"Within less than five minutes. As soon as he had taken his drink, I took off my disguise and said to him, 'Jean Garnier, behold Pierre Gaudon!' He gave one look, put down his half-empty glass on the table, sank back in his chair, his jaw dropped, his eyes bulged, and in three seconds, I should think, he was dead."

"Then, my friend, he died from the shock. He had a weak heart, so the doctor at the inquest told me, and though morally speaking, perhaps, you hastened his end by the sudden shock you gave him, you were not his murderer. That poison will not take effect under half an hour, so that, though you had the intent to murder, you did not actually murder. It may be stretching a point as to whether I should lay information; but, after all, Jean Garnier was wanted for another crime in France which would have brought him to the guillotine, and I do not think he is worth troubling over. As for me, I am a Frenchman and a man, and I applaud you, Pierre Gaudon, for what you have done. It was wrong, it was wicked, it was foolish of you, of course; but it was also very human. Shake hands with me, Pierre Gaudon, and go your way!"

Monsieur Poiret took off the handcuffs and pointed to the door. Pierre Gaudon sat silent for a moment, his face working, and then, with true French emotion, he threw his arms round Monsieur Poiret and kissed him on both cheeks.

"Yes, I go," he said, "and I shall never forget Monsieur Poiret."

The fat old man showed Pierre Gaudon to the door and watched him until he had turned the corner on his way to the Strand, a free man, never to return again, either as the seamstress or the waiter, to Judd Lane.

Monsieur Poiret went back into his sitting-room and indited in a neat hand in his diary the heads of this his latest experience.

"And now, my little ones," he said as he laid down his pen, "come along and sing to your Papa Poiret."

And the fat old detective opened the door of his canaries' cage, and one by one the little yellow birds hopped out on to the stick held for them, and, forgetful of everything else, the great crime investigator leant back in his chair, listening, with half-closed eyes, to the melodious tunes of his little birds.

"My faith," he said drowsily, "this is not such a bad old world, after all! And now, my children, back to your little home, for Papa Poiret would sleep!"

In a few minutes prolonged snores proclaimed that the great detective was asleep.

Water Running Out

Ethel Lina White

Ethel Lina White (1876–1944) was born in Abergavenny and—as a woman who eschewed personal publicity during her lifetime—she would no doubt be astonished to discover that her birthplace in Frogmore Street is now marked by a blue plaque. This recognition highlights the intrinsic merit of her novels of domestic suspense, but there is more to it than that. Her writing was vivid and atmospheric and ideally suited to adaptation for film or television. Of all the screen versions of her work, the most famous is the classic Hitchcock movie *The Lady Vanishes*, based on *The Wheel Spins*, which has also been adapted for television and the stage. *Some Must Watch*, set in Welsh border country, was also memorably filmed as *The Spiral Staircase*.

Ethel's father William was a successful builder. His experiments with cement and bitumen led to his inventing Heigia Rock, a waterproof building material which was used for construction work on the London Underground and made him a rich man. He built a new family home, Fairlea Grange, in Belmont Road, and Ethel was still living there in her mid-thirties at the time of the 1911 census. For a few years thereafter she worked in the Ministry of Pensions before concentrating on writing. She died of ovarian cancer in 1944, and because of her fear of being buried alive (reflected in her novel *The First Time He Died*) she bequeathed her entire estate to her sister "on condition she pays a qualified surgeon to plunge a knife into my heart after death." This story first appeared in *Crime Mysteries* on 28 October 1927.

———

"Many happy returns of the day," said Charles.

"Thanks, old chap," said Harvey quietly.

"Have you killed Aunty yet?" enquired Charles, who was a humorist.

"No. But I'm going to."

Everyone laughed. For all that, Harvey meant what he said. This evening, he was going to kill Aunty.

All his friends liked Harvey. He was such a nice little man. He had kind blue eyes and a chubby shrimp-pink face. When he was twenty, he contrived to grow a moustache of which he was very proud. Everyone said it made him look much older. Recently, he had shaved it off, although he was as proud of it as ever.

It was Harvey's birthday, and he was celebrating it by a tea party in his flat. His pink-iced cake had candles on it; if the candles did not quite correspond to his years, it must be remembered that candles are dearer than they used to be.

He shared the flat with Aunty. No, "shared" is not the word.

Aunty pervaded it. Although she was not in the little sitting room, everyone felt her presence. Aunty was an enormous woman, of vast swollen bulk with tiny features smothered amid the flaps of her white face. Her little eyes, set close together, were blank as boot buttons. She had no brain—only a fester of malice. Even today she dominated the conversation.

"Will Aunty come to the tea party?" asked Miss Lemon. Miss Lemon was a competent brunette and arch-gossip of a little town, where tongues were those of adders.

"No," answered Harvey. "She doesn't alter her habits. To the dot is Aunty. She takes her saltrated bath at six thirty, to the tick."

"And then she dresses and reads her Bible till bedtime," said Annie Reed. There was a tinge of bitterness in her gentle voice. Annie had become engaged to Harvey when she was eighteen. Now she was thirty-four.

"Perhaps," said the curate, "it would be more accurate to say that Aunty sits with the Bible on her knee."

"Unless," remarked the witty Charles, "she makes up her own Bible. 'Give us this day our daily bread, for tomorrow it will be stale.'"

"That's not funny," said Annie. "Tom, dear," she turned to Harvey, "shall Mother pour out?"

"If she feels equal to it."

The widowed Mrs. Reed took the place of honour, with dignity. She was very superior. She looked white and frail, as though fashioned out of eggshell. But—believe me—she had her pride.

They all sat down to tea. It was a special feast. Besides the pink-iced cake, there was plum and plain; today, both plum and plain had names, in honour of the occasion. They were called "Genoa" and "Madeira."

But Annie's brow was furrowed as she noted the appointments of the table. The jam was set out in glass dishes which had been bought at Woolworth's. The silk poppies in the vases were dirty. There were no doilies.

Annie had a whole box of beautiful mixed flowers, fresh from the fingers of The Crippled Girls. She had numerous cushions, doilies, and tablecloths. For sixteen years she had been filling her bottom-drawer.

When love for Harvey had induced her to offer him some of the treasures she should, rightly, be sharing, she was grateful for Aunty's curt refusal. Aunty didn't hold with rubbish to make dust. Not that Aunty dusted anything. Annie could write her name in the dust on the mantel. But she didn't want to write her name. After thirty-four years, she was too sick of it.

When Annie became engaged, she had a rose-tinted childish face, infantile blue eyes, and pale-yellow crinkled hair. The years had altered her very little. But of late, her hair seemed to be losing its colour and, in a strong light, her face showed unsuspected lines.

As he looked at her, she reminded the curate of the roses still blooming in September gardens. They were beautiful today—but what of tonight's frost? Any night, while they slept, Annie would turn to a sapless old maid, unless she could be kept in the sun.

All this made the curate very angry. He was an intensely human person, and he loved his flock. Annie was such a good girl. She taught in the Sunday school and helped at the Band of Hope, every Monday night. She was also an officer in the Girls' Guides.

Mrs. Reed, in her pride of a clergyman's widow, approved her daughter's parochial labours, just as she approved the fact that Annie was no longer a typist at Short's, the corn merchants.

Annie now took dictation only from the head of the firm. She received the same salary, though she never left to time, like the other clerks. But Mrs. Reed could now allude to her daughter as a "private secretary."

The curate, who knew how hard Annie worked, wanted to see her busied in her own home. She and Harvey were the nicest couple in his parish; regular communicants, good worthy young people. It enraged him to think that their union was impossible because of Aunty.

Aunty was a Sacred Trust. She was the sister of Harvey's mother. At a time of financial stress, she had saved the parental fortune, by a timely loan of £50 from her post office savings book. She had been repaid, but she continued to make her home with the family.

When Harvey's parents were both dead, the children continued the tradition of Aunty; but, one by one, they fell out of the race, by reason of marriage or discard of responsibility. Finally, Harvey—at the age of twenty—was left, alone faithful to the Trust.

The curate knew that this was praiseworthy. No one should ignore the claim of an aged relative. Only, Aunty was so much more than that. She was selfish and venomous. She was an organism that absorbed everything. She seemed a fungoid growth, which preyed on matter, in order to add to its bulk.

Increase of salary was useless to Harvey. Every small addition to his income—that of a bank clerk—was met inevitably by a fresh claim on the part of Aunty.

Gradually, the curate—when he prayed for those in trouble—had grown to think definitely of Harvey and Annie, at the clause, "granting them patience under their sufferings and a happy issue out of all their afflictions."

He thrust aside gloomy thoughts to beam upon the cake. Annie had lit the candles and they shone on the circle of faces. The curate liked both Mrs. Reed and Annie. Miss Lemon, the gossip, stimulated him, by reason of her designs on himself. Charles, Harvey's fellow clerk, could be depended on to make things hum. There was also a pretty girl, but, in Mrs. Reed's presence, she did not count, being a mere typist. Altogether, a pleasant company and a splendid tea.

They talked of Saturday's football. Miss Lemon introduced a bright young scandal, but the curate crushed it. They confided to each other their likes and dislikes, where food was concerned. But—very soon—they were back to Aunty.

"I'm sorry your aunt was not well enough to grace the festive board," said Mrs. Reed, who was not sorry at all.

"It's the time for her bath," repeated Harvey. "You could set a clock by Aunty."

"Does she suffer much from rheumatism?" enquired Mrs. Reed.

"She doesn't complain," replied Harvey dutifully.

He wondered if Aunty were capable of physical feeling.

He knew she wore a triple strand, of sewing cotton around her waist, as a cure for lumbago. He knew, also, that the daily packets of saltrates cost good money.

"She's something chronic," he confided. "Every evening, at six-ten, she dissolves a packet of saltrates in exactly the same quantity of boiling water. She gives it twenty minutes to cool and then she soaks in it for fifteen minutes. Annie will bear me out; eh, Annie?"

"Yes." Annie nodded. "At six-forty-five, to the tick, you hear the gurgle of the water in the waste pipe. She's like clockwork."

"Cheer up!" said the privileged Charles. "One day, the clock will run down. And then you two young people will have your innings."

One of the young people—Harvey—felt a sharp contraction at his heart at the sight of the setting sun glinting on Annie's head. Her hair was of minted gold. Today, for the first time, he detected a slight depreciation in the currency—silver! He breathed hard. Then he recovered himself. "Come, Miss Lemon!" He passed the brown bread and butter. "Last piece. It's lucky."

Miss Lemon looked at the curate. Annie pressed her elbows on the table.

"It's a birthday," she said, "and it's all among friends, so you may as well know my plans. I've decided not to wait any longer for Aunty to die."

"Hear, hear!" cried Charles.

"I am self-supporting, and Mother is not dependent on me."

"Indeed, no!" murmured Mrs. Reed proudly.

"So we've practically decided—Tom and I—to do like the Pearces."

There was a little gasp of approval. The Pearces, newcomers to the sleepy town, had inaugurated a novelty in the marriage institution. When Pearce went on half-time, Mrs. Pearce had retained her post as head milliner, at Jones', the drapers.

"With our joint incomes," went on Annie, "there is no reason why we should not set up housekeeping. Of course, it can't be perfect with Aunty. But I'm sick of waiting. I'll wait no longer."

Harvey groped desperately for the comfort of his vanished moustache. Why had she uttered those damning words?

She little knew. None of them knew exactly how Aunty hated Annie. Annie was the menace to her supremacy. So far, she had kept her out, by sheer economic pressure.

Ever since Harvey had first broached their plan of pooled incomes, Aunty had sat silent, her little dark eyes inscrutable, her mouth sucked in—spinning plots. When he watched her, Harvey felt that the inside of her head must be interlaced with foul black cobwebs.

And at last she had trapped Annie. Hour by hour, Aunty had sat, spinning. Presently, she worked back to the last summer holiday, which Harvey had spent with the Reeds, as usual, at Eastbourne.

According to custom, they had stayed at the Marigold Tea Rooms Boarding Establishment. The ladies had occupied a double room, and Harvey had slept in the adjoining single room. When Mrs. Reed had been obliged to curtail her holiday by a day, the engaged couple had stayed on the extra time.

Aunty threw out some more thread. She established the fact that the Harvey's "daily" had a cousin, who, during the season, was cook at the Marigold Tea Rooms Boarding Establishment.

In Harvey's absence, the cook was invited to the flat and plied with gin and questions as to the adjoining bedrooms. Thus was established the ominous fact—the door of communication.

The poor frustrated lovers had known nothing at all of that door. On Harvey's side, it was barricaded with furniture; on Annie's, it was shrouded with a chintz curtain. Had they known of its existence, in their innocence, they would never have questioned whether it were open or locked.

But, in the slimy depths of Aunty's mind, it became the symbol of Annie's loss of character. She had the lovers in the hollow of her hand. She knew the timid souls could never face her music.

"Every one shall know her for what she is," she told Harvey. "Your precious Sunday school Annie! Couldn't wait! Couldn't wait for poor old Aunt to be buried decently. Now the whole town shall know that she is a hussy!"

At first, Harvey had weakly thought of putting off his party. But that action was akin to leashing Niagara with a dog muzzle. Short of cutting out her tongue, nothing could silence Aunty. So, following precedent, Harvey had his birthday party.

But he alone knew that today, the clockwork routine would be broken. Behind that closed door, Aunty was waiting. She was waiting for the last drop of tea to be swallowed and the last crumb of cake devoured. True to timetable, Aunty had informed him of her programme.

At seven, precisely, Aunty would address the tea party. Harvey's watch told him that it was now six-thirty-five.

He glanced at Mrs. Reed. She looked frail, as though she would be wafted to another planet did any one sneeze. In half an hour, the pride which had sustained her in every trial would be shattered in the sight of all. Ten minutes later, the official herald of the town, in the person of Miss Lemon, would have the freedom of the streets. Harvey felt something thick upon his lip. It was not the ghost of his lost moustache.

"Hot for September," observed the curate. "You're sweating, Harvey."

"I do perspire rather freely," replied Harvey.

"He's thinking of his little job," said the humorist Charles. "The thought of work always affects him like that. By the way, *when* are you going to murder Aunty?"

"Very soon."

"Shall we all be present at the ceremony?"

"I can't promise that. But you shall certainly hear the victim's last cry."

They all laughed at the joke. It was all among friends.

Harvey turned to Mrs. Reed.

"Talking of Aunty, she had a bad choking fit, two days ago. I had to call in the doctor."

"She eats too much," said Annie.

"And just a teeny bit too fast, I'm afraid," said Mrs. Reed.

"And her false teeth fit none too well, I'm sorry to say," said Harvey.

Thereupon, they all began to talk of teeth.

A sandy-and-white kitten scrambled from the pretty girl's lap onto the table. Its mother was a plain-looking female, and the kitten took after mother.

Miss Lemon, in order to disprove her predestined spinsterhood to the curate, screamed shrilly. But the burly curate wound the kitten round his neck.

"Fond of animals, Harvey?" he asked.

"Yes, I like all dumb creatures. Aunty is always at me to drown the kitten; thinks it might trip her up; but I couldn't be so cruel."

"I'll find it a good home," cried Miss Lemon, putting her arm round the curate's neck to disengage the kitten.

Charles was humorously shocked at her action. "If I could have snapped you two then, I'd never do another stroke of work. Say, Padre"—like Harvey, he clung to the old war title—"listen! If you were in a boat with your child and another man's child, and the boat leaked, and you could only save one child—"

Harvey listened no further. He gazed dreamily out of the window, noting how the setting sun gilded the roofs of the old town. A pigeon on the mellowed coping preened itself against the blue sky. A horse chestnut tree near the window hung golden fans among its green. Harvey loved the old town. He loved it in every season. He could have been so happy, but for Aunty.

A roar of laughter told him that Charles had "caught" the curate.

"Say, Padre," said Harvey suddenly, "I've one for you. This isn't a catch. It's a moral problem. Suppose you were in a boat with your wife and another man, and the boat upset, and there was only room for two to cling to, and the man tried to pull off your wife, would you be justified in holding his head under the water? Or would it be murder?"

"I should certainly consider it murder, if I were the miserable man," said the curate. "But it is conceivable that you might shelter under the moral law."

"Only, it wouldn't help your wife if you got found out," said Annie. "You can never tell how a jury will look at things."

Harvey vaguely felt that there was something wrong about that sentence. But it sounded all right, and Annie was a Sunday school teacher.

"Will you cut the cake?" he asked the curate. "There's a thimble, a ring, and a threepenny bit inside."

The curate rose and, from his height of six feet, smiled down at Annie. "I hope it will be Annie's turn next, to cut the wedding cake. With all my heart, I hope that day will come soon."

"It all depends," said Harvey, looking at the clock. Six-forty. Yes, it all depended on the next few minutes.

He turned to the pretty girl. "Raspberry or strawberry jam?"

"But they are both my favourite," she wailed.

He politely waited for her to make up her mind. Then he apologised to the party. "There's the postman's knock. If you will excuse me for two minutes, I would like to see if any one has sent me a birthday card."

On his way to the door, he stooped and kissed Annie. She coloured, looking prim, but pleased. After all, it was all among friends.

When the door closed, Miss Lemon, feeling the warm breath of incipient matrimony, smiled dreamily at the curate. "Isn't he a nice little man?"

The curate assented briskly.

Within three minutes, Harvey returned from his journey down to the front door. The corners of two letters showed from his pocket.

"Two," he said. "I wonder if Aunty would like any cake."

"No," said Annie, "she's still in the bath room, for she's only just let out the water. We heard the gurgle of the waste pipe a second ago."

Harvey looked at the clock. "Six-forty-five. You could set a clock by Aunty."

They sat long over the cake. Miss Lemon got the fatal thimble and didn't care one little scrap. It was simply laughable. The curate got the threepenny bit and said he would save it for the collection. And Annie got the ring.

Then Miss Lemon, still savouring the bliss of domesticity, proposed that they should all wash up. "It will save the girl in the morning. After all, she is human like the rest of us."

Harvey again felt the beaded outline of his phantom moustache. "No. I've something better to propose." He turned to Charles. "Charles, old man, I was thinking of winding up with a game of cooncan, but I've only one pack of cards. What about your asking us all down to your apartment?"

Charles had rooms on the lower floor of the old family house, which had been roughly converted into flats.

"Righto," sang Charles. "Come below decks, my hearties. Ladies, remember to descend the ladder backwards!"

Harvey shepherded his guests out onto the landing and then thriftily turned out the gas of the sitting room.

As they passed Aunty's bedroom, Miss Lemon laid her fingers on the handle of the door. "Aunty will be dressed by now. Do you think she would mind if we ladies slipped inside to tidy up?"

The gas on the landing was unlit, so no one saw Harvey's face. He laid clammy fingers on Miss Lemon's sleeve and whispered in her ear. "I think the padre expects you to sit by him, at cards."

She took the hint. Harvey drew a long breath as he saw her break away down the stairs, well in advance of the rest of the field.

It was very pleasant in Charles's room. There was a red-caked coal fire, instead of the inhospitable Japanese umbrella which had blocked the Harvey grate. The incandescent light was cheery under its green cardboard shade. They shut out the autumn twilight, which was growing misty and sad, and settled down in shabby chairs around the old red tablecloth.

"Harvey's eaten too much tea," remarked Charles. "He looks as if he'd seen a ghost."

"If I met a ghost, I—I'd invite it to have some of my birthday cake." Harvey laughed in excellent spirits, as he rose from the table.

"I've known you for seven years, Charles, old man, and been not so much the worse for it, so I can poke your fire."

His back was towards them as he broke up the caked coals. No one noticed that he stirred into the leaping flames the two letters which he had just received.

But when one considers the point that they were blank sheets of paper enclosed in envelopes which had never gone through the post, the matter is of no consequence, other than the waste of good stationery.

Cooncan proved hilarious. As it was a birthday, they played for money, twelve counters a penny. Fortunes were won and lost.

At nine o'clock, Charles offered bachelor refreshment of beer and cocoa.

Harvey started up guiltily. "I've quite forgotten Aunty. She'll be in bed by now. I'd better see if she wants her Benger's."

"I'll go!" said Miss Lemon, as Harvey knew she would. Miss Lemon could never resist a visit to a bedroom. She wanted to know if the pillowslips were clean.

When she returned, her face was red, and her eyes crescent moons of excitement. Her whole being was drunk with drama. *"Aunty's dead!"*

The inquest was a tame affair. One bright young spirit on the jury tried to introduce a flicker of life by the suggestion of foul play, but it was crushed by Harvey's voluntary statement that the faint marks on Aunty's throat were probably made by his own fingers. During her previous choking fit, he had had great difficulty in unfastening the stud of her stiff linen collar, and, in his haste, had used slight force.

According to the medical evidence of old mossy Dr. Plume, deceased had been suffocated by her false teeth, which had been forced down her throat, presumably in another fit of choking. She had been dead about two hours. It was proved by all those present at Mr. Harvey's birthday party that the deceased had taken her bath as usual and was alive at six-forty-five. As she was fully dressed when discovered by Miss Lemon, it was presumed that she had died immediately after completing her toilet. It was proved that no one had entered the house, or had access to the upper storey, after the party had descended to Charles's flat, which—together with total absence of motive—ruled out any suggestion of foul play. The deceased was penniless and dependent on the generosity of her nephew.

The jury returned a verdict of "death by accident." The coroner proposed a vote of sympathy to the nephew of the deceased.

Harvey and Annie were married the following May. They spent the honeymoon at Eastbourne, staying at the Marigold Tea Rooms Boarding Establishment. They had glorious weather and enjoyed every minute of their holiday.

On their last night, Harvey advanced to the window to close it the customary six inches.

"Annie," he said suddenly, "did you know that this room and the next had a communicating door?"

"No," she replied. "Why are you looking so funny, Tom?"

"Aunty knew!"

He saw the horror dawn and deepen in her eyes as she listened.

"She called you vile names, Annie. She did. She said you wouldn't wait—"

"Oh, Tom, stop! Suppose, only *suppose* if she had accused me of that! The awful disgrace! The Sunday school—and all. You know what people are. They'd have talked—and talked. It would have killed Mother!"

"I know. And you—Annie?"

"Me? I could never have held up my head again. I should have gone to the river and got it over!"

"Well," said Harvey, "it didn't come so there's no call for you to cry."

"No." Annie wiped her eyes. "But—suppose! Oh, Tom, it was the direct intervention of Providence that she died when she did."

"Well, yes, I suppose, in a way, it was. It all fitted in so well."

He pondered for a minute. No one but he knew that the gurgling sound to which—true to his promise—he had invited the attention of his guests, had not been caused by water passing through a waste pipe. Aunty had taken no bath that night.

He looked at Annie, illumined in the electric pendant which hung over the bed. She was wearing the trousseau nightdress which she had made herself—white crêpe-de-Chine, embroidered with bulky pale-blue butterflies. Her hair was a golden fleece on the pillow. In the dim light, she looked exactly like the girl he had wooed. For the sun was shining on her.

He set his lips. Of course, Aunty had got in before him and had carried her tale to God. But—according to the padre—He would wait to hear Harvey's version before pronouncing judgment.

Harvey snapped off the light. He stood for a moment, looking at the silver streak of moonlight over the sea.

"Annie," he said, "I've thought of a text for Aunty's stone. 'Blessed are the peacemakers.'"

"But Tom!" Annie protested through the darkness. "You couldn't call Aunty *that*!"

"Perhaps not. But—it's all so happy and peaceful now. And—it sounds kind."

He was a nice little man.

A Busman's Holiday

Francis Brett Young

Francis Brett Young (1884–1954) studied medicine at Birmingham University and qualified as a doctor, practising in Brixham from 1897. He married a singer and composed songs for her, and in 1913 he published his first novel, *Undergrowth*, in collaboration with his brother Eric. His first solo effort followed a year later. He served as a medical officer during the First World War only to be invalided out. No longer able to work as a doctor, he concentrated on writing and travel. His loosely linked "Mercian" novels were set around the area associated with the ancient kingdom of Mercia, which incorporated parts of present-day Wales, and his love of the Welsh border country is evident in much of his work. The Mercian books helped to secure his reputation as a storyteller of considerable prowess, and to this day, a Francis Brett Young Society celebrates his writing with a range of activities. His ashes were interred in Worcester Cathedral.

Young's most famous novel is probably *My Brother Jonathan*, which was filmed in 1948 and adapted for BBC

TV in 1985. He is not usually associated with crime fiction, but this accomplished story, which appeared in *Pall Mall Magazine* in 1930, was chosen by Dorothy L. Sayers for inclusion in the third of her magisterial anthologies of mystery fiction (did its title, one wonders, inspire that of the final Lord Peter Wimsey novel, *Busman's Honeymoon*?). As is so often seen in Young's work, the protagonist is a medical man.

————

IF THERE WAS ONE THING THAT DOCTOR MALCOLM detested and dreaded more than another it was a busman's holiday—in other words, the intrusion of medicine, that science to which his name had added so much lustre, into those precious weeks when sea trout were on the run.

When a celebrated lawyer or stockbroker goes away for a holiday and the man who is sitting next to him in the train reads his name on his baggage, edges up to him, slips gradually into polite conversation, then drops in a casual question about some hypothetical case of law or the future of International Nickels or General Motors, that lawyer or stockbroker is within his rights if he changes his seat or turns the subject in the direction of golf, cocktails, or fishing tackle.

Neither litigation nor speculation is a matter of life and death; neither the lawyer nor the stockbroker has a duty towards humanity. But a doctor has. Hence the nobility and some of the prime disadvantages of his profession. That was one of the reasons why Henry Malcolm had chosen this remote retreat, the Forest Arms at Felindre, on the Welsh border, for his summer holiday. And that was why he felt an

acute and justifiable annoyance when, just as he was pulling
on his waders after breakfast, the landlord announced a lady
to see him.

"Miss Morgan of Bryntyrion," he said. "She says that she
knows you, sir."

"Miss Morgan? I don't remember anyone of that name.
What does she want?"

"She wants to see you, sir. She didn't say why."

"Well, show her in, Jones," said Henry Malcolm resignedly.
"No peace for the wicked!"

He pulled off his waders and put on his shoes again. Miss
Morgan... It was difficult for a physician with an extensive practice to remember the name of everyone who had
consulted him. The remoteness of the Forest Arms had its
disadvantages; in tiny places of this kind every stranger was
conspicuous. The fact that he had been run to earth like this,
within a few days of his arrival, might be taken as a compli-
ment to his celebrity as a neurologist—but that was small
consolation for the loss of a morning's sport.

"Miss Morgan," the landlord announced.

Miss Morgan entered. She came in with a nervous smile,
an odd little woman of fifty or thereabouts, dressed primly,
severely, in a fashion of twenty years since. In her face, in her
smile, there was something vaguely familiar to Malcolm, half
recalling a memory too remote to be fixed. When she spoke,
her speech was, quite obviously, that of a lady.

"I'm afraid you don't remember me, Doctor," she said.
"It's hardly to be expected. Thirty years... You were only
a boy when last I saw you. But my sister Agatha and I have
followed your wonderful career with the greatest interest and

pride, and when I heard, last night, that you were staying in the village"—tears welled into her eyes—"it seemed like an act of Providence. Ah, I'm afraid you've forgotten."

Miss Morgan? Miss Agatha Morgan? And thirty years ago? At last he had it! Two old maids, the Miss Morgans! Of course, he remembered perfectly! They lived in a tiny house, as neat as a bird's nest, at the corner of the street where Malcolm had spent his childhood. Their father was a retired colonel, a Crimean veteran, who went stumping past the schoolroom window every afternoon on his constitutional—a precise, grey-whiskered figure with an Indian cheroot in his teeth.

He remembered, above all, the smell of the Miss Morgans' sitting room, a chamber as small and orderly as a ship's cabin. It was a composite odour of furniture polish, potpourri, and cigar smoke, enveloping a confused and exotic collection of furniture: a spinet, tortured carvings of ebony, Benares brass. He remembered the red and gold of a Crown Derby tea set, the richness of Miss Agatha's fruit cake, the flavour of the guava jelly which the Colonel imported from Jamaica and which the Miss Morgans insisted on calling not "jam" but "preserve," and, even more awe-inspiring, their father's Crimean sword, which hung, in a place of honour, above the mantelpiece. Thirty years...

"Why, of course I remember," he said. "You must be Miss Susan."

She flushed, almost prettily. "How clever of you to remember my name!"

"But what are you doing here, in Felindre?" he asked. "You must tell me all about it. And how is Miss Agatha?"

"She isn't Miss Agatha any longer; she's married—her

name's Mrs. Peters. And she's not very well. That's why I have taken this…liberty."

"Liberty indeed!" He encouraged her. "Sit down and make yourself comfortable. Since I've settled in Harley Street, I rarely see old friends. I should never have forgiven you if you hadn't looked me up. I shall want to know everything that's happened since last I saw you."

She sat down nervously. "It's a very long story," she said. "If it weren't that your dear mother had been so kind to us in the old days, I should almost hesitate…"

He shook his head smilingly; the poor little withered thing was pathetic. "I can see you're in trouble," he said. "Tell me all about it. First of all, how on earth did you get here?"

She smiled, with a wan, appealing gratitude. "Perhaps," she said, "I had better begin at the beginning." She straightened her back and composed her thin hands on her lap, but Malcolm could see, by the nervous twining of her fingers, that her mind was agitated.

"About fifteen years ago," she began, "long after you had gone to London, dear Father died. He was a wonderful man, a true soldier and gentleman, and the best of fathers. We had always lived modestly, well within our income, as everybody should; but when Father died, you see, his pension died with him, and Agatha and I were left in very reduced circumstances. If we hadn't been used to careful living, I really don't know how we should have got on. But Agatha, of course, was a marvellous housekeeper—the very soul of thrift—so we managed to keep up appearances and go on living in accordance with dear Father's station. It wasn't easy, though!" She shook her head slowly.

Malcolm could see what that meant; the little room, cosy no longer; the economies of fuel in winter; the diet, which verged on starvation, of bread and margarine, the makeshift dressmaking. How many spinsters of this kind were prepared to pay this price for their faded gentility!

"However," she went on cheerfully, "we managed to pull through. Of course, from time to time we had to sell little bits of furniture. Some of the most lovely things that Father had brought from India fetched next to nothing. It was a crying shame that we had to part with them; but what could we do? If I had had my own way, I should have tried to get a post as a lady's companion or governess; but Agatha would never consent to it. 'We may be poor, Susan,' she said, 'but we're proud. Nobody in our family has ever done a thing like that. I think Father would turn in his grave,' she said, 'if we ever forgot that we are gentlewomen.' So there it was! Of course Agatha is much more strong-minded than I am. And, as I've said, we *did* manage to pull through, hard though it was, until Agatha came into the property."

"The property?" Malcolm repeated. "Come, that sounds better!" He felt a considerable relief to know that this harrowing tale of hardships would not be prolonged.

"Yes, it was most fortunate in a way," Miss Susan continued demurely, "and quite unexpected. You see," she explained, "our family is a very old one; the Morgans have been squires of Felindre for hundreds of years. When you go to church on Sunday, you'll see all our ancestors' monuments."

"Shall I?" Malcolm thought grimly. "Not if I know it! I'm on a holiday!"

"Bryntyrion, the family seat," Miss Susan went on, "had

gone to dear Father's cousin, Howell Morgan. He was very proud of it; and so, when he died, he left it to Agatha, who was his eldest living relative. Quite properly, too. It would have been dreadful to think of it going out of the family.

"Of course, it all came as a wonderful surprise to us. I'm afraid, if I had my own way—I mean, if it had been left to me—I should have wanted to sell it and settle down in some nice neighbourhood where Father's service reputation was known. But Agatha is extremely determined and has a high sense of duty. She said we were bound, out of respect for dear Father's memory, to keep up the family tradition and go and live there, even though it *was* so dreadfully out of the way."

"The property is near here?"

"Just three miles from Felindre. Quite alone in the country, and over ten miles from a railway station. Please don't misunderstand me—the property is not very valuable. Cousin Howell had sold the greater part of the estate. Apart from the house there were only a couple of farms, which were let, at the time when Agatha inherited, to tenants who run sheep on them. My sister, who is terribly courageous, would like to have taken them over and set up farming herself. But really, you know, we had lived all our lives in town, and hadn't the necessary experience; besides which, the payment of the death duties and the expense of moving into Wales left us with very little capital to spare for an adventure of that kind. Our lawyer, very wisely I think, dissuaded Agatha from embarking on it, but nothing and nobody could persuade her that it wasn't our duty to live at Bryntyrion."

"So you came there, all alone?" Malcolm asked. The hues

of romantic prosperity were already beginning to fade from the picture.

"Well, no. Not exactly alone," said Miss Susan nervously. She threw an anxious glance behind her, as though she suspected that somebody was listening, then continued in a voice that was almost lowered to a whisper:

"Not exactly alone," she repeated. "You see, it was like this. Our lawyer, who was the soul of wisdom and kindness and consideration—I cannot blame *him*—our lawyer impressed upon us most strongly the necessity of *not* being alone. At first Agatha laughed at him—she's a typical soldier's daughter, very different from me, I'm afraid—but eventually even she was forced to admit that he was right. 'You can't go out living in the wilds of Wales,' he told her, 'unless you have a capable man in the house.' The mere mention of a man was enough to make Agatha obstinate. Apart from one rather unfortunate love affair, nearly forty years ago, Agatha had never had anything to do with men. She despised them, in fact, and was almost scornful whenever I made any gentlemen friends; she said that dear Father's society was surely enough for us."

"How jealous these old maids are!" Malcolm thought, while Miss Susan continued:

"At first she refused point blank to entertain the idea. She despised me, you know, for my lack of self-reliance; but really the idea of living right out in the country like that got so much on my nerves that I'm afraid I was guilty of playing a trick on her. I told her that I was sure it would be more in keeping with the family dignity if we had a butler—not a *real* butler, of course, but a man of all work—the kind of man who was used to good service, who could open the door and take messages when our new neighbours called."

"I think that was very wise of you and entirely reasonable," Malcolm agreed.

"Yes, in principle I'm sure I was right. Of course I never dreamed..." She shook her head sadly. "I suggested that our lawyer should find a suitable man," she went on, "but Agatha would not be beholden to anybody. She said that she herself was a sufficiently good judge. So she put an advertisement in the paper and interviewed all the applicants personally. Mr. Peters was the last of the lot. From the moment when he entered the room, I could see that Agatha had made up her mind. She engaged him at once.

"And really, I must confess," Miss Susan admitted, "I completely agreed with her choice. To begin with, Peters was an extremely handsome man—the kind of figure who would lend dignity to any house. You would have said at once that he was a man who knew his place. We liked the way he said 'Madam' whenever he addressed us, and stood with his feet together. In spite of his perfect manners, there was nothing servile about him. As Agatha said at the time, it almost seemed as though he must have gentle blood in his veins. So different, in every way, from the servant type!

"Indeed, though he had been a butler once, Peters had not been in service for years. That was why he didn't bring any references with him. He had been keeping a bicycle shop ever since the war. It seemed just like fate when he told us he had served in Father's old regiment. He was wearing cycling stockings on the day when he came to apply for the post, and really, as Agatha said—his limbs were most shapely! We felt sorry for him, too: he had lately lost his wife. He said he'd been born in the country and was handy with his fingers. He could knock up a hencoop or anything like that, you know; and it quite touched our hearts when he suggested bringing his fowls along with him to Bryntyrion. There's nothing like having a hobby, Agatha said; and it would be such a change to have new-laid eggs for breakfast!"

Miss Susan sighed. Once more the tears came into her eyes. She dabbed them with her handkerchief.

"So I gather," said Malcolm encouragingly, "that this man Peters wasn't exactly a success?"

Miss Susan shook her head. "I must try," she said, "not to do him any injustice. In a sense, you see, I was responsible for him coming to us, although it was actually Agatha who chose him. At first, I must say, I thought he was marvellous. To begin with, even for such a fine man, he's exceptionally strong. All the work of moving the furniture—he made it seem just like child's play. Then again, having been brought up in the country, he knew far more than we did about farming and that sort of thing. And it was a relief, I can't deny it, to hear him whistling and singing about the place, even though the words he sang were sometimes excessively vulgar. He knew just how a house should be run, and 'bossed up' the other servants, as he used to call it. Indeed, I don't know what we should ever have done without him. As I've told you already, there was something superior about him that singled him out from the ordinary run of his class. You couldn't help thinking of him more as a bailiff than as a butler. He dealt with the tenants, collected the rents, and kept his accounts so exactly and in the most beautiful copperplate handwriting."

"Ah, now I begin to see," said Malcolm sympathetically.

"Oh, no, you don't," Miss Susan hurriedly interrupted him. "As far as money is concerned, Mr. Peters is the soul of honour. It was because of that—his reliability, I mean—that we became so dependent on him, and passed over little things that otherwise we might have objected to."

"You mean he became too familiar?"

"Well, so I thought at the time..." She hesitated. "What I noticed first of all was that he seemed to have taken a dislike to me personally. I used to hear him saying terrible things about me behind my back. The other servants must have heard."

"Of course you told your sister?"

"Of course. Up till then we had always shared our confidence. It came as a great shock to me"—her lips trembled—"when Agatha appeared to be taking his side against me. So unlike her...and so humiliating!"

"So that's it!" Malcolm thought: "Persecution mania. Poor old thing!"

"But it's no good arguing with Agatha," Miss Susan went on pitifully, "she's so strong-minded. I felt—oh, so terribly isolated: Mr. Peters and Agatha on one side and me on the other! Do you know, if I'd had a penny of my own at that time, I really believe I should have left Bryntyrion. But I hadn't even expectations. Of course, later on," she continued mysteriously, "I understood just what it meant..."

"Which was...?"

"Let me tell you in my own way. Last autumn, you see, we both of us had influenza. I took it lightly—I'm very much stronger than I look—but Agatha was left with a sort of bronchitis. It always rains here, you know. That makes the house damp, and we hadn't enough money to repair it. Well, one night I woke up and thought I heard Agatha talking. I wondered if she were wandering—delirious, you know—so I lit a candle and put on my slippers and went out on to the landing; and I saw—oh, I hardly like to tell you...!" She put her hands to her eyes—"I saw Mr. Peters coming out of Agatha's room.

"That night I didn't sleep a wink, as you can imagine. Next morning, to my surprise, Agatha got up for breakfast. I felt so ashamed that I couldn't look at her. All through the meal she never spoke a word. Then, at the end of it, she got up, folded her napkin, and said, most terribly calmly: 'Susan, I have some news for you: I'm going to marry Mr. Peters.'"

"So she isn't mad after all," Henry Malcolm thought with relief. "Well, what did you say to that?" he asked encouragingly.

"Why, of course, I protested; I said it was quite impossible. I asked her what dear Father, who was so exclusive, would have thought of a union of that kind; and that set poor Agatha off in a terrible rage: she said that she wasn't going to stand there and see her fiancé insulted. Outside of her presence, she said, I could say what I liked about Mr. Peters; but anyway he was a *Man*. Then Mr. Peters himself came in, and I had to stop."

"And she carried it through?"

"They were married three weeks later. Since that moment, Dr. Malcolm, my life has been one long agony. I can't even attempt to describe it. You see, poor Agatha lost her head completely; he could do no wrong; and Peters, who'd been bad enough before, became quite unbearable. All his beautiful manners—which, really, had been unexceptionable—were thrown to the wind. He went on with the housework, cleaning the silver and things like that; but when he sat down to table with us, he was quite disgusting. He ate like a wolf, and when he had indigestion he made no attempt to conceal it. Indeed, he used to wink at me as though he took pride in it. And Agatha—poor dear Agatha—seemed quite blind to his disgusting coarseness. He ordered her about like a slave, and she'd only smile as if she thought it was a privilege. Why, would you believe it? She didn't even protest when he brought a big brass spittoon into the drawing room! Although I always carefully called him Mr. Peters, he insisted on calling me 'Sue.' And he called her 'Aggie'—such a vulgar abbreviation! It got so much on my nerves—his vulgarity and the way in which Agatha seemed to delight in it—that I couldn't bear sitting with them. I used to go up to my bedroom and freeze there: you see, Mr. Peters wouldn't allow us to have fires upstairs. 'Coal costs money,' he said, 'and if you think I'm going to chop wood for you, you're damn well mistaken!' You must excuse the word, Dr. Malcolm, but that's what he said and that's nothing, *nothing* to the language he generally uses!"

"Well, people of that kind, you know…" Henry Malcolm began.

"Oh, of course; I know only too well; it's unbelievable. But where was I? Oh, yes. The fires…that was part of his plan. Apart from his food—he's excessively particular about that—he thinks about nothing but money. He's so mean. You can have no idea of his meanness. In the very first week after the marriage, he dismissed our maids. He said it was ridiculous to have two able-bodied women (he never calls us ladies) in the house just eating their heads off. So Agatha, if you please, just had to do the cooking and me the house-work, and if anything isn't just to his liking, you should hear the language. You've only to look at my hands, Dr. Malcolm, to see what that means!"

And she held out her pitiful, toil-stained delicate fingers.

"So now that poor Agatha's ill in bed," she went on pathet-ically, "the whole of it falls on me. I'm no better than a slave, Dr. Malcolm; yet what can I do? I ask you, what can I do?" She wrung her hands helplessly. "It's not *that* I mind," she said, "it's just Agatha's illness. In spite of all her cruelty, she's still my sister, and I simply can't bear to see her wasting away like this!" Miss Susan composed her working features rapidly. "That's why," she went on, "I've slipped away without telling them, and dared to ask you, as an old friend of Father's to come and see her. Will you come?" she entreated.

"Why, of course, I'll be glad to consult with your local doctor," Malcolm told her. "What does *he* say about her?"

She shook her head. "They won't even allow me to call him in. You see, Dr. Meredith, our nearest doctor, lives ten miles away. His visits would be expensive, and Mr. Peters has persuaded Agatha that we can't afford them. He's had some experience of nursing, he says—I think he was an attendant in an asylum at one time—and really, to do the man justice, he *is* most attentive. He prepares all her food, and washes her, and makes her bed. Agatha herself is quite satisfied; she thinks he's wonderful; but, after all, Dr. Malcolm, Peters is an ignorant man, and if you *would* be so kind…"

"Of course, I'll come," Malcolm told her. "I'll walk up to Bryntyrion this afternoon. You'd better warn them."

"Oh, I don't think I dare do that," said Miss Susan

tremulously. He watched her, a poor little shrunken figure, as she went fluttering away.

The road to Bryntyrion ran upward through lanes so deep and suffocating, between banks of over-arching hazel and insurgent bracken, that Malcolm was only aware at intervals of the line of mountain which dominated the sky like a hanging thunder cloud. The air was all dead and dense, the blank sky so white with heat, the torment of wood flies so incessant, that it was with a sense of relief that he emerged on to a higher plateau, a shelf upon the mountain's flank, and saw before him the gloomy mass of stucco that the older Miss Morgan had inherited. It was a tall house, whose rectangular building had a low-pitched roof; an ugly, eerie-looking place, whose blank, uncurtained windows gave an impression of deadness and desolation. He approached it through an unkempt avenue of wind-tortured beeches that led to a sweep of moss-grown gravel skirting a pillared portico from which the plaster had fallen in flakes that gave it an aspect of disease. It was hard to imagine that any living soul inhabited it. The bell, which Malcolm rang, seemed to echo in utter emptiness.

For a long while his summons remained unanswered; then heavy hobnails rang on the stone flags, and the warped door was pulled open with a screech. The man who opened it and glowered at him with grudging, suspicious eyes, was obviously Mr. Peters.

From that first glance Malcolm took a dislike to him. He was, as Miss Susan had indicated, by certain standards, a fine figure of a man; six feet of bulky masculinity. But the eyes of the physician saw more than that. They saw the body of a strong man who had gone soft with idleness and indulgence;

an unruly paunch; pouched eyes; cheeks above whose lax muscles a fine network of congested blood vessels showed a ruddiness that was not that of health. It was the body of a man who slept too much, ate too much, drank too much. The small eyes, set like a pig's in shallow orbits, were suffused with angry red at the inner corners. They were full of resentment, obstinacy; prepared to bluff. And yet, behind all their suspicion, fear was lurking. "This man is a coward," Malcolm thought. "I have his measure."

"Well, what do you want?" Mr. Peters asked him gruffly. He stood in the doorway, blocking it with his bulk. He was not inviting.

"You are Mr. Peters?" Malcolm asked.

"Yes. That's my name. What is it?"

"I have come to call on your wife. My name is Malcolm. I knew her when she was Miss Morgan."

"You can't see her," said Peters stolidly. "She's ill in bed."

"I'm sorry to hear that," said Malcolm blandly. "However, I'm glad I came. You see, I'm a doctor."

"A doctor?" Peters repeated. ("Yes, he's afraid," Malcolm thought.) "That makes no difference," the man went on. "It's nothing serious. I'm a bit of a nurse myself," he continued, with a smile that was not meant to be ugly. "What's more, Mrs. Peters has a great dislike to doctors. She refuses to see one, though I've pressed her again and again. Besides, she's asleep just now, and that's what she needs. I'm not going to wake her for you or anyone!" he added obstinately.

"Don't you think it's a pity to miss this opportunity?" Malcolm urged. "You see, I'm a very old friend of the family's: I knew her father, Colonel Morgan. I'm leaving the district tomorrow, and I think both she and Miss Susan would be disappointed if I missed seeing them."

"I don't know where Susan is," Peters answered. "And as for my wife, I've told you I'm not going to wake her."

"And I tell you I'm going to see her," said Malcolm firmly.

"Look here, I'd have you know this is my house," Peters blustered.

"It is not your house…not yet. And I'm going to see her."

The gross man went red in the face. His shoulders went back. It looked, for one moment, as if he intended violence. Then his pig-eyelids fluttered, his protruded lips relaxed into an uneasy smile; his truculence vanished; he became, in one moment, that mixture of dignity and obsequiousness, which is the well-trained manservant. With the manners of a perfect butler, he bowed and stood aside for Malcolm to enter.

"Perhaps you are right, sir," he said. "It's not very often Mrs. Peters has the chance of seeing old friends. And to tell you the truth," he admitted, "I *am* a bit worried about her. Will you be so good as to wait here a minute?"

He showed Malcolm into a dank drawing-room, in which, among the relics of the Colonel's house, he recognised traces of Mr. Peters's occupation: the big brass spittoon, of which Miss Susan had told him; an odour of stale shag tobacco; a copy of the *Police Budget*, and a barrel of beer supported on an eighteenth-century love seat. Within a few moments Peters lumbered in again.

"She's awake," he said, "and says she'll be pleased to see you. Only, if you'll take my advice, as one who knows her in and out, you'll be wise not to mention her illness. It only upsets her. All the same, I should take it as a great kindness on your part," he added, "if you'd just run your eye over her as a doctor, like, and give me any hints that come into your mind when you're alone with me afterwards. I don't say there's anything to worry about, but you never know..."

"No, you never know," Malcolm agreed. "Perhaps it would be just as well if you told me her symptoms beforehand?"

"Well, you see," Mr. Peters confided, "it's this indigestion. It's been troubling her for months. It's what I should call the acidity. She can't peck no more than a bird; and, of course, that means she's lost flesh. Seeing the way she was, I've taken no risks. A milk diet, just slops, nothing solid to bring on the pain. And no morsel of food has passed her lips, sir, that I haven't prepared with my own hands. Then she's had some trouble with her nerves as well; but I think that's just the result of lying in bed. One thing I will say, though, I couldn't have paid her more attention if she'd been my own child. And she'll tell you the same."

"Well, she *is* your own wife, isn't she?" Malcolm suggested.

Mr. Peters preceded him upstairs; through their creaking progress Malcolm became more than ever oppressed by Bryntyrion's dank emptiness. He wondered wherever that poor little Miss Susan had got to; he pictured her trembling in her bedroom, aware of his presence. Mr. Peters, with admirable decorum, knocked at the door. They entered.

"Here's Dr. Malcolm, love," said Peters kindly.

"It's very good of him, I'm sure," a feeble voice answered.

Even Malcolm, who was used to such sights, was shocked by the woman's appearance. Instead of the Miss Agatha he remembered, a strong, dark creature with a certain grim hardness about her firm, handsome features, he saw a frail wisp of a woman with scanty grey hair, yellow and wasted. He took a seat at her bedside and pressed her thin hand. She gave a little gasp: "Oh, you hurt me!" she said. "My fingers are so tender I can scarcely bear any one to touch them. Edward"—she beamed wanly on her husband—"is always very gentle with me. I'm so glad you have met him."

Malcolm was curiously touched by the humble gratitude of the glance which she gave Mr. Peters. Her eyes dwelt on him tenderly; it was obvious that she wanted the visitor to see the best of him. If ever he had seen love, blind devotion in a woman's eyes, Malcolm thought, he could see it in those. And Peters himself seemed different, gentle, solicitous. He wondered if, after all, he had done the man an injustice. But that tenderness in the fingers...? His medical mind was at work.

All through their talk, which was of old times, his boyhood, the Colonel, his mind kept on working, his eyes were never at rest. Miss Agatha, as he still thought of her, went on talking with a gentle dreaminess, eagerly contriving to draw Mr. Peters into their conversation, displaying his unapparent virtues with the care of a mother showing off an uncomely child. Only when he happened to mention Miss Susan's name did her voice, her features, harden.

"I hardly like to tell you," she said, "but Susan has not behaved well. She objected to our marriage. You can see for yourself how unreasonably," she added, with a loving glance at Mr. Peters. Mr. Peters, embarrassed, smiled and cleared his throat.

That tenderness of the fingers...that history of dyspepsia...that queer pigmentation of the skin...

Tactfully, almost without letting her know it, Malcolm

diverted the conversation in the direction of Miss Agatha's illness. "She doesn't like to talk about it," Peters protested. "It always upsets her."

"Still, it does seem like missing an opportunity when the doctor's here," Miss Agatha replied.

Yes, for a long time she had been suffering from indigestion; she'd always had that tendency, but lately it had become much worse. Indeed, she couldn't imagine what she would have done without Edward. In times of sickness Susan was absolutely useless. But Edward—would he believe it?—was a perfect invalid cook. Such delicious, light, appetising food he prepared for her. And all with his own hands! If she'd had a trained nurse in the house, she couldn't have been more comfortable. Apart from the indigestion, there wasn't much wrong with her—nothing except that queer tenderness which had made her jump when they shook hands. Oh, no, it wasn't only in the fingers, it was in the arms as well. And in her legs, too; she could scarcely bear the touch of the bedclothes. And an odd tingling and numbness—as if they had gone to sleep! But that wasn't anything serious, really, was it?

"If you'd let me examine you for a moment," Malcolm suggested, "I'll try to be just as gentle with you as your husband."

"I'm not going to have you upset, love," said Peters, with a flash of the old stubbornness.

"I'd like him to, Edward darling," his wife entreated. By this time, whether she liked it or no, Malcolm meant to have his way. A perfunctory examination was enough to confirm his conjectures. The case was quite simple—a general peripheral neuritis. Three causes—three only, for alcohol was out of the question. Lead, antimony, chronic arsenical poisoning.

How...why? The answer to both of these questions seemed fairly obvious.

"It isn't serious?" Miss Agatha was saying. "It will be a great comfort to my dear husband if you can tell him that."

Malcolm smiled. "It's not serious at all. If you follow my instructions religiously, you'll be well in a month. I'm ready to promise you that, if you do what I tell you."

"You may be sure we'll do that," said Peters, with humble gratitude. "I'm sure we're much obliged to you. This is a great relief."

"I'll talk to you downstairs. There's no point in tiring her further," said Malcolm.

Mr. Peters had spoken truly when he said that the verdict was a great relief. He seemed almost boyish and excited as he led Malcolm into the drawing room and offered him a glass of beer.

"You've taken a great weight off my mind, Doctor," he said. "Now what shall we do? I'll drive into town this evening and fetch out the medicine."

He spoke boisterously, confidently; the fear had gone out of his eyes; he was the perfect picture of a relieved, a devoted husband.

Malcolm chose his words carefully:

"Mr. Peters, I've said that this case is not serious. Well, it isn't—it won't be—if you obey my prescription to the letter. The person I'm most concerned about is not your wife but yourself."

"Why, Doctor, you're wrong. I was never better in my life."

"Ah, there you're mistaken, my friend. As a doctor I know better. I'm being quite candid when I tell you that your life is in danger. Wait a moment—let me go on. All this long anxiety, all this watching at your wife's bedside, all this delicate invalid cookery—unless we do something about it, I won't answer for the consequences. Your obvious anxiety has been getting on the poor woman's nerves. You play on each other. You're having a bad effect on her. This isn't a matter of medicine, it's plain common sense. Now listen to me. There's no time to be lost. You must leave Bryntyrion this evening. Go right away from here!"

"But, Doctor!" Mr. Peters was pale as a sheet, his thick lips quivered. "No doubt she will miss you," Malcolm continued smoothly. "But it's you who have to be considered, Mr. Peters. You leave Bryntyrion this evening. If you don't come back, I guarantee she'll be better in a month. Miss Susan will have to take up the invalid cookery; she's perfectly capable of doing so, don't you worry. Now remember," he went on sternly, "you are going away this evening. I advise you not to tell anyone when or where. If you don't come back—well, that will be even better for you. If you *do* come back, I shall know. Be quite sure of that! So I warn you, here and now, it's a matter of life and death. Understand?"

From the blanched terror in Peters's eyes Malcolm knew that he understood.

He left Bryntyrion, that ghastly house, without another word. Midway on his journey homeward a frail black figure fluttered out of the hedge. It was little Miss Susan, who had run down the hill to intercept him.

"You've seen him…and her?" she gasped. "Oh, is it all right?"

"It's all right, Miss Susan," he told her. "You'll have to get busy. Your brother-in-law is going on a holiday."

"A holiday? Where?" she stammered.

"I haven't the least idea where. But he's going. That's all that matters. I want you to promise me one thing," he went on calmly. "I am returning to London tomorrow by the first train; I shan't see you again. Now if Mr. Peters has not left Bryntyrion by then, or if he comes back—which I don't think he will—or if anything happens that you think I'd like to know—and I want to know everything—will you promise to send me a wire to my house in Harley Street? Number forty-seven. Be sure you remember."

"Yes, yes, I'll remember," she said eagerly. "But Agatha, Doctor…?"

"I promise you that Agatha will be as well as you are in a month."

"Oh, how can I thank you?" she cried.

"You needn't thank me," he laughed. "But don't forget what I've told you. Now run along home to your sister; she may be needing you."

Next evening, when Malcolm opened the door of his house in Harley Street, he found a telegram awaiting him in the hall. Although he guessed what was inside it, he opened it eagerly.

"*Terrible accident,*" he read, "*Peters shot dead accidentally this evening while cleaning gun. Susan Morgan.*"

With a smile of satisfaction on his face, he tore the telegram into fragments. The last day of his holiday, he reflected, had been the most profitable of all.

1936

Change

Arthur Machen

Arthur Llewellyn Jones was born in Caerleon,
Monmouthshire, in 1863. His father, a vicar, adopted the
name Machen in order to inherit a legacy (which sounds rather
like the premise for a mystery story in itself) and the boy was
baptised under the name Jones-Machen. He went to London,
but failed to get into medical school and drifted around the
fringes of the publishing world for several years, writing under
the name Arthur Machen. He developed an interest in the
occult, and his breakthrough novel, *The Great God Pan*, published in 1894, was inspired by memories of visiting the ruins
of a pagan temple in Wales. Together with *The Three Imposters*
(1895), it remains his most famous work, but he continued to
write prolifically for many years. He died in 1947.

Over the years, Machen's reputation has had something of
a roller-coaster ride, but it is now widely agreed that he was
a major figure in the history of popular fiction. His admirers
have included T. S. Eliot, John Masefield, Jorge Luis Borges,
and George Bernard Shaw as well as other gifted exponents

of macabre fiction such as H. P. Lovecraft, Peter Straub, and Stephen King. His Welsh background and fascination with Welsh mysticism are key elements of his work. And although, if one has to label his work, it is horror rather than crime fiction, an anthology of Welsh mysteries would surely be incomplete if it excluded Machen. This story comes from *The Children of the Pool*, published in 1936.

———

"Here," said old Mr. Vincent Rimmer, fumbling in the pigeon-holes of his great and ancient bureau, "is an oddity which may interest you."

He drew a sheet of paper out of the dark place where it had been hidden, and handed it to Reynolds, his curious guest. The oddity was an ordinary sheet of notepaper, of a sort which has long been popular; a bluish grey with slight flecks and streaks of a darker blue embedded in its substance. It had yellowed a little with age at the edges. The outer page was blank; Reynolds laid it open, and spread it out on the table beside his chair. He read something like this:

a	aa	e	ee	i	e	ee
aa	i	i	o	e	ee	o
ee	ee	i	aa	o	oo	o
a	o	a	a	e	i	ee
e	o	i	ee	a	e	i

Reynolds scanned it with stupefied perplexity.

"What on earth is it?" he said. "Does it mean anything? Is it a cypher, or a silly game, or what?"

Mr. Rimmer chuckled. "I thought it might puzzle you," he remarked. "Do you happen to notice anything about the writing; anything out of the way at all?"

Reynolds scanned the document more closely.

"Well, I don't know that there is anything out of the way in the script itself. The letters are rather big, perhaps, and they are rather clumsily formed. But it's difficult to judge handwriting by a few letters, repeated again and again. But, apart from the writing, what is it?"

"That's a question that must wait a bit. There are many strange things related to that bit of paper. But one of the strangest things about it is this; that it is intimately connected with the Darren Mystery."

"What Mystery did you say? The Darren Mystery? I don't think I ever heard of it."

"Well, it was a little before your time. And, in any case, I don't see how you could have heard of it. There were, certainly, some very curious and unusual circumstances in the case, but I don't think that they were generally known, and if they were known, they were not understood. You don't wonder at that, perhaps, when you consider that the bit of paper before you was one of those circumstances."

"But what exactly happened?"

"That is largely a matter of conjecture. But, anyhow, here's the outside of the case, for a beginning. Now, to start with, I don't suppose you've ever been to Meirion? Well, you should go. It's a beautiful county, in West Wales, with a fine sea-coast, and some very pleasant places to stay at, and none of them too large or too popular. One of the smallest of these places, Trenant, is just a village. There is a wooded height above it called the Allt; and down below, the church, with a Celtic Cross in the churchyard, a dozen or so of cottages, a row of lodging-houses on the slope round the corner, a few more cottages dotted along the road to Meiros, and that's all. Below the village are marshy meadows where the brook that comes from the hills spreads abroad, and then the dunes, and the sea, stretching away to the Dragon's Head in the far east and enclosed to the west by the beginnings of the limestone cliffs. There are fine, broad sands all the way between Trenant and Porth, the market-town, about a mile and a half away, and it's just the place for children.

"Well, just forty-five years ago, Trenant was having a very successful season. In August there must have been eighteen or nineteen visitors in the village. I was staying in Porth at the time, and, when I walked over, it struck me that the Trenant beach was quite crowded—eight or nine children castle-building and learning to swim, and looking for shells, and all the usual diversions. The grown-up people sat in groups on the edge of the dunes and read and gossiped, or took a turn towards Porth, or perhaps tried to catch prawns in the rock-pools at the other end of the sands. Altogether a very pleasant, happy scene in its simple way, and, as it was a beautiful summer, I have no doubt they all enjoyed themselves very much. I walked to Trenant and back three or four times, and I noticed that most of the children were more or less in charge of a very pretty dark girl, quite young, who seemed to advise in laying out the ground-plan of the castle, and to take off her stockings and tuck up her skirts—we thought a lot of Legs in those days—when the bathers required supervision. She also indicated the kinds of shells which deserved the attention of collectors: an extremely serviceable girl.

"It seemed that this girl, Alice Hayes, was really in charge of the children—or of the greater part of them. She was a sort of nursery-governess or lady of all work to Mrs. Brown, who had come down from London in the early part of July with Miss Hayes and little Michael, a child of eight, who refused to recover nicely from his attack of measles. Mr. Brown had joined them at the end of the month with the two elder children, Jack and Rosamund. Then, there were the Smiths, with their little family, and the Robinsons with their three; and the fathers and mothers, sitting on the beach every morning, got to know each other very easily. Mrs. Smith and Mrs. Robinson soon appreciated Miss Hayes's merits as a child-herd; they noticed that Mrs. Brown sat placid and went on knitting in the sun, quite safe and unperturbed, while they suffered from recurrent alarms. Jack Smith, though barely fourteen, would be seen dashing through the waves, out to sea, as if he had quite made up his mind to swim to the Dragon's Head, about twenty miles away, or Jane Robinson, in bright pink, would appear suddenly right away among the rocks of the point, ready to vanish into the perilous unknown round the corner. Hence, alarums and excursions, tiring expeditions of rescue and remonstrance, through soft sand or over slippery rocks under a hot sun. And then these ladies would discover that certain of their offspring had entirely disappeared or were altogether missing from the landscape; and dreadful and true tales of children who had driven tunnels into the sand and had been overwhelmed therein rushed to the mind. And all the while Mrs. Brown sat serene, confident in the overseership of her Miss Hayes. So, as was to be gathered, the other two took counsel together. Mrs. Brown was approached, and something called an arrangement was made, by which Miss Hayes undertook the joint mastership of all three packs, greatly to the ease of Mrs. Smith and Mrs. Robinson."

It was about this time, I suppose, that I got to know this group of holiday-makers. I had met Smith, whom I knew slightly in town, in the streets of Porth, just as I was setting out for one of my morning walks. We strolled together to Trenant on the firm sand down by the water's edge, and introductions went round, and so I joined the party, and sat with them, watching the various diversions of the children and the capable superintendence of Miss Hayes.

"Now there's a queer thing about this little place," said Brown, a genial man, connected, I believe, with Lloyd's. "Wouldn't you say this was as healthy a spot as any you could find? Well sheltered from the north, southern aspect, never too cold in winter, fresh sea-breeze in summer: what could you have more?"

"Well," I replied, "it always agrees with me very well: a little relaxing, perhaps, but I like being relaxed. Isn't it a healthy place, then? What makes you think so?"

"I'll tell you. We have rooms in Govan Terrace, up there on the hill-side. The other night I woke up with a coughing fit. I got out of bed to get a drink of water, and then had a look out of the windows to see what sort of night it was. I didn't like the look of those clouds in the south-west after sunset the night before. As you can see, the upper windows of Govan Terrace command a good many of the village houses. And, do you know, there was a light in almost every house? At two o'clock in the morning. Apparently, the village is full of sick people. But who would have thought it?"

We were sitting a little apart from the rest. Smith had brought a London paper from Porth, and he and Robinson had their heads together over the City article. The three women were knitting and talking hard, and down by the blue, creaming water Miss Hayes and her crew were playing happily in the sunshine.

"Do you mind," I said to Brown, "if I swear you to secrecy? A limited secrecy: I don't want you to speak of this to any of the village people. They wouldn't like it. And have you told your wife or any of the party about what you saw?"

"As a matter of fact, I haven't said a word to anybody. Illness isn't a very cheerful topic for a holiday, is it? But what's up? You don't mean to say there's some sort of epidemic in the place that they're keeping dark? I say! That would be awful. We should have to leave at once. Think of the children."

"Nothing of the kind. I don't think that there's a single case of illness in the place—unless you count old Thomas Evans, who has been in what he calls a decline for thirty years. You won't say anything? Then I'm going to give you a shock. The people have a light burning in their houses all night to keep out the fairies."

I must say it was a success. Brown looked frightened. Not of the fairies; most certainly not; rather at the reversion of his established order of things. He occupied his business in the City; he lived in an extremely comfortable house at Addiscombe; he was a keen though sane adherent of the Liberal Party; and in the world between these points there was no room at all either for fairies or for people who believed in fairies. The latter were almost as fabulous to him as the former, and still more objectionable.

"Look here!" he said at last. "You're pulling my leg. Nobody believes in fairies. They haven't for hundreds of years. Shakespeare didn't believe in fairies. He says so."

I let him run on. He implored me to tell him whether it was typhoid, or only measles, or even chicken-pox. I said at last:

"You seem very positive on the subject of fairies. Are you sure there are no such things?"

"Of course I am," said Brown, very crossly.

"How do you know?"

It is a shocking thing to be asked a question like that, to which, be it observed, there is no answer. I left him seething dangerously.

"Remember," I said, "not a word of lit windows to anybody; but if you are uneasy as to epidemics, ask the doctor about it."

He nodded his head glumly. I knew he was drawing all sorts of false conclusions; and for the rest of our stay I would say that he did not seek me out—until the last day of his visit. I had no doubt that he put me down as a believer in fairies and a maniac; but it is, I consider, good for men who live between the City and Liberal Politics and Addiscombe to be made to realise that there is a world elsewhere. And, as it happens, it was quite true that most of the Trenant people believed in the fairies and were horribly afraid of them.

But this was only an interlude. I often strolled over and joined the party. And I took up my freedom with the young members by contributing posts and a tennis net to the beach sports. They had brought down rackets and balls, in the vague idea that they might be able to get a game somehow and somewhere, and my contribution was warmly welcomed. I helped Miss Hayes to fix the net, and she marked out the court, with the help of many suggestions from the elder children, to which she did not pay the slightest attention. I think the constant disputes as to whether the ball was "in" or "out" brightened the game, though Wimbledon would not have approved. And sometimes the elder children accompanied their parents to Porth in the evening and watched the famous Japanese Jugglers or Pepper's Ghost at the Assembly Rooms, or listened to the Mysterious Musicians at the De Barry Gardens—and altogether everybody had, you would say, a very jolly time.

It all came to a dreadful end. One morning when I had come out on my usual morning stroll from Porth, and had got to the camping ground of the party at the edge of the dunes, I found somewhat to my surprise that there was nobody there. I was afraid that Brown had been in part justified in his dread of concealed epidemics, and that some of the children had "caught something" in the village. So I walked up in the direction of Govan Terrace, and found Brown standing at the bottom of his flight of steps, and looking very much upset.

I hailed him.

"I say," I began, "I hope you weren't right, after all. None of the children down with measles, or anything of that sort?"

"It's something worse than measles. We none of us know what has happened. The doctor can make nothing of it. Come in, and we can talk it over."

Just then a procession came down the steps leading from a house a few doors further on. First of all there was the porter from the station, with a pile of luggage on his truck. Then came the two elder Smith children, Jack and Millicent, and finally, Mr. and Mrs. Smith. Mr. Smith was carrying something wrapped in a bundle in his arms.

"Where's Bob?" He was the youngest; a brave, rosy little man of five or six.

"Smith's carrying him," murmured Brown.

"What's happened? Has he hurt himself on the rocks? I hope it's nothing serious."

I was going forward to make my enquiries, but Brown put a hand on my arm and checked me. Then I looked at the Smith party more closely, and I saw at once that there was something very much amiss. The two elder children had been crying, though the boy was doing his best to put up a brave face against disaster—whatever it was. Mrs. Smith had drawn her veil over her face, and stumbled as she walked, and on Smith's face there was a horror as of ill dreams.

"Look," said Brown in his low voice.

Smith had half-turned, as he set out with his burden to walk down the hill to the station. I don't think he knew we were there; I don't think any of the party had noticed us as we stood on the bottom step, half-hidden by a blossoming shrub. But as he turned uncertainly, like a man in the dark, the wrappings fell away a little from what he carried, and I saw a little wizened, yellow face peering out; malignant, deplorable.

I turned helplessly to Brown, as that most wretched procession went on its way and vanished out of sight.

"What on earth has happened? That's not Bobby. Who is it?"

"Come into the house," said Brown, and he went before me up the long flight of steps that led to the terrace.

There was a shriek and a noise of thin, shrill, high-pitched laughter as we came into the lodging-house.

"That's Miss Hayes in blaspheming hysterics," said Brown grimly. "My wife's looking after her. The children are in the room at the back. I daren't let them go out by themselves in this awful place." He beat with his foot on the floor and glared at me, awe-struck, a solid man shaken.

"Well," he said at last, "I'll tell you what we know; and as far as I can make out, that's very little. However… You know Miss Hayes, who helps Mrs. Brown with the children, had more or less taken over the charge of the lot; the young Robinsons and the Smiths, too. You've seen how well she looks after them all on the sands in the morning. In the afternoon she's been taking them inland for a change. You know there's beautiful country if you go a little way inland; rather wild and woody; but still very nice; pleasant and shady. Miss Hayes thought that the all-day glare of the sun on the sands might not be very good for the small ones, and my wife agreed with her. So they took their teas with them and picnicked in the woods and enjoyed themselves very much, I believe. They didn't go more than a couple of miles or three at the outside; and the little ones used to take turns in a go-cart. They never seemed too tired.

"Yesterday at lunch they were talking about some caves at a place called the Darren, about two miles away. My children seemed very anxious to see them, and Mrs. Probert, our landlady, said they were quite safe, so the Smiths and Robinsons were called in, and they were enthusiastic, too; and the whole party set off with their tea-baskets, and candles and matches, in Miss Hayes's charge. Somehow they made a later start than usual, and from what I could make out they enjoyed themselves so much in the cool dark cave, first of all exploring, and then looking for treasure, and winding up with tea by candlelight, that they didn't notice how the time was going—nobody had a watch—and by the time they'd packed up their traps and come out from underground, it was quite dark. They had a little trouble making out the way at first, but not very much, and came along in high spirits, tumbling over molehills and each other, and finding it all quite an adventure.

"They had got down in the road there, and were sorting themselves out into the three parties, when somebody called out: "Where's Bobby Smith?" Well, he wasn't there. The usual story; everybody thought he was with somebody else. They were all mixed up in the dark, talking and laughing and shrieking at the top of their voices, and taking everything for granted—I suppose it was like that. But poor little Bob was missing. You can guess what a scene there was. Everybody was much too frightened to scold Miss Hayes, who had no doubt been extremely careless, to say the least of it—not like her. Robinson pulled us together. He told Mrs. Smith that the little chap would be perfectly all right: there were no precipices to fall over and no water to fall into, the way they'd been, that it was a warm night, and the child had had a good stuffing tea, and he would be as right as rain when they found him. So we got a man from the farm, with a lantern, and Miss Hayes to show us exactly where they'd been, and Smith and Robinson and I went off to find poor Bobby, feeling a good deal better than at first. I noticed that the farm man seemed a good deal put out when we told him what had happened and where we were going. 'Got lost in the Darren,' he said, 'indeed, that is a pity.' That set off Smith at once; and he asked Williams what he meant; what was the matter with the place? Williams said there was nothing the matter with it at all whatever but it was 'a tiresome place to be in after dark.' That reminded me of what you were saying a couple of weeks ago about the people here. 'Some damned superstitious nonsense,' I said to myself, and thanked God it was nothing worse. I thought the fellow might be going to tell us of a masked bog or something like that. I gave Smith a hint in a whisper as to where the land lay; and we went on, hoping to come on little Bob any minute. Nearly all the way we were going through open fields without any cover or bracken or anything of that sort, and Williams kept twirling his lantern, and Miss Hayes and the rest of us called out the child's name; there didn't seem much chance of missing him.

"However, we saw nothing of him—till we got to the Darren. It's an odd sort of place, I should think. You're in an ordinary field, with a gentle upward slope, and you come to a gate, and down you go into a deep, narrow valley; a regular nest of valleys as far as I could make out in the dark, one leading into another, and the sides covered with trees. The famous caves were on one of these steep slopes, and, of course, we all went in. They didn't stretch far; nobody could have got lost in them, even if the candles gave out. We searched the place thoroughly, and saw where the children had had their tea: no signs of Bobby. So we went on down the valley between the woods, till we came to where it opens out into a wide space, with one tree growing all alone in the middle. And then we heard a miserable whining noise, like some little creature that's got hurt. And there under the tree was—what you saw poor Smith carrying in his arms this morning.

"It fought like a wild cat when Smith tried to pick it up, and jabbered some unearthly sort of gibberish. Then Miss Hayes came along and seemed to soothe it; and it's been quiet ever since. The man with the lantern was shaking with terror; the sweat was pouring down his face."

I stared hard at Brown. "And," I thought to myself, "you are very much in the same condition as Williams." Brown was obviously overcome with dread.

We sat there in silence.

"Why do you say 'it'?" I asked. Why don't you say 'him'?"

"You saw."

"Do you mean to tell me seriously that you don't believe that child you helped to bring home was Bobby? What does Mrs. Smith say?"

"She says the clothes are the same. I suppose it must be Bobby. The doctor from Porth says the child must have had a severe shock. I don't think he knows anything about it."

He stuttered over his words, and said at last:

"I was thinking of what you said about the lighted windows. I hoped you might be able to help. Can you do anything? We are leaving this afternoon; all of us. Is there nothing to be done?"

"I am afraid not."

I had nothing else to say. We shook hands and parted without more words.

"The next day I walked over to the Darren. There was something fearful about the place, even in the haze of a golden afternoon. As Brown had said, the entrance and the disclosure of it were sudden and abrupt. The fields of the approach held no hint of what was to come. Then, past the gate, the ground fell violently away on every side, grey rocks of an ill shape pierced through it, and the ash trees on the steep slopes overshadowed all. The descent was into silence, without the singing of a bird, into a wizard shade. At the farther end, where the wooded heights retreated somewhat, there was the open space, or circus, of turf; and in the middle of it a very ancient, twisted thorn tree, beneath which the party in the dark had found the little creature that whined and cried out in unknown speech. I turned about, and on my way back I entered the caves, and lit the carriage candle I had brought with me. There was nothing much to see—I never think there is much to see in caves. There was the place where the children and others before them had taken their tea, with a ring of blackened stones within which many fires of twigs had been kindled. In caves or out of caves, townsfolk in the country are always alike in leaving untidy and unseemly litter behind; and here were the usual scraps of greasy paper, daubed with smears of jam and butter, the half-eaten sandwich, and the gnawed crust. Amidst all this nastiness I saw a piece of folded notepaper, and in sheer idleness picked it up and opened it. You have just seen it. When I asked you if you saw anything peculiar about the writing, you said that the letters were rather big and clumsy. The reason of that is that they were written by a child. I don't think you examined the back of the second leaf. Look: 'Rosamund'—Rosamund Brown, that is. And beneath; there, in the corner."

Reynolds looked, and read, and gaped aghast.

"That was—her other name; her name in the dark."

"Name in the dark?"

"In the dark night of the Sabbath. That pretty girl had caught them all. They were in her hands, those wretched children, like the clay images she made. I found one of those things, hidden in a cleft of the rocks, near the place where they had made their fire. I ground it into dust beneath my feet."

"And I wonder what her name was?"

"They called her, I think, the Bridegroom and the Bride."

"Did you ever find out who she was, or where she came from?"

"Very little. Only that she had been a mistress at the Home for Christian Orphans in North Tottenham, where there was a hideous scandal some years before."

"Then she must have been older than she looked, according to your description."

"Possibly."

They sat in silence for a few minutes. Then Reynolds said:

"But I haven't asked you about this formula, or whatever you may call it—all these vowels, here. Is it a cypher?"

"No. But it is really a great curiosity, and it raises some extraordinary questions, which are outside this particular case. To begin with—and I am sure I could go much farther back than my beginning, if I had the necessary scholarship—I once read an English rendering of a Greek manuscript of the second or third century—I won't be certain which. It's a long time since I've seen the thing. The translator and editor of it was of the opinion that it was a Mithraic Ritual; but I have gathered that weightier authorities are strongly inclined to discredit this view. At any rate, it was no doubt an initiation rite into some mystery; possibly it had Gnostic connections; I don't know. But our interest lies in this, that one of the stages or portals, or whatever you call them, consisted, almost exactly, of that formula you have in your hand. I don't say that the vowels and double vowels are in the same order; I don't think the Greek manuscript has any *aes* or *aas*. But it is perfectly clear that the two documents are of the same kind, and have the same purpose. And, advancing a little in time from the Greek manuscript, I don't think it is very surprising that the final operation of an incantation in mediaeval and later magic consisted of this wailing on vowels arranged in a certain order.

"But here is something that is surprising. A good many years ago I strolled one Sunday morning into a church in Bloomsbury, the headquarters of a highly respectable sect. And in the middle of a very dignified ritual, there rose, quite suddenly, without preface or warning, this very sound, a wild wail on vowels. The effect was astounding, anyhow; whether it was terrifying or merely funny, is a matter of taste. You'll have guessed what I heard: they call it 'speaking with tongues,' and they believe it to be a heavenly language. And I need scarcely say that they mean very well. But the problem is: how did a congregation of solid Scotch Presbyterians hit on that queer, ancient and not over-sanctified method of expressing spiritual emotion? It is a singular puzzle.

"And that woman? That is not by any means so difficult. The good Scotchmen—I can't think how they did it—got hold of something that didn't belong to them: she was in her own tradition. And, as they say down there: *asakai dasa*: the darkness is undying."

1938

Error at Daybreak

Carter Dickson

Carter Dickson was the principal pen-name used by John
Dickson Carr (1906–1977), one of the leading exponents
of Golden Age detective fiction and a grand master of the
locked room mystery. Carr was American by birth, but he
married an Englishwoman and spent much of his adult life in
Britain. He created several memorable detective characters,
most notably Dr. Gideon Fell and Sir Henry Merrivale, but
also Henri Bencolin and Colonel March of Scotland Yard.

March only appeared in short stories, gathered in the volume *The Department of Queer Complaints*, but their quality is
high, and a single season of twenty-six television episodes star-
ring Boris Karloff was broadcast in the U.S. from December
1954 and subsequently in the UK. Many of the episodes
were written specifically for the series, but some were based
on original stories. "Error at Daybreak" first appeared in *The
Strand Magazine* in July 1938, and the TV adaptation is cred-
ited to Leslie Slote. Slote was a political spokesman who had
a curious literary sideline; his obituary in the *New York Times*

explains that he fronted as a screenwriter for writers who had been blacklisted for alleged Communism. The cast for the episode included two actors who would become well-known: Adrienne Corri and a very young Richard O'Sullivan.

———

UNDER THE WHITE LIGHT OF DAYBREAK, THE BEACH seemed deserted for a full half-mile towards the headland. The tide was out, showing a muddy slope at the foot of smooth sand. But it had begun to turn, and flat edges of surf moved snakily back towards the beach.

A narrow lane led down to it, between the high and crooked banks which closed it off from the road. Until you were well out on the sands it was impossible even to see Norman Kane's cottage some distance up towards the right. But one landmark showed in a dark wedge against sand and sea. For several hundred yards out into the water a line of rocks ran in humped formation, curved at the end, in a way that suggested the paw of an animal. It seemed to catch at the incoming tide. Bill Stacey knew it at once for the Lion's Paw, and he set off down the lane towards the beach.

It is to Stacey's credit that he still felt moderately cheerful after having just tramped two miles on an empty stomach, carrying a heavy suitcase. Norman Kane had specified the train he was to take from London, and the wayside station at which it would land him. But Kane had said nothing about a certain lack of transport at that hour of the morning.

The prospect of seeing Marion—Kane's niece and secretary—so cheered him that he forgot the matter. He did not know whether Kane knew he was in love with Marion. Norman Kane had for him the slightly amused tolerance with which Kane would naturally regard an easy-going journalist like Stacey. And Stacey, in turn, had concealed from a hero-worshipping Marion his belief that Norman Kane was an imposing, dignified, and strenuous crook.

For in his way Kane was a great man, a power in the City and a company-juggler of skill. And he was genuinely fond of Marion, as he was of all his dependants. With his theatricalism went tireless energy; it was only at Dr. Hastings's orders, when he had developed signs of a bad heart, that he had been dragged off for the summer to South Wales.

Heart trouble, Stacey knew, was often the case with these ex-athletes who have run to fat. Kane's worried looks, Marion's worried looks, had disturbed him the last time he saw them. But, as he came out on the beach in the morning light, he felt that nothing ever could happen to Kane.

There was the man himself. Even at a distance he recognised Kane's bulky figure, jauntily wrapped in a dark-red bath-robe with white facings, striding along with a towel over his arm, kicking the sand out of his way with rubber slippers. His bath-robe made a spot of colour against that lonely shore, where the Lion's Paw stretched out into the tide.

And Kane strode out briskly along the Paw. He was not going to bathe. He was going out along the rocks to dive.

"Here!" Stacey said aloud. Swimming, in that sea, with a bad heart? The mutter of the surf was growing as it drove in, and the farther end of the Paw was already awash.

"Ahoy there!" he yelled. "Kane! Hoy!"

The cry seemed to linger in emptiness across the sands.

But it reached Kane, who turned round. He was some fifty yards out on the ridge, but he lifted his towel and waved it.

"Ahoy, my lad!" he bellowed back. "I didn't expect you so early. Come for a dip! The water's fine. Everything is—"

Then it happened.

Stacey never forgot that big, greyish-haired figure, framed against the sea and the dark crook of the Lion's Paw. He was too far away to catch the expression on Kane's face. But Kane's voice died away in a gulp, a puzzled kind of gulp, and his shoulders drew together. For a moment he stood looking at the beach, swaying a little and pressing his arms as though he were cold. Then he pitched forward on his face like a bag of sand.

It was a second or two before Stacey began to run. As he did so he noticed other figures moving on the beach. From some distance away to the right, in the direction of Kane's cottage, he saw Marion running towards him. There was a gleam on her yellow hair; she wore a bathing-suit and a beach-robe blown out by the wind. Behind her lumbered Dr. Hastings, in a white linen suit.

But Stacey did not wait for them. He knew instinctively that something had happened to Norman Kane, something that was worse than a faint.

Along the top of the Lion's Paw there had been worn a natural sunken path some two feet wide. Picking his way out across this, he found Kane's great bulk wedged into it. Kane's right hand, still clutching the towel, was doubled under him; his left hand lay limply outstretched ahead. Stacey took his pulse, but there was no pulse.

He stood staring down, listening to the slap and swing of the water against the rocks. Heart gone: just like that. At that moment he did not notice the small hole or tear in the back of the dark-red bath-robe, just over the heart. He was too dazed to notice anything more than the fact of death. He hurried back to the beach, where he met Marion and Dr. Hastings.

"Steady," he said, as the girl tried to push past him. "You'd better go out there, Doctor. But I'm afraid he's done for."

None of them moved. He could not quite estimate the effect of his words on Kane's niece. He realised, too, that he had never before seen Marion without her glasses, which had added a business-like and almost prim touch to her good looks. Over her shoulder towered Dr. Hastings, whose wiry, close-cut hair had a Teutonic look, and his expression a Teutonic heaviness.

"Oh!" said the girl. She was looking at him curiously, and she breathed hard. "Was it—suicide?"

"Suicide?" repeated Stacey, startled. "No. His heart gave out. Why should you think it was suicide?"

"Oh!" said Marion again. She put her hand on his arm and pressed it. "I want to see him. No, I'm quite all right. I hope I can move. I can't think very well."

Dr. Hastings, who seemed about to launch a violent pro-test, checked himself and pushed past. They went with him to the body, and watched while he made his examination. Then he urged them back towards the beach.

"Look here," Hastings began heavily. He cleared his throat, and tried again. "Yes, he's dead right enough; but possibly not for the reason you think. Do you know if Lionel is up yet, Marion?"

So that fellow was at the cottage, thought Stacey. He had never liked the supercilious and aesthetic Mr. Lionel Pell. Norman Kane had once courted Lionel's mother, in the days before she had married the late Mr. Pell; and this seemed to give Lionel the idea that he had some claim on Kane, particularly with regard to sponging.

"Lionel?" repeated Marion. "I—I haven't seen him. I got up and went out for an early bathe at the other side of the bay. But I shouldn't think he was up yet. Why?"

"Because," replied Dr. Hastings with his usual directness, "he'll have to get out his car and drive to the village and get the police. I'm afraid this is murder."

The surf was driving in now, with deepening thunder. A wave veered against the rocks and flung up a ghostly mane of spray. A cold wind had begun to blow from the south, fluttering Marion's beach-robe. She looked at the doctor with rather blind blue eyes, winking as though to keep back tears.

"We had better go up to the house," Hastings went on heavily, "and get something to use as a stretcher: he's a weight to move. There are some bad cross-currents out at this distance when the tide rises, and we don't want him washed out to sea before the police get here."

Then Stacey found his voice.

"The police? Good God, what do you want with the police? His heart—"

"His heart was as sound as yours or mine," said Hastings.

"So," said Marion, "you knew that."

"I should hope I knew it, my dear girl. I happen to be his doctor. Now keep your chin up and let's face the facts. He's been murdered. What little blood there is doesn't show up well against that dark-red bath-robe; but you probably noticed it. And you may have seen the cut in the back of the bath-robe just over the heart."

Stacey put his arm round Marion, who had begun to tremble. He spoke with restraint.

"Look here, Doctor. I don't like to suggest that you're out of your mind, but you might come aside and talk nonsense to me instead of talking it to her. Murdered? How could he have been murdered? He was all alone in this path. There wasn't anybody within a hundred yards of him. You must have seen that for yourself."

"That's true," put in Marion suddenly. "I was sitting up at the top of the beach, up under the bank, getting dry; and I saw him go past. That *is* true, Doctor."

"Yes. It is true. I saw him from the verandah of the cottage," agreed Hastings.

"Then why all this talk about murder?" asked Stacey. "Hold on! Are you saying he was shot with a long-range rifle, or something of the sort? It would have to be very long range. His back was towards the sea when he was hit, and there were several miles of empty water behind him."

"No, I am not saying that."

"Well?"

"He was killed," answered Dr. Hastings slowly, "with some kind of steel point like an old-fashioned hat-pin. That's what I think, anyhow. I haven't removed it. And I can't swear to the exact nature of the weapon until the post-mortem."

That afternoon, while the grey rain fell, Superintendent Morgan tramped up to the cottage. He had joined the quiet group assembled inside the verandah—Marion, Dr. Hastings, Lionel Pell, and Bill Stacey sat there. Outside, the sea looked oily and dangerous, as though by its restless movements it were about to burst against the cottage. Superintendent Morgan wore a sou'wester and an oilskin cap; the expression of his face was a contrast to his soft voice.

He glared at Dr. Hastings.

"And that's that," he said. "I'm suggesting to you, Doctor, that you did this deliberately."

"You mean," asked Hastings, examining all sides of the matter, "that I killed Mr. Kane?"

"That is not what I mean. I mean, that you deliberately allowed that body to be washed out to sea. Don't worry. We'll find it. Indeed we will. That was an incoming tide, and it's somewhere along the beach." The superintendent's light eyes opened. His sing-song voice was more disturbing than violent. "I say you deliberately let it be carried off so that we shouldn't find out how Mr. Kane was killed."

"Miss Kane and Mr. Stacey," said Hastings shortly, "will tell you I warned them. I wanted to get a stretcher and move him in time. We were too late, that's all. Why shouldn't I want you to find out how he was killed?"

"Because it's an impossible thing you tell us. The man was alone. No one could have touched him. And yet he was stabbed. There was a way of doing that. If we had found the body, we should have known how it was done."

"Probably you would have," agreed Hastings.

There was an ominous silence, broken by the flat drizzle of the rain. Bill Stacey, sitting beside Marion, did not look at the superintendent. He found himself more curious about another person, a man who lounged across the verandah near the doorway.

The stranger weighed some seventeen stone and his

waterproof made him seem even larger. From under a sodden tweed cap a bland blue eye surveyed the company; and from under a cropped moustache, which might be sandy or grey, there projected a large-bowled pipe, at which he seemed to be sniffing. Stacey had heard the superintendent address him as Colonel March. Colonel March listened, but so far had said nothing.

"Meantime," said Superintendent Morgan, taking out a notebook, "there are more queernesses here. I want to hear about them, if you please. Miss Kane!"

Marion glanced up briefly. She had been holding herself in well, Stacey thought, and preserving her blank, "secretarial" manner.

"We've heard a good deal, hereabouts," Morgan went on, "about Mr. Kane and his bad heart. You tell us you knew he didn't have a bad heart at all."

"I guessed it. So did Dr. Jones in the village, I think."

"Then why did he keep on saying he had?" demanded Morgan.

"I—I don't know."

"Then tell me this, miss. When you first heard this morning that Mr. Kane was dead, you asked whether it was suicide. Why did you ask that?"

"I—"

"Truth, miss!"

"I've been worried about him," answered Marion. "He's been threatening suicide, if you must know. And he's been acting queerly."

Lionel Pell intervened. Lionel's way of speaking, which sometimes made him as unintelligible as a gramophone running down, now became almost clear. His long legs were outthrust; and his usual expression of supreme indifference was now replaced by one almost helpful. He sat back, long of nose and jaw, and laid down his pronouncement.

"The word, I believe, is 'childish,'" he decided. "The poor old boy—Norman, of course—has been playing with toys. Tell them about the cardboard soldiers, Marion. And the air-rifle."

Marion gave him an almost malevolent look.

"There's nothing very funny or childish about the air-rifle. It's a powerful one, hardly a toy at all. You've used it yourself. But I admit I don't understand about the soldiers.

"You see," she appealed to Morgan, "only the night before last my uncle came home with a huge box of cardboard soldiers. He bought them in Cardiff. They were gaudily painted, each of them five or six inches high. In the bottom was a wooden cannon, painted yellow, that fired a hard rubber ball. My uncle went back to his study and unwrapped them, and set them all up on the table."

At this point, Stacey noticed, the man called Colonel March stirred and glanced across with sudden interest. They all saw it; it brought a new atmosphere of tension. The superintendent looked at her with quick suspicion.

"Did he, Miss Kane? Did he seem to be—er—enjoying himself?"

"No," she replied quite seriously. "He looked ill. Once he came out, for no reason at all, and begged my pardon."

"Miss Kane, do you mean your uncle was insane?"

Dr. Hastings interposed. "Norman Kane," he said, "was one of the sanest men I ever met."

"Now I will tell you something myself," said Superintendent

Morgan. "He 'begged your pardon,' you say. You talk of suicide. I have heard of your Mr. Kane from my cousin, Morgan David. My cousin tells me that your Mr. Kane was not much better than a swindler. My cousin says his companies are crashing, and that he was going to be prosecuted. Is *that* a reason for suicide? I think it is."

"I know nothing of my uncle's private affairs," said Marion. And yet it was, Stacey felt, the thing she had been fearing. Marion wore a print frock, and she seemed less like a secretary than a nurse—a nurse at the bedside of a patient who she had determined should not die.

"Is that, I ask you, a reason for suicide?"

"It may be a reason for suicide," snapped Dr. Hastings. "But it won't explain how a man could run himself through the back at an angle his hand couldn't possibly reach—and in full sight of three witnesses as well."

"Murder or suicide, it is still impossible!"

"And yet the man is dead."

"One moment," said Colonel March.

It was an easy, comfortable voice, and it soothed tempers frayed by rain and fear. His presence was at once authoritative and comfortable, as though he invited them to a discussion rather than an argument; and his amiable eye moved round the group.

"It's not my place to butt in," he apologised, "but there are one or two things here that are rather in my line. Do you mind, Superintendent, if I ask a question or two?"

"Glad," said Morgan fervently. "This gentleman," he explained, throwing out his chest, "is the head of D3 Department at Scotland Yard. He is down here—"

"—on not a very exciting errand," said Colonel March sadly. "A matter of a curious thief who steals only green candlesticks, and therefore comes under the head of our special investigation department. Excuse me: Miss Kane, two days before he died your uncle bought a box of cardboard soldiers. Will you get me that box of soldiers now?"

Without a word Marion got up and went into the cottage. Dr. Hastings looked up suddenly, as though on the defensive.

"We have also heard," Colonel March continued presently, "that he bought an air-rifle. I think you used that air-rifle, Mr. Pell?"

Lionel sat up. With the superintendent he had been friendly and helpful. With Colonel March he had adopted his usual indifference, the air of ease and right with which he (at twenty-three) had called Kane "Norman" and conferred a favour by accepting loans.

"I *have* used it," he said. "It was not my property. Are you under the impression that our late good host was killed by being shot with one of those microscopic pellets out of a toy air-rifle? Or, for that matter, by a little rubber ball out of a toy cannon?"

"Where was the air-rifle kept?"

You could not shake Lionel's placidity.

"I believe I kept it in my room. Until last night, that is. Then I lent it to Marion. Hadn't you better ask her?"

Marion returned in a few moments, with a large and bright-coloured box, which she handed to Colonel March. She seemed to feel that her name had been mentioned; for she looked quickly between Lionel and Bill Stacey. Colonel March opened the box, sniffing at his pipe.

"And yet," he said, with a sharpness which made Stacey uneasy, "the rubber ball is gone. Where, I wonder, is the air-rifle now? You borrowed it, Miss Kane?"

"Look here—" interrupted Dr. Hastings, with an oddly strained expression. He got up from his chair and sat down again.

"Yes, I borrowed it," Marion answered. "Why? Didn't I tell you? I took it out with me when I went to swim this morning, at the other side of the cottage. I shot a few meat-tins and things, and then put it down. When I came back to this side of the beach, I must have forgotten it."

She stared at them, her eyes widening.

"I'm afraid it'll be ruined, in all this rain. I'm sorry. But what of it? Is it important?"

"Miss Kane," said Colonel March, "do you usually go out for a swim as early in the morning as that?"

"No. Never. Only I was horribly worried about my uncle. I couldn't sleep."

"You were fond of him?"

"Very fond of him," said Marion simply. "He had been very good to me."

Colonel March's expression seemed to darken and withdraw. It was as expressionless as his ancient cap or his ancient pipe; and he said nothing. But he closed the box of soldiers with great care, and beckoned the superintendent to one side. They had not long to wait for the result.

Late that afternoon a body was washed up on the shore two miles below Barry Island. And Marion Kane was detained for questioning at the police station, as a prelude to formal detention on a charge of murder.

Stacey spent one of the worst nights of his life. He told himself that he must keep calm; that he must resist the impulse to telephone wildly for solicitors, invade the police station, and generally make a nuisance of himself. He realised, wryly, that he was not a strong, silent man like Dr. Hastings. In difficulties he wanted to do something about them, if only to adopt the dubious course of hitting somebody in the eye.

Things would be all right, he assured himself. Kane's own solicitor was coming from London, and the police were fair. But this very feeling that the police were fair disturbed him worst of all. After a sleepless night at the cottage he dozed off at dawn, and came downstairs at ten o'clock. Lionel Pell was coming up the verandah steps with a newspaper. It was still raining, and so dark that Dr. Hastings had lighted the oil-lamps in the living-room.

"Here's their case," said Lionel, holding up the newspaper. "Our superintendent has been talking indiscreetly. It's plastered all over the world."

"Their case? Their case against—?"

Stacey had to admit that his opinion of Lionel had changed. Lionel had no affectations now; under press of trouble, he was only lanky and awkward and human.

"Well, they don't mention her name, of course. She's not officially under arrest. It's very carefully worded. But they appear to have found that air-rifle buried in the sand at the top of the beach under the bank. They found it at the exact place where Marion says she was sitting when old Norman fell, and in an almost direct line with the Lion's Paw."

Against the lamplight from one of the living-room windows appeared Dr. Hastings's head. It was only a silhouette with wiry cropped hair, but they saw his knuckles bunch on the window-sill.

"*I* don't know anything about it," Lionel urged hastily. "I was in bed and asleep when it happened. But you recall, Bill, that until you came well out on the beach yesterday morning you couldn't see Marion at all. You were in the little lane. Dr. Hastings couldn't see her either. He was on the verandah here, and this cottage is set well back behind the line of the bank.

"If Norman were shot in the back, particularly with a weapon like that, he wouldn't feel it the moment he was hit. People don't, they say. He would hear a hail from Bill Stacey, and turn round. Then he would fall forward with the weapon in his heart—"

From the window Hastings uttered a kind of growl.

"The weapon?" he said. "As a matter of academic interest, will you tell me just what an air-rifle has to do with this, anyhow?"

"Oh, come! You won't be able to dodge responsibility like that, Doctor," said Lionel, who always dodged responsibility.

"Dodge—?"

"Yes. It's your fault. You were the one who suggested that the wound was made by a point and shaft like an old-fashioned hatpin?"

"Well?"

"Those air-rifles, you know; they're pretty powerful. Hardly like a toy at all. But sometimes the lead pellets stick in the barrel and clog it. So as a rule the makers give you a very thin, light rod to clean the barrel with. If you cut off about three-quarters of the rod, and sharpen the other end to a needle-point, you would have a short missile that could be fired with very damaging force in the ordinary way."

There was a silence, except for the noise of sea and rain. Stacey walked to the end of the verandah.

"I've heard rot before," he said, as though making a measured decision. "But never in my life… Do you realise that there's no air-rifle powerful enough to carry any kind of missile with enough force to kill at a distance of well over fifty yards?"

"Yes, I know," admitted Lionel. "But you see the trouble?"

"No, I don't."

"It's just plausible," said Lionel. "I don't believe it. It only worries me."

"I want my hat," said Dr. Hastings suddenly. "Where's my hat? This can't go on; I won't have it. I'm going down to the police station and tell them what really happened."

Outside the cottage there was a rustle of footsteps, stumbling footsteps in the gloom. It was so dark that they could barely see the two persons who came up the steps, but Dr. Hastings picked up a lamp inside the window and held it so that the light fell on Colonel March and Marion Kane.

Colonel March was wheezing a little, but as bland as ever. Marion's expression could not be read. There was relief in it, and disillusionment, and even peace; despite the signs of recent emotion, she was smiling.

"I should like a cigarette, please, Bill," she said. Then she took his arm. "Thank heavens," she added, "for an ordinary decent human being."

"The superintendent and I," said Colonel March, "have come to apologise. Of course, we did what we did entirely with Miss Kane's consent. We have concocted a fiction and kept on the lee side of libel. We have set a trap and heard it snap. We have given you all, I fear, a bad night. But it was the only way we could bring the corpse back to tell his own story... You had better come up now, Mr. Kane."

It was a very muddy, shamefaced, and glowering corpse who walked up the steps behind Superintendent Morgan. Norman Kane, whose heart had stopped beating more than twenty-four hours ago, was now very much alive; and looked as though he wished he weren't.

Norman Kane's grey-haired dignity did not sustain him. He seemed undecided whether or not to hide behind Superintendent Morgan. For a moment he stood opening and shutting his hands. Then he caught sight of Dr. Hastings standing in the window, holding up the lamp.

"You traitor," he roared, and flung himself at the doctor.

"He was dead," insisted Stacey. "His heart had stopped; I'll swear to that. How did he manage it?"

On a clear, cool morning after the rain, Marion, Stacey, and Colonel March stood on the beach looking at a new tide. Colonel March frowned.

"You had better hear the story," he said. "Kane was wrong in nearly everything; he was wrong in the way he flared out against Dr. Hastings. Hastings is his friend, and only tried to help him when his pig-headed piece of deception would have been discovered in two minutes.

"You will already have guessed the fact which Miss Kane feared: Norman Kane was heading for a bad financial smash. It might not necessarily mean prison, but it would mean ruin and penury. Kane did not like such embarrassments. So he planned to stage a fake death and disappear, with a good sum laid by. Other financiers have been known to do it, you know," Colonel March added dryly.

Marion shied a pebble at the water and said nothing.

"He was going to 'die' and have his body washed out to sea—never to be found," the colonel went on. "But he did not want either the stigma of suicide or the prying investigation of a murder. So, with the assistance of Dr. Hastings, he arranged to die of heart failure on the Lion's Paw. There had to be an independent witness there to swear to his death: you, Mr. Stacey. You were summoned for that purpose. Hastings had to be there to corroborate you. Then Hastings would shepherd you to the cottage, many hundred yards away, as the tide rose. Kane, a supremely powerful swimmer, could let himself into the water, swim out and round to the headland, and disappear.

"So for a long time he gabbled everywhere about his weak heart. But he would not listen to Hastings, who told him it was very risky. Miss Kane knew that his heart was not weak. Even the village doctor knew it. If Kane, therefore, suddenly dropped dead of a complaint he did not have, there would be a strong suspicion of fraud at the start. It was altogether a foolish plan. Even so it might have gone through if, on the very morning chosen for the 'death' Miss Kane had not decided to get up for an early swim.

"She was not accustomed to getting up early, as she told us. Norman Kane and Dr. Hastings thought they would have the whole beach to themselves at that hour—except for their special witness: a young man of—er—unsuspicious nature."

Stacey looked at him gloomily.

"For 'unsuspicious,'" he said, "read 'imbecile.' Very well; but I was in full command of what faculties I have, Colonel. I know when a man is dead. And I tell you his heart had stopped."

"I beg your pardon," beamed Colonel March. "His heart had not stopped. But his pulse had stopped."

"His pulse?"

"You will recall how he was lying. Flat on his face, with his right hand doubled under him, but his left hand stretched out invitingly. He was also lying wedged in a kind of trough; and you know his enormous weight. To move him and get at his heart would be difficult and awkward. You would never try to do it, with that limp hand stretched out towards you. You would automatically feel the pulse at his wrist. And there was no pulse."

"But how the dickens can you stop a pulse? It's the same as a heart."

"You stop it," said Colonel March, "by means of a small, hard, rubber ball, such as the little one supplied with the toy cannon in the box of soldiers. It is a good trick, which was exhibited before a group of doctors in London some time ago—and it worked. At the same time it is so simple that I suggest you try it for yourself. Kane, of course, got it from Dr. Hastings. The small rubber ball is placed under the armpit. The arm is pressed hard against the side; the flow of blood is cut off; and the man is 'dead.' Kane lay with his upper arm against his side, but with his lower arm from elbow to wrist extended for your inspection. That is all.

"Even so, the whole plan almost crashed, because Miss

Kane appeared on the scene. You, Mr. Stacey, had found the body and announced death from heart failure. But Hastings knew that this would never do. Miss Kane strongly suspected that the weak heart was a sham.

"If the body had already been swept out to sea, if she had come on the scene only afterwards, she might have wavered. She might have been uncertain. She might have thought it was suicide, which they tried to conceal from her under a mask of heart failure. But there was the body. If something were not done quickly, she would have insisted on examining it. And it would never do for her to find a living man."

Marion nodded. She was still shaken from the after-effect of a somewhat bitter hoax, but she thrust out her chin.

"I certainly should have!" she said. "Only the doctor—"

"Diverted your attention. Exactly. He is an ingenious fellow, Hastings; and no wonder he was upset that morning. He diverted it in the only possible way, with a sudden clap of violence and murder. He drew you hastily back to the beach, so that Kane should not overhear. He shocked you out of your wits, which made it easy for him to put ideas into your mind.

"Remember you never actually *saw* any trace of a wound or a weapon. All you saw was a very minute tear in the back of the dressing-gown, where it had been skagged on a nail.

"That tear (he admits) put the idea into his mind while he was making his 'examination.' To account for such a very small puncture, and such a complete absence of blood, he had to think of some weapon corresponding to that description; so he postulated something like an old-fashioned hatpin. He could have said it was suicide, of course. But he knew that a man could neither stab himself in the back at that angle, in the presence of witnesses, nor press such a weapon so far into the flesh as to be invisible. Whereas it was just possible that a thin blade might have been projected or fired by a murderer. It was altogether too possible. Dr. Hastings had acted wildly and unwisely on the spur of the moment, to prevent the discovery of his friend's hoax. But he must have grown somewhat ill when he saw the case we spun out of a completely harmless air-rifle."

Colonel March smiled apologetically.

"It was a very weak case, of course," he said, "but we had to bring the corpse back. We had to have something—suggestive, but non-committal and non-libellous—to stare at Kane from the Welsh newspapers. It had to be done before he got away to the Continent, or we might never have caught him. The discovery of a drowned body, washed up at Barry, was very helpful; it aided the illusion with which we might snare Kane. The matter was suggested to Miss Kane, who agreed…"

"Agreed?" cried Marion. "Don't you see I had to know whether… I have looked up to him all my life. I had to know whether he would cut and run just the same if he thought I might be hanged for his murder."

"Which he did not do," said Colonel March. "Mr. Norman Kane, I think, has had a refreshing shock which will do him no harm. I should like to have seen him when he crept into town last night; when he found that he was not dead of heart failure and washed out to sea, but that his murdered body has been found and his niece was accused of having killed him. No wonder he burst out at Hastings. But what did he do? He must have realised, Miss Kane, that this charge against you would sooner or later be shown as nonsense; and yet he came back. It was a decent thing to do, as decent as the thing you did yourself. I think it likely that, if he faces his difficulties now, he will save himself as he thought he was saving you."

Murder in Church

G. D. H. and M. Cole

George Douglas Howard Cole (1889–1959) was a prominent economist who wielded considerable political influence. His students included two Labour Party leaders, Hugh Gaitskell and Harold Wilson, but some of his published comments about the relative advantages of a Europe dominated by Nazi Germany or Soviet Russia are disturbing to read today. Cole's wife, Margaret (1893–1980), was a fellow left-wing intellectual, and she published a posthumous biography of her husband.

Cole's first detective novel, *The Brooklyn Murders*, appeared in 1923 and was a solo effort. Thereafter, he and Margaret wrote in collaboration, and over time Margaret's role in the partnership seems to have become dominant. The Coles' novels enjoyed popularity in their day, and the pair remain the only husband and wife who have both been elected to membership of the Detection Club. Their principal detective was Superintendent Wilson, and this story was included in

Wilson and Some Others, a collection published by Collins Crime Club in 1940.

———

"WHAT PUZZLES ME, KINSEY, IS TO FIND YOU WASTING your time in an out-of-the-way corner of the world like this."

Derek Kinsey had been one of Dr. Michael Prendergast's most brilliant contemporaries at the hospital. It had therefore surprised the eminent Harley Street consultant not a little, after losing sight of Kinsey for a number of years, to receive a request from him to come down and advise concerning the correct treatment for a patient in the rustic village of Wilstone, on the Welsh border beyond Clun, where Kinsey was apparently, from his letter, now in practice as a rural G.P. The letter had been forwarded to Prendergast while he was on holiday in Central Wales with his friend, Superintendent Wilson, of Scotland Yard; and he had announced that he would call in at Wilstone on his way back in a few days' time. Rejecting an invitation to both of them to be the doctor's guests, they had gone to the village inn, which looked friendly but bony; and Prendergast, who valued his creature comforts more than Wilson, was already regretting their rejection of the doctor's invitation when Kinsey was shown into the inn parlour.

Kinsey had been introduced to Wilson, who had strolled out, leaving the two doctors alone, before Dr. Prendergast made the remark cited above. Kinsey answered, "My dear fellow, why not? One place is as good as another to a wise man. Besides, this happens to be my native heath. I was born here, and my fathers before me. In fact, my people used to own the whole place, till the Jenkyns bought most of it a couple of hundred years ago."

"The Sir Mortimer Jenkyn you want me to have a look at is one of them?"

"Yes; and you'll find him a very queer customer indeed. In fact, I should say he's mad."

"My dear Kinsey, I'm not an alienist."

"Oh, quite. It's his guts, not his brains, I want you to have a go at. If it were only a brain case, I should feel fully capable of dealing with it myself." Kinsey plunged into a description of Sir Mortimer's illness, which it is fortunately unnecessary for us to reproduce.

"That seems clear enough," Dr. Prendergast commented when he had done. "But I'd be glad if you'd tell me a thing or two about the mental side of his affliction."

"H'm, I suppose he's not mad, in any ordinary sense of the word. Religion's his trouble."

"Religious mania?"

"Say rather, fanaticism. The chap's a fanatical Protestant."

"Aren't most of the people round here? I thought this was a strict Calvinist neighbourhood. This village has got two of the ugliest chapels I ever saw."

"Four, Prendergast. And the two you missed are uglier. But Jenkyn's not a Calvinist—he's C. of E. He calls himself a Low Church Evangelical. He hates the local Calvinist ministers almost as much as he hates the parson… But not quite. He and the parson really do hate each other—like hell."

"The parson's got a little gem of a church, anyway, Kinsey. I was looking at it early this morning. It's one of the most unspoilt bits of eleventh-century building I've ever seen. That doorway is magnificent. From the decorations, I conclude that the parson is 'High.'"

"I should say so. Anglo-Catholic, and then some. And he calls himself a Christian Anarchist into the bargain. Always having rows with the bishop, as well as the squire. This village is just one damn row after another. Might be Kilkenny. He's the squire's cousin, too, which makes it worse."

"Who presents to the living?"

"The parson does. He presented himself. And he owns a tidy slice of the estate too. Sir Mortimer's grandfather had no sons—only two daughters. He divided the estate, giving one the big house and the other the Dower House and the living. Both the sons-in-law took their wives' names, and the parson one took the living, and his son succeeded him. The little bit of property that's stayed in my family is the only part of the village they don't own between them."

"Then you aren't a simple village G.P."

"No, I've got enough to live on in a quiet way, even without what I earn. But I like having a bit of a practice, besides keeping up with my research."

"You still stick to your medical psychology?"

"Yes, that's my line. P'raps I'll publish some day. This place gives me all the clinical material I need."

"I'm rather surprised Sir Mortimer Jenkyn will have you for his doctor, unless you've changed your views, or become more discreet about expressing them."

"I assure you I haven't. I'm still the blatant blasphemer. Jenkyn employs me because I'm the only competent medico in fifty miles. He tried the other local man, who's blind and nearly ninety-three; but he'd soon had enough. He'd have been dead long ago, if he hadn't had me to look after him."

"Are you the parson's doctor too?"

"He doesn't hold with doctors. He just prays. The chap's as strong as a horse, so he can stand it. But we're very good friends. We're both so cocksure about being right that we enjoy hearing each other talk nonsense. Of course, the parson's mad too. You'll see, if you stop over Sunday. He's running a special Christian Anarchist Festival in the churchyard. You ought to go and hear one of his sermons. Sheer raving lunacy, all about the Revolution and the Kingdom of Heaven on Earth that'll arrive as soon as we bump off all the squires and bishops, and have all things in common like the Apostles. Wouldn't suit me."

Prendergast laughed. "Any other lunatics about the place?" he inquired.

"Oh, yes, three hundred and seventy odd. That's the local population. But one more specially so. I mean Caradog Jenkyn."

"Who's he? Not the parson?"

"No, the parson's David—'Father David,' he likes being called. Caradog's the heir."

"Sir Mortimer's son, or the parson's?"

"Neither. He's Sir Mortimer's nephew. But he's the nearest relative. He lives with Sir Mortimer most of the time. They get on fine. In fact, Caradog manages the estate for the old man. He's the last word in squeezing rent out of a tenant in arrears. And he's prudent enough to share the squire's religious views. Goes about all dressed in black, like a Methodist minister, and can't look you in the face."

"You don't love him."

"He's easily the worst of the lot. But he's away just now. You won't have the pleasure of meeting him. But I've got to be off and see an old woman t'other end of the village. You two chaps had much better think again, and put up with me while you're here. This pub is a rotten hole, and I can promise you decent cooking and a really good bottle of claret. Not port; I can't abide the stuff."

Michael Prendergast thanked Kinsey, but said he would have to consult Wilson before accepting. At that moment the superintendent's tall figure was seen strolling down the village street. They went out to meet him, and it did not take much persuasion to induce him to change his quarters. Kinsey, who had his car, said he would pick them up on his way back from his visit to the old woman, guide them to his house, and then take Michael on to visit his patient at the Castle.

The two friends, having finished their simple packing and settled their modest bill, strolled out again into the village street. Towards them came striding, a minute or two later, an immensely tall, strongly built figure, in a long, rusty black cassock, with flowing white hair waving in the breeze. He brandished a heavy stick as he walked.

"Here comes the parson, Harry," Michael whispered. "He lives up to Kinsey's description."

The tall clergyman appeared to be talking aloud to himself as he strode down the street. As he came near them, he waved his stick, and said, "Good-morning. Kinsey was telling me… Which of you is the doctor?"

"I am," Michael answered.

"Kinsey has sent for you because he does not understand. You will not understand either. Shall I tell you what is wrong with Sir Mortimer?"

"I shall be seeing him this morning," Michael answered, rather at a loss.

"You will do him no good. Nothing will do him good, unless he sees the error of his doings and ceases to batten on the wretchedness of the poor. Tell him from me that I have laid a curse on him because of the widow Williams, whom he has driven from hearth and home against the Lord's will."

"I... I am afraid that is rather off my line."

"Tell him, if he will give her back her home, I will remove the curse immediately," the parson continued. "But let him beware. If he repeats his offence, the pains will come on again."

Superintendent Wilson interposed. "You have a fine church here, Father. Perhaps, some time, you would tell us about it."

The parson's tone changed at once. "The finest in the country," he said. "In my perhaps prejudiced view the finest, for its size, in the whole world." He plunged into an enthusiastic description. "You must come with me. I will show you its treasures."

"Dr. Kinsey promised to call for us after he had made his visit," said Michael doubtfully.

"He will come to us. We will leave a message at the inn."

Dr. Prendergast turned to his companion. "What do you say, Harry?"

"The opportunity is much too good to be missed."

Accordingly, having left their message, the two friends accompanied "Father David" to the little church, which stood on a small eminence at one end of the village street. They approached by way of the Rectory, which adjoined it, and entered not by the main door but by a private way, which led to a magnificent carved doorway, on which were depicted in stone the triumphs of the Church Militant over the forces of evil, represented by a series of grotesquely horrible monsters. The priest's eyes were afire as he explained the significance of the scenes, not omitting to mention how far short the Church had fallen in modern times of the glorious mission which was symbolised in these early medieval sculptures.

The two friends duly admired, and were guided at last into the church itself. It was very small, and entirely simple in structure—a mere oblong of building, with a raised altar at one end, gaily decorated with flowers, flags, and a fine crucifix, clearly of ancient design. Down one side, however, there was a high pew in plain oak, now dark with age—a pew so high as to screen completely any persons who sat, or even stood, within it. The priest's eyes flashed as he pointed to it in scorn.

"God's house is defiled," he exclaimed, "by that squirearchical abomination. The date is 1743. I had it removed; but the powers of darkness, headed by the bishop, compelled me to put it back. I comfort myself that it is fitting for such as Sir Mortimer to be hidden in their own blindness, when they visit this place."

"Then Sir Mortimer attends your services?" Dr. Prendergast was surprised.

The Rector nodded. "He comes in hate, and in hate he departs," he said. "There is no other church for many miles. To go to Chapel would be beneath his dignity. He comes…and I do my best to chastise him." There seemed to be a glimmer of laughter at the back of the Rector's words, though he spoke gravely. It was plain that chastising the squire in church was one of his favourite recreations.

On the opposite side of the little church there was a tiny gallery, also built in oak, but heavily carved, and evidently of much earlier date than the great private pew. It looked as if it had been used to contain the musicians, in the days before the small organ nearer the altar had been installed. Hard by the end of this gallery was an old stone pulpit, carved with scenes from the gospels, and reached by steps from the floor of the church; and over the pulpit hung a great canopy of wrought metal—a fine example of English ironwork, probably of the sixteenth or early seventeenth century.

"The interior," the Rector was explaining, "is a sad mixture of styles and periods. I would clear it all away, if I were free to do as I wish. But behind these vulgarities of later times, the old medieval building is miraculously intact. Try to imagine this church as it was before the hand of the desecrator had been laid upon it…"

The Rector was still dilating on the beauties of his church when Dr. Kinsey came to look for his guests. They had not been bored—far from it; for David Jenkyn was an expert as well as an enthusiast, and the building really deserved his laudations.

"Come off it, Father," said Kinsey, laughing, when the Rector attempted to continue his lecture in face of the new arrival. "Dr. Prendergast's nearly due at the Castle now, and I haven't taken him round to my place yet."

"But I haven't finished." There was a childlike simplicity in the Rector's tone of expostulation.

Wilson said, "If you have to run off, Michael, perhaps I may be allowed to remain and hear the rest. I can drive Michael's car to the doctor's in time for lunch, if he'll tell me where to go; and you, Doctor, can take Michael to the Castle in your car, if that suits you all right."

So it was arranged; and Wilson stayed behind and completed his knowledge of the history, antiquities and present condition of Wilstone Church, while Michael Prendergast went away with Dr. Kinsey to visit Sir Mortimer Jenkyn.

After a while, they climbed up a narrow, wooden stair into the little gallery, in order the better to study the tracery of the vaulted roof. This done, Wilson found himself staring at the great metal canopy which overhung the pulpit.

"This thing must be an enormous weight," he observed. "How is it supported?"

"I really never considered the matter," the Rector answered abruptly. "Now, you see that curving carved capital over there…"

While he spoke, Wilson was continuing his inspection of the canopy. The entire affair seemed to depend on a huge iron hook, screwed into a great beam which formed part of the roof. It looked, to Wilson's keen eyes, as if the part of the hook on which the weight rested had worn very thin with the years."

"I suppose," he said, "you're sure that canopy's quite safe. It looks to me a bit dangerous, as if that hook up there were badly worn. It'd be awkward if it came down some day while you were in the middle of your sermon."

The Rector glanced indifferently upwards. "I would that the Lord would make it fall," he said. "It would prove the bishop's error in refusing me leave to remove it."

"There wouldn't be much left of you to explain that to the bishop," Wilson said with a smile.

"I am in the Lord's hands," said the Rector. "I fear it is quite safe. It has hung there for some hundreds of years."

"That doesn't make it any safer," said Wilson.

"Let us go down," the Rector answered. "There are things I should like to show you at the Rectory. It is not often I find any one to appreciate my treasures." He smiled ruefully.

Dr. Kinsey's house was a delightful, timbered building, dating from the sixteenth century, but equipped with every modern comfort. It stood a mile or so from the village, at a crossing of roads, and the front door opened straight on to the highway. The doctor's car was standing outside when Wilson drove up in Dr. Prendergast's Packard, and Dr. Kinsey greeted him with the remark that he was late for lunch, but he wasn't surprised. "The old boy'll go on talking for ever, if you let him," he added. "I suppose he gave you a lecture on Anarchism when he'd finished showing off his church."

"He did not so much as mention the subject," Wilson answered. "He was much too busy showing me the Rectory. I promised to go and lunch there tomorrow and see the rest."

Dr. Kinsey made a face. "If you like dry bread and water— and wooden platters to eat it off," he said, "and probably a turnip or two for company, you'll be in your element. I can promise you a better lunch here, any day."

Wilson laughed. "I'm quite ready to sample your hospitality

now," he said. "Sight-seeing is hungry—and thirsty—work, especially in this weather."

"Then wash your hands, and come along. I've got a bottle of Montrachet I hope you'll appreciate."

In the matter of food and drink, Dr. Kinsey was plainly a connoisseur. The lunch which he offered his guests was excellent, and carried with it the promise of a pleasantly somnolent afternoon. For it had been decided that the visitors should remain in Wilstone over the week-end; and Dr. Kinsey had proposed that, after lunch, they should take chairs out on the lawn.

Nothing was said over lunch, or over coffee afterwards, about Dr. Prendergast's visit to Sir Mortimer Jenkyn. But presently Dr. Kinsey was called away; and Wilson lazily asked his friend what he had made of the squire.

"He's as mad as a hatter, Harry. Physically, there's nothing very seriously wrong with him—nothing that can't be put right by the proper treatment, if he'll only stick to it—which I doubt. It's not his guts that are amiss; it's the man himself. Really, Harry, he is a quite remarkably nasty piece of goods."

"From you, Michael, that means a lot. I've seldom heard you so vehement about anybody. What's the matter with him?"

"Well…to begin with, his manners are abominable. He very nearly ordered me out of the house when I said he drank too much."

"I conclude he's a secret drinker—probably brandy."

"You're absolutely right. He's sodden with it. His nerves are all anyhow. Then, he's intolerably sanctimonious. Guess what he did when Kinsey had introduced me, and I was just about to start examining him."

"I won't try."

"He fell on his knees, and prayed I might be guided to a right opinion of his condition."

Wilson laughed. "That must have made you uncomfortable, Michael."

"I got my own back by telling him how much I admired the church. That provoked a tirade. It appears that churches ought to be as ugly as possible, so as not to distract the worshippers' thoughts. And the church here is not merely beautiful, but idolatrous. The Reverend David, according to the squire, is own brother to the devil himself. He is worse than a Papist, and a—Bolshevik into the bargain. I heard quite a lot about this forthcoming Christian Anarchist Festival. It seems the Rector proposes to preach an extra-special sermon, all about the duty of Christians to be Anarchists, tomorrow morning; and Sir Mortimer says he is coming to interrupt. He intends to denounce the proceedings in his capacity as a magistrate, and to demand that the Rector be unfrocked, or inhibited, or tarred and feathered, or I'm not quite sure what—except that there's boiling oil in it."

"Really, Michael, I think you and I must go to church for once in a way, even if we do shock Dr. Kinsey. I should like to see an encounter between our St. George and your dragon."

Kinsey came back at that point; and Wilson announced his intention of attending service next morning in the village church. "What about you, Doctor?"

Kinsey shook his head. "It'd give my patients too much of a shock. Besides, I never get up on Sunday morning, unless I have to. You're sure you fellows wouldn't sooner breakfast in bed, like decent Christians?"

"I loathe breakfast in bed," said Wilson feelingly. "It makes me feel crumby all day long."

The two friends breakfasted excellently the following morning, without seeing any sign of their host. But the manservant who brought in the coffee threw a quite different light on Dr. Kinsey's habits. So far from lying late abed, the doctor, he said, had been at work in his laboratory from an early hour, and had given special orders that he was not to be disturbed. A breakfast tray had been taken over to him there, and left outside the door. The man said that Dr. Kinsey always rose very early on Sundays, and put in a long morning in his laboratory. Nothing would be seen of him until lunch-time, at half-past one, when he hoped to meet his guests again, unless they preferred the Rector's hospitality. Wilson said he was not sure—he had half-promised the Rector to stay to lunch. The man answered, "In that case, sir, I had better keep something for you when you get back." Michael Prendergast said he would be in to lunch in any event. Michael had no desire to forsake Dr. Kinsey's fleshpots for the Rector's alleged dry bread and water.

In due course Wilson and his friend strolled down into the village in good time for church. There were quite a number of people walking in that direction. It seemed as if all the village meant to attend, and as if there could be few left to furnish congregations for the four Calvinist chapels Dr. Kinsey had spoken of. Wilson and Prendergast entered the little church and took places right at the back, near the main door. Soon the church began to fill up, but there was no sign of life from the great private pew. Wilson wondered whether its occupants had a private entrance which he had failed to notice the day before, or had to reach their seclusion by way of the public entrance.

At length the service began. It was by far the most ritualistic Wilson had ever attended, except in a Catholic place of worship. There was much chanting, genuflexion, and soon the smell of incense pervaded the little building. The Rector had a fine voice, and used it to good effect; and someone had evidently taken pains in training the choir. Wilson, who had been brought up a Wesleyan, felt ancient anti-papist prejudices stirring within him, contending with a real appreciation of the music, and sending him off into trains of thought that every now and then distracted his attention from what was happening.

Presently the Rector, standing behind a carved reading-desk, and speaking in his ordinary tone of voice, made certain announcements. The first two or three were trivial. But then came the announcement that at half-past two there would be a Christian Anarchist assemblage in the churchyard. A contingent, with banners, was expected from a neighbouring village; and the great Russian Anarchist leader, Madame Balakirov, was coming from Shrewsbury, where she was staying, to deliver a short address.

The Rector was about to say more, when the door of the private pew suddenly opened, and a little old gentleman in a black frock-coat bounced out like a jack-in-the-box and exclaimed in a high, squeaky voice:

"In the Lord's name, I protest against this sacrilege. This is the Lord's house; but you"—he pointed a quivering finger at the Rector—"you would make it a den of thieves. I shall appeal to the bishop. I shall bring an action. I forbid you…"

The Rector's voice boomed out, drowning the interruption. "Peace, babbler. Be silent in the presence of One whose shoestring thou art not worthy to unloose. If you say one word more, I will hurl you with these hands into the outer darkness." He spread out his great arms with a gesture full of menace.

"I have said what I came to say," Sir Mortimer squeaked back. "I forbid this iniquity, in the name of the Lord."

The Rector gave an inarticulate roar; but Sir Mortimer was already scuttling back into his private pew. The door banged behind him.

"The service will now proceed as usual," said the Rector.

A few minutes later the Rector ascended the high pulpit and began his sermon. It was an astonishing performance, more like something out of Blake's Prophetic Books than anything Wilson had ever heard in a church. Most of it Wilson found quite unintelligible; but there were sundry references to the torments of the damned which he could not help regarding as directed especially at Sir Mortimer, still presumably immersed in his private pew. The Rector was particularly insistent on the point that these torments were to be suffered, not so much in a future existence, as on earth, and that without any undue delay.

The parson's voice boomed on, and his speech was accompanied by the most remarkable series of gestures. Sometimes he was speaking with his arms waving high above his head; then one arm would be thrust suddenly forward, as if pointed at a physical enemy; and, more than once, he leant so far forward over the high pulpit, still gesticulating wildly, that Michael Prendergast had to suppress an impulse to dash forward in order to catch him as he fell headlong into the body of the church.

Suddenly, at the height of one of the Rector's periods, there was a loud cracking sound, and then a second, following hard upon it. Even as the congregation was leaping to its feet by a common impulse, came a resounding crash, as the great metal canopy over the pulpit fell hurtling down and settled over the top of the pulpit itself like a gigantic candle-extinguisher. A moment before, the Rector had been standing bolt upright, denouncing with outstretched arms the sin of those who would not busy themselves about the Lord's work. But now, in an instant, he had been snuffed out; and for a brief space a dead silence of sheer astonishment filled the little church. It was followed by a hubbub of confused shouts and screams; for flying fragments of stone from the pulpit had struck several members of the congregation, and the screams of the wounded and the frightened mingled with the clamour of those farther off shouting advice and crying out to know what had happened. There was a stampede from the pews farther back towards the scene of the disaster; and some of those nearer the front collided with the oncoming tide in their attempts to escape.

At the very moment of the catastrophe, Michael Prendergast was aware of Superintendent Wilson slipping from his side. As for Michael, he knew full well where his duty, as a doctor, lay in such an emergency. He hurried forward down the narrow aisle towards the pulpit, crying as he went, "I am a doctor," in order that those who were crowding out of their seats might make room for him. He was just conscious, as he ran, of a high, cracked voice crying from somewhere within the church that God had delivered His judgment upon the wicked and the idolater.

Dr. Prendergast pushed his way to the front of the group of persons already gathered round the pulpit. The canopy, in its fall, had sent splinters of the stonework of the pulpit flying in all directions; and somewhere Michael could hear someone whimpering as if hurt. But he felt that his first business must be with the parson, or what was left of him. The canopy, falling vertically, had settled down over the top of the pulpit, and what was within was hidden completely from view. It would be clearly out of the question to move the canopy without mechanical power, or at all events an arrangement of block and pulleys that would take long to fit up. The only way of discovering what had happened to the unfortunate Rector was to ascend the pulpit steps and creep inside through the narrow space which remained open where the entrance to the pulpit had been. Pushing the people aside, and making sure that he had his matches, Dr. Prendergast, who was a big-built man, set himself to crawl in through the narrow opening.

He got his head and shoulders through, and then managed to wriggle his arms in, and to strike a match. Its flicker showed him the Rector's body, lying all of a heap on the floor of the pulpit. His head was crushed in like an eggshell: there was no doubt at all that he was past all help. Michael stayed still for a second, thinking. The Rector's body had better remain for the time being where it was: his next duty was to offer his aid to any member of the congregation who had been hurt by the splinters of stone sent flying by this ghastly accident.

He heard Wilson, calling from just behind him, "Well, Michael?" His voice made a curious muffled sound as he called back, "He's dead. Nothing to be done. I'm coming out to see if any one else is hurt." He squeezed his body back out of the aperture and stood up on the steps of the pulpit, shaking himself free of the stone-dust he had collected in his passage.

Wilson said, softly, "I've locked the church—both doors. I'll just have a look in, while you do your job; and then we must set to work quickly."

Dr. Prendergast nodded; but he barely heard what his friend was saying. He called out, "Is there anybody else hurt?" A surge of voices inquired what had happened to the Rector. Michael answered that he was dead and past human aid, and he heard a number of people sobbing and crying out as he repeated his inquiry whether any one else had suffered hurt.

It appeared that remarkably little damage had been done, most of the flying fragments having been stopped by the high pew. But one old woman had been struck on the head by a splinter of stone. She sat moaning, with a cluster of neighbours round her. Michael hastily examined the wound, and called for water and a cloth. He could see that nothing serious had happened, beyond the shock.

A middle-aged man in a rusty cassock—probably the verger—came bearing a basin of water and some pieces of cloth that seemed to be fragments of a surplice. As Michael bathed the wound, and spoke soothingly to the old woman, he became aware of Sir Mortimer standing beside him, and noticed that all the others had drawn away at the squire's approach.

Sir Mortimer looked at Michael, and at the wound. "Tchah!" he said, "nothing to fuss about there." He paused, and then said, "He's dead, is he? It is God's judgment on him."

Michael merely grunted; and Sir Mortimer went on with relish. "He died saying that the wicked should be punished in this world. I say they shall be burned eternally in the next world also."

"Be quiet!" said Michael. He deftly bound up the old woman's head with a bandage made of a piece of surplice, told her she would soon be quite all right, and handed her over to her own friends. He turned to see what Wilson was doing, just as a loud hullabaloo broke out at the back of the church. Some of the congregation, attempting to get out, had discovered that the door was locked, and were raising angry protests against their imprisonment.

Sir Mortimer strutted down the aisle and, pushing past the people in the doorway, rattled at the door-handle. He came back into the church, fuming.

"Who locked this door?" he shouted angrily.

Wilson faced him. "I did."

"Who the devil are you?"

"I am Superintendent Henry Wilson, of Scotland Yard."

Sir Mortimer's jaw fell. He appeared very completely astonished. But in a moment, with an effort, he recovered himself. "I don't care who you are. By what right do you presume to lock the door?"

"I am investigating a murder, Sir Mortimer," Wilson answered.

"Murder! What in God's name do you mean? The thing fell on him. It was an accident—a judgment of God."

Wilson shook his head slowly. "No, no," he said. "It was deliberate murder. Every one must stay in this church until there has been time to summon the local police."

"Do you realise that I am a magistrate?" Sir Mortimer was saying.

"If you please, sir," said a red-faced man in a dark blue suit, "I am the local police. I'm Constable Chaney. Only I ought to go home and get me uniform."

Wilson said, "I will let you out, Constable. But never mind your uniform just now. Go to the nearest telephone and tell the County Police to send out an inspector and some men at the earliest possible moment. Tell them I will hold every one until they come." He took a huge key from his pocket and made ready to unlock the door. "Now, then, every one will please stand back, except the constable and Dr. Prendergast. Michael, you and I are to see that nobody else gets out."

"I insist on my right to go through that door when I please," said the squire angrily.

Chaney put in his word. "Better stay where you are, Sir Mortimer, if the superintendent thinks it best."

"Mind your own business," the squire answered furiously. "Come, Superintendent, if that's what you are, I insist that you have no right to detain me."

"Every citizen has a right to detain a suspect in a case of murder, sir. You, as a magistrate, ought to know that."

Sir Mortimer fell back a pace. His face was livid. "You accuse me of murder?"

"No. I merely include you, among others, as a person who ought to remain here until the police arrive. I am only doing my duty, Sir Mortimer. Yours is to set a good example to the rest by sitting down quietly until the police are here."

"Aren't you the police?"

"My presence is a mere accident. The responsibility for

investigating this matter will fall on the County Police as soon as they come."

Michael put in, "But, Harry, what makes you think it is murder? You told me yourself that canopy looked dangerous. Surely it was just a dreadful accident."

"No, Michael—far from it. You must have heard the shot just before the canopy fell."

Dr. Prendergast was taken aback. In the turmoil he had forgotten all about the sounds he had heard. "I heard two sounds that might have been shots," he said. "But..."

"Exactly," said Wilson. "Now, I want to know this. Where did they seem to you to come from?"

"I'm not sure I know," said Michael slowly. "At least, I think the second came from over there." He pointed in the direction of Sir Mortimer's private pew.

"And the first?"

"I really don't know. From somewhere different. From the other side of the church, I should say."

Sir Mortimer, after his passage of arms with Superintendent Wilson, had stalked away up the aisle. But now he came hurrying back. "Did you also lock the door leading to the Rectory?" he exclaimed angrily.

"No," said Wilson. "I did not need to. I found it was locked already."

"Then where is the key?"

Wilson shrugged his shoulders. "Most probably in the Rector's pocket."

"You persist in holding me your prisoner?"

"Until the police come, Sir Mortimer. As soon as they take charge, my responsibility is at an end."

There was further altercation after that; but at last both the squire and the congregation were induced to accept the inevitable, and most of them went back to their pews and stayed there, quietly awaiting the next move. Sir Mortimer, however, remained standing near the main doorway, as if he were determined to get the first word with the local constabulary when they appeared on the scene.

Wilson, leaving him there, walked back slowly up the aisle, with his friend beside him. "What are you suggesting, Harry?" Michael asked.

"I am not suggesting. I am prepared to state facts. As I told you, the metal hook that held the canopy was worn nearly through. I shall discover later whether that was ordinary wear and tear or deliberate damage. I only wish that I had looked at it more carefully yesterday; for then perhaps this tragedy could have been prevented. At all events, whether the hook was worn thin by time or filed by man's deliberate action, what happened this morning was that what was left of it was deliberately shot away. It was a revolver shot, I feel nearly sure; and the revolver must be somewhere in the church. That is why I dare not let any one leave the building until it has been found."

"Do you mean to search everybody's person?"

"No, I shall leave that to the locals. But you and I may as well have a look round, in case it is anywhere obvious." As he spoke he pushed open the door of Sir Mortimer's great private pew.

"What's that?" cried Michael, pointing to an object lying on the floor in the far corner.

Wilson walked over to it and stood looking down in silence. Michael followed him. On the floor, in the far corner of the pew, lay a big service revolver. Without thinking, he bent down to pick it up.

"No, leave it where it is, Michael. Let the locals have it. And it mustn't be touched, because of fingerprints."

There was a sound behind them, and they turned to find Sir Mortimer facing them.

"What are you doing in my pew?"

"At the moment, discovering a service revolver on the floor," said Wilson.

Sir Mortimer gave a bellow, and tried to break past; but the others stood solidly in his way.

"That revolver must not be touched until the police come," said Wilson. "If you will promise not to touch it, you may look at it and tell me whether you have ever seen it before. Do you own a service revolver?"

"That's no business of yours."

"As you please, Sir Mortimer. It will be easy enough to find out."

"Well, I do, then; but it's safe at home in my study. Here, let me see." He brushed past, and this time Wilson did not restrain him, though he stood ready to seize him if he should attempt to touch the weapon.

The squire made no such attempt. He stood limp, staring close at the revolver with goggle eyes. "I swear I never put it there," he said hoarsely. The discovery seemed to have cowed him.

"Then it is your revolver, is it?"

"It—it looks like mine. But I have not touched it for weeks."

"All that will be gone into later," said Wilson sternly. "Have you a key to this pew?"

"Yes."

"Then please lock it up after us."

They filed out, and Sir Mortimer, with trembling hands, locked the pew. At Wilson's demand, he handed over the key.

"Were you alone here in your pew this morning?" Wilson inquired.

"Yes."

"No one else has been in here, to your knowledge?"

"No one. But I suppose someone must have been."

Wilson made no comment. He turned to Michael Prendergast. "And now, Michael, we had better see about arresting the murderer."

Michael looked questioningly at his friend. What did he mean? Was he intending to arrest Sir Mortimer Jenkyn without waiting for the local police?

Sir Mortimer cried out in affright. "I swear I did not touch him. Nobody touched him. It was a judg... an accident."

"Come, Michael," said Wilson shortly, and strode away, leaving the squire gaping, towards the opposite end of the church. Michael, after a moment's bewilderment, went after him. "Harry, I don't understand."

"If the parson locked the door leading to the Rectory," said Wilson, "there is no possibility of the murderer having got away. That shot came from the gallery. The murderer must have fired at close range, in order to be sure of not missing. It would have been much too difficult a shot to attempt from any distance."

"But the revolver was in Sir Mortimer's pew."

"Yes, because it was thrown there from the gallery. I saw the dent in the woodwork where it hit the back of the pew before it fell where we found it."

"But the second shot! I'm sure that came from the direction of the pew."

"There was no second shot."

"But I heard it. I distinctly remember hearing two shots."

"Yes, Michael. You heard two *sounds*—the shot and the echo. Naturally, the echo came from the opposite side of the church."

"Then you think the murderer is still lurking in the gallery?"

"I don't know, Michael. I am just going to look. I think he must be somewhere in the church. That is, unless he made his getaway by the door to the Rectory, and locked it after him. And I feel sure he didn't, because there wasn't time."

"If he has the key, he could have got away later, surely. Nobody's been watching that door."

"Oh, no, Michael. I took the precaution of jamming the keyhole with something he wouldn't be able to get out in a hurry. It will very likely take a locksmith to open that door now."

"Then the gallery is the only place where he can be. Unless he joined the congregation in the confusion."

"We shall see, Michael. There is one other place—the organ loft, or, beyond it, up the tower. If he's there, he can stay there till help arrives. It's a winding narrow stair one armed man could hold against a dozen. I shall try the gallery first."

So saying, Wilson led the way, at a run, up the wooden steps leading to the gallery. It did not take long to make sure that there was no one lurking there.

"He is not here," Michael exclaimed, stating the obvious.

"Then he must be in the tower, or somewhere among the

congregation. What do you say, Michael, shall we be heroic and risk the tower, or shall we leave the locals to get him out, if he's there?"

"I don't feel heroic, Harry—even though I feel sure you would insist on going first."

"Wisely said, Michael. I don't feel heroic either. Our lives are too valuable to be thrown away. If he's there, he must be feeling pretty desperate. And he's safe enough, for the time being. He can't possibly get away."

They were standing in the gallery as they spoke, looking down on the congregation huddled beneath. Suddenly there was a hammering at the main door.

"If that is the police, they've been remarkably quick," said Wilson. He darted down the stairs from the gallery and reached the door almost at the same moment as Sir Mortimer. Michael was close behind him.

"Stand back!" Wilson exclaimed. "Who's there?"

"It's me, sir, Constable Chaney. And Dr. Kinsey."

Wilson inserted the huge key and unlocked the door. He opened it just enough to admit the newcomers, and re-locked it behind them.

"Inspector Currie is on his way, sir. I met Dr. Kinsey in the village, and he came along. There's a crowd outside, sir; but I told them they couldn't come in."

While Wilson was speaking with the constable, Kinsey was clamouring to Dr. Prendergast for information about what had happened. Michael told him, in short, breathless sentences. He ended by saying that the superintendent believed that the unknown murderer was still hiding in the church tower.

"Then Sir Mortimer didn't do it?"

"Wilson says not. There's no doubt he was in his own pew when it happened, because he bobbed out immediately afterwards, and said it was the judgment of God."

"Then who on earth…? Every one else hereabouts loved the poor old Rector, even if they did think he was off his head. It beats me." Kinsey paused. "You say this chap's up the tower."

"Wilson thinks he must be."

"Then we'll have him out of it in half a jiffy. Don't say a word to the superintendent, though. I'll collect a chap or two I know, and rout him out for you in no time."

"You mustn't run any risks. Wilson says we'd better leave it to the local police."

"Lord bless you, I'm much too fond of my skin to run risks. Don't you worry." Kinsey slipped away; and Michael saw him talking excitedly to one or two members of the congregation, who proceeded to follow him up the aisle in the direction of the organ.

Despite Kinsey's injunction, Dr. Prendergast thought he ought to tell Wilson. But he was delayed a minute or two, as he did not want to speak until he could get his friend out of earshot of Sir Mortimer. He had just drawn Wilson aside, when suddenly, over their heads, the church bells pealed out—no regular peal, but a horrible, discordant jangle.

"Stop that!" Wilson shouted, and ran towards the organ.

The tower of Wilstone Church, later than the rest of the edifice, was unusually placed to the side of the raised altar place, and its lower part accommodated the organ. Behind the organ was the space for the bell-ringers, and a narrow winding stair in one corner led up to the belfry. The organ loft, at the top of this stair, was a wooden platform, in full view of any one standing on the floor of the tower among the bell-ropes.

Wilson and Prendergast dashed into the space behind the organ and found a little group of men, under Kinsey's direction, tugging hard at the bell-ropes. As they entered, Michael, looking upwards, saw a figure stagger out suddenly on to the wooden platform, as if in a blind panic. The man seemed to fling himself wildly at the wooden railing, which gave way under the impact. An instant later, he came hurtling down from the platform and fell with a heavy thud on the stone floor of the tower.

Michael was bending over the body in a moment. The man was clad in what looked like clerical black. It took but a second to be sure that his neck was broken. Life was not yet extinct, but he was dying—would be dead in a few minutes at most.

Kinsey, too, was bending over the body. "My God, it's Caradog," he exclaimed. "I thought he was away somewhere."

The dying man breathed heavily, but he was past speech. A couple of minutes later all was over. Sir Mortimer meanwhile had come, and he was among the group that stood looking down upon the broken body.

Superintendent Wilson said, "It is better so, Sir Mortimer. I am always glad when there need be no execution."

"Then he…killed him," Sir Mortimer murmured brokenly. "But why? I cannot believe it. He had no reason. Did he— kill himself?"

"In a sense. But not intentionally. Dr. Kinsey knew no one could remain in the belfry while the bells were ringing. He staggered out, lost his head, and crashed through the rail."

"Then Dr. Kinsey killed him."

"If so, it was a merciful death."

Dr. Kinsey, Prendergast, and Superintendent Wilson had drawn their chairs up to the study fire after an excellent dinner. It had been a lovely day; but the evening had turned chilly, and the warmth was pleasant.

"Well, Harry, this has been another of your one-day non-stop records," Michael observed. "But I still don't see what motive this nephew of the squire's had for killing the parson. If Sir Mortimer had killed him, that would have been intelligible—a clear case of *odium theologicum* moving a madman to the point of murder. But this chap who did it, from all I can hear, wasn't a madman, but merely a very nasty piece of goods. He had nothing to gain by the murder that I can see."

"That's because you weren't with me when I helped the local police search the Rectory this afternoon. We found a letter there, addressed to the Rector, alleging that Caradog Jenkyn had been embezzling Sir Mortimer's property. You know he had the management of the estate in his hands. Then we learnt from the Rector's housekeeper that Caradog had been at the Rectory the day before yesterday, and there had been a stormy interview. It looks as if the Rector had sent for him and threatened to expose him unless he repented and made restitution. That is indicated by a prayer for some unnamed sinner we found written out in the Rector's hand in his study. Caradog had no intention of repenting, and couldn't have made restitution even if he had been prepared to. His first idea was to prevent the exposure by shutting the Rector's mouth. And then, I imagine, he got the notion that he might be able to kill two birds with one stone—kill the Rector and, if it didn't get turned off as an accident, get Sir Mortimer charged with the murder. Of course, he expected to inherit the estate when the old man died.

"So he must have got into the church, and filed away the hook that held the canopy of the pulpit until it was only just strong enough to hold. I blame myself for not having made certain that the hook hadn't been tampered with when I noticed its weakness yesterday, while the Rector was showing me over the church. But Jenkyn had darkened the place over, so that it couldn't be seen that it had been filed away until it was examined carefully from close to."

"You can't blame yourself for that, Harry. There was absolutely no reason to suspect foul play until it had actually happened."

Wilson made a wry face. He said, "There so seldom is. That's the trouble of it. That is why the police are so much better at detecting murder than at preventing it."

"At all events, no one can hold you to blame, Harry."

"Perhaps not. But I ought to have gone to more trouble when I had noticed that the thing was dangerous. I do blame myself."

"That's nonsense, Harry."

Wilson shrugged his shoulders. "In any case, the mischief's done. Well, the murderer must have hidden himself in the gallery well before the service began, and in the middle of the sermon he fired a round from Sir Mortimer's revolver, which he had bagged from the Castle, at point-blank range at the metal hook, shattering it and bringing the canopy down. Then immediately, while every one's attention was distracted by the fall, he flung the revolver across into the private pew. Possibly he threw it so quickly that the sound was drowned by the crash of the falling canopy. Sir Mortimer, you remember, rushed out almost as soon as the canopy fell. At all events, it seems clear he knew nothing of the revolver being in his pew."

"But, Harry, if the murderer was up in the gallery, how did he mean to escape without being noticed?"

"Easily enough, Michael. Only his plan went wrong. He supposed he had simply to let himself down from the end of the gallery, sliding down the wooden pillar right behind the pulpit. That in fact was what he evidently did, as nobody saw him. Then he meant to escape from the church by the door leading to the Rectory; but he found it locked, as the Rector had left it—even apart from the fact that I must have bunged up the keyhole before he could get there. We found the key in the Rector's pocket, by the way."

"You must very nearly have run into him, Harry."

"Yes, he may even have seen me bunging up the keyhole. If so, that must have given him a pretty fright. At all events, when he found that way barred, he didn't dare to attempt the main door, or mix with the congregation, for fear of being spotted. So the only place he could hide in was the belfry. You know the rest."

"Another of your triumphs, Harry."

"Not a bit of it. There was nothing for me to do, except use plain common sense."

"If you hadn't noticed that damaged hook, the whole thing might have passed off as an accident."

"Aren't you forgetting the shots?" Dr. Kinsey put in.

"Would any one have known they were shots, if Wilson

hadn't been there? I'm sure I should have forgotten all about them," said Michael Prendergast indignantly.

Kinsey laughed. He raised his glass. "Have it how you like. Here's to that nonpareil hero, Superintendent Wilson, of Scotland Yard."

"The claret is so excellent," said Wilson, raising his glass in turn, "that I propose to drink that toast myself."

The three men drained their glasses, and there was a silence—a heartfelt tribute to the excellence of Dr. Kinsey's wine.

1951

Brother in the Barrow
Ianthe Jerrold

Ianthe Bridgeman Jerrold (1898–1977) came from a literary family. Her grandfather Douglas was a playwright and her father, Walter, a journalist and author. She published a book of verse in her teens, and her macabre story "The Orchestra of Death" appeared in *The Strand Magazine* when she was twenty. Jerrold was a versatile writer whose work spanned genre and mainstream fiction. Two detective novels, one (*Dead Man's Quarry*) with a well-evoked setting in the England-Wales border country, featured the amateur sleuth John Christmas. Writing as Geraldine Bridgman, she produced *Let Him Lie* (1940) and *There May Be Danger* (1948), a whodunit and a thriller respectively. *The Stones Await Us* (1945) was a fantasy set in 1985 in an isolated Welsh community which is "an oasis in a sea of death and destruction."

Jerrold and her husband, George Mendes, bought and restored Cwmmau Farmhouse, situated in Herefordshire but close to Wales and boasting breathtaking views of the Black Mountain and Brecon Beacons; the property now belongs to the National Trust. This story first appeared in *The London Mystery Magazine* in 1951.

———

At the time Corney Dew buried his brother-in-law in the Celtic barrow, locally called the tump, hardly anybody had heard of the Aymesley Antiquarian Club. But when Gwyn Griffith became the Club's secretary, he started hiking round the country-side looking for Roman or Celtic remains or anything else he could find to make Saturday outings for his members; and he soon started pestering Corney to let him open the tump and see if what was inside was a Druid or a Roman. Corney could have told him what was inside—his brother-in-law Davy—but, of course, he didn't; just put on a wooden face and said the tump was nothing but an old heap of road-clearings, and he remembered his grandfather heaping them there. Gwyn Griffith said that, in that case, there surely to goodness would be no harm in the Antiquarian Club having a look! When Corney went on looking wooden, Gwyn Griffith concluded that his reluctance must be due to superstition, and assured him that if they found any bones in the tump they'd treat them reverently, just photograph them and put them back. Corney could hardly keep a straight face at the notion of Davy being reverently photographed and put back; but at least he had an idea now of what to say, and told Gwyn confidentially that the fact was, there was a tradition in his family that a curse would come on any Dew who tampered with the tump or let anybody else tamper with it.

Gwyn Griffith gave it up for the time being, and Corney

was left in a fine state of perturbation. Suppose it should occur to Gwyn Griffith to come poking round in the tump while Corney was asleep? Davy being only about two feet down could hardly escape notice; and although Corney had very little respect for antiquarians, he doubted if Gwyn Griffith would be soft enough to take Davy for a Druid.

Corney had buried his brother-in-law in the tump because it was a place he'd never want to plough up, where digging was quick and easy, and where the brambles and thorns conveniently hid both his operations and the scar left by them. He'd tucked Davy away in the early hours of the morning and gone home to make a hearty meal of fried bacon and strong tea, for he'd never liked Davy—a poor sort of chap who'd driven Corney's sister Marion to her grave with his shiftlessness—and he was not going to pretend to himself that he was sorry the chap was dead. His only regret had been that it was all for nothing, for he still didn't know where his Aunt Ann's gold ring was! He'd searched all Davy's pockets through and through, and the lining of his jacket, and inside his shoes. But although Davy had been wearing the ring when he first arrived that evening—it was just like the silly beggar to come trying to borrow money wearing a gold ring that didn't belong to him but had been loaned to him years ago to marry his wife with, on condition he gave it back after the honeymoon—it was nowhere to be found. After the tea and bacon, Corney had gone all over the floor with a bicycle-lamp, but it was no use. Davy must have hidden the ring somewhere when they started quarrelling about it. At any rate, if Corney hadn't the ring, neither had Davy, and there was some satisfaction in that!

Corney was not the man to be depressed for long, and until the visit of Gwyn Griffith, he'd scarcely given a thought to Davy, except to wonder sometimes, when he was out rabbiting, how the rabbits got on with him. After all, his conscience was clear—pretty clear. Goodness knew why the chap had died! His head had hit the flags a bit hard, maybe: but if he'd handed over Corney's property when Corney asked for it, Corney wouldn't have hit him.

Corney was well aware, though, that it would look bad for him if anybody ever found out about Davy, for people don't usually bury their relations secretly in old heathen tumps, and Corney wouldn't have done it, very likely, if he hadn't been too busy with his harvest and a cow with mastitis to spare time for inquests and that kind of thing. Yes, it would look bad for Corney if anybody found Davy; and after Gwyn had gone, Corney felt quite depressed, for he didn't trust Gwyn, no, he didn't trust him at all—a roaming, inquisitive chap like that, with all his time on his hands! Corney went quite off his food thinking about it, and Mrs. Thomas the Cwm[1] started telling the neighbours that old bachelors never made old bones, and trying to reckon to herself how much Corney's grandfather clock would fetch in an auction sale, and whether she'd have enough saved up when the time came. And when, one evening, Gwyn Griffith came back again, Corney only wished he could put Gwyn in with Davy and have done with him! But it was no use thinking of that; for, apart from it being sinful, Gwyn Griffith was a man with a place in the world, and people would enquire after him, whereas nobody had

---

1   Welsh, meaning Mrs. Thomas of the Vale.

enquired after poor Davy for fear of seeing him again! Gwyn
started all his persuasions once more, telling Corney how the
owners of such old ancient things only held them in trust for
humanity and so on. But Corney, having found a good line,
stuck to it, and just went on saying that he was sorry, but he
couldn't go against the curse, until Gwyn had to give it up
again. But just as Gwyn was going, he said something that
threw Corney into quite a panic. He said that as far as he
could see, the only way to get the tump opened would be to
get a police order to do it.

"What?" gasped Corney, hardly believing his ears.

"Only a joke, mun!" said Gwyn Griffith. "But Lloyd the
police is one of our new members, look you! Sure you hav-
en't got somebody tucked away in there the police ought to
know about?"

He went off laughing like anything at his own jocosity,
but it was no joke to Corney, who spent all that night cutting
faggots and lugging them into his back kitchen. And the next
evening, after dark, he went out to the tump with a wheel-
barrow and a spade. It was a moonlight night, so though he
took a lantern he didn't need to use it except at the end, to
make sure he hadn't left any bits behind. For there was nothing of Davy now but bones.

However, Corney got home without meeting anybody,
and only had to stop once to pick up some finger-bones which
had come loose and had dropped over the edge of the barrow.
He had lit the fire in the bread-oven early in the evening, and
when he opened the little door the dome-shaped oven was
full of swirling flame, so he made no delay and got Davy in
as best he could, feet-end first, shovelling the loose pieces in

after him. He didn't at all like the look on Davy's face as it went in, but then, he never had liked the look on Davy's face.

He shut the oven door, put a kettle on for a cup of tea, and sat there thinking about his sister's wedding-day and how everybody had said the marriage would come to no good, and wishing he hadn't been such a softie as to loan Davy his Aunt Ann's gold ring, for he might have known he'd never get it back. It was when he went out to the back kitchen to get last week's newspaper from the top of the copper to see how much a gold sovereign was worth now, that he realised that Davy was ending up as he'd lived—in a stink. My goodness! said Corney to himself, what'll I do now; the neighbours will be thinking my place is on fire! And he opened the oven door, though the smell nearly choked him, and bundled in as much more brushwood as would go, hoping to hurry matters up.

Sure enough, before long there was Thomas the Cwm at the door wanting to know what was the matter, and his missis sticking her sharp nose forward as usual. But Corney was ready for them and said his week's batch of bread had caught fire owing to him not having raked the oven out properly. Mrs. Thomas squeaked with glee at that, as a woman always does at a man's mistakes, and said she'd rake the lot out on to the floor if she was Corney, and pour cold water over it.

"What, and crack the flags?" said Corney, looking astounded, although goodness knew the flags around his oven had been cracked to atoms since his great-grandmother's day. "Let them bide!" said he, but before he could prevent her, Mrs. Thomas had the oven door open a crack and her long nose poking in.

"My Goddie, what was the matter with your yeast?" she squeaked. "The batch has run all over the place!" and she shut the door quick and started telling Corney about how the same thing had happened at her sister's three winters ago, and it was all owing to some yeast they'd got from the new baker in Huntingly.

This set Corney laughing like anything, when they'd gone, thinking of Mrs. Thomas's sister with her brother-in-law in the bread-oven! And then he went on to consider how little neighbours and relations knew of one another, when you came to think of it, and how, after all, if Mrs. Thomas's sister *had* had a relation in her bread-oven, Mrs. Thomas need not have known anything about it, any more than she knew about Davy, even after smelling and seeing him! And he cut himself a slice of fat bacon, and sat enjoying his own sentiments.

Well, now that the tump had been cleared of his property, Corney felt it would be un-neighbourly to go on denying Gwyn Griffith the treat of digging for a Druid. So after a few months' delay, to be respectful to Davy and give his grave time to heal over, he withdrew his objections to having the tump opened. And Gwyn brought all his Antiquarian Club over on a Saturday morning early, with spades and sieves and picks and a book he'd picked up secondhand in Presteign about how to open tumps and what you might expect to find in them. They started by clearing away the brushwood and brambles, and then Gwyn made a very nice speech about Corney, saying what a public-spirited man he was; and after a lot of argument about where to start, they began digging, putting all the earth through sieves, because that was what the book said they ought to do. They didn't start at the side, though, as the book said, cutting a bit out of the tump as if it were a cake, because the tump was a lot harder than any cake. So they started at the top, where it was crumbly and easy, and before long there was a great outcry and everybody was gathering round one of the sieves. And there—would you believe it?—was Aunt Ann's gold ring!

"My goodness!" thought Corney. "The dirty blackguard must have swallowed it!" and he started forward to grab his property. But then he stopped, because for the life of him he couldn't see how he was going to explain his Aunt Ann's ring without encouraging people to ask a lot of silly questions. And before he could think of what to say, there was Gwyn Griffith locking it up in a tin case and everybody discussing whether it belonged to the Bronze Age or the Roman!

Well, they didn't find anything more that day, and all the next week it rained, so the digging had to wait, and Corney didn't see anything of Gwyn. He was often on the point of going over to Aymesley to get his ring back, but he couldn't see how to explain his Aunt Ann's ring being in the tump, without getting a lot too near the truth.

The ring went up to the Crown as treasure-trove, and the Crown was very polite about it, but returned it, saying the owner of the ground could have it, for all it cared. You would think the matter would have been settled then. But not a bit of it! Gwyn Griffith took it for granted that Corney wanted nothing better than to loan the ring to the new Folk Museum he was starting in Aymesley, where he already had a lot of queer-shaped flints, an old ox-plough and three patten-irons; and Corney thought about Davy, and didn't know how to refuse.

The Antiquarian's Club didn't find anything else in the tump, except some large flat stones, which Gwyn said were the remains of a cyst. He said there had been bones in them, right enough, but somebody must have filched them out a long while ago. Corney reflected that he was not the only man in history who'd found it convenient to alter his mind about the best place for his brother-in-law.

But when a year or so afterwards, the Ancient Monuments Act was passed, and he had a paper sent him with the Government's seal at the top of it, telling him if he so much as touched the tump with the side of a spade, he'd be sent to prison or fined, it gave Corney the worst turn he'd ever had in his life; and he was a more serious man from that day forward, and took to paying very nearly as much income-tax as he owed, and made a will leaving his Aunt Ann's gold ring to the Aymesley Museum for ever. He'd had no idea the Government had means of knowing so much about him!

1954

The Way up to Heaven
Roald Dahl

It is tempting to say that Roald Dahl (1916–1990), whose books have sold more than 300 million copies worldwide, needs no introduction. He was born in Llandaff, Cardiff, to parents who had come to Wales from their native Norway, and his first language was Norwegian. At the age of six he met Beatrix Potter, an encounter which gave rise to a TV drama in 2020, and today he is best-known as a writer of children's books. He moved in celebrity circles and was married to the American actress Patricia Neal. However, he was also a notable fighter pilot, author of macabre short fiction (which earned three Edgar Awards from the Mystery Writers of America), and film screenplays, adapting two very different novels by his friend Ian Fleming, *You Only Live Twice* and *Chitty Chitty Bang Bang*.

Dahl introduced early episodes of the ITV anthology series *Tales of the Unexpected*, which originally concentrated on adaptations of his own stories before its popularity— eventually it ran to nine series—meant that the work of other writers ranging from Robert Bloch to Peter Lovesey was also utilised. This story was originally published in *The New Yorker* on 27 February 1954, and the TV screenplay, first aired on 19 May 1979, was written by Ronald Harwood; the cast included Julie Harris and Roland Culver.

———

ALL HER LIFE, MRS. FOSTER HAD HAD AN ALMOST pathological fear of missing a train, a plane, a boat, or even a theatre curtain. In other respects, she was not a particularly nervous woman, but the mere thought of being late on occasions like these would throw her into such a state of nerves that she would begin to twitch. It was nothing much—just a tiny vellicating muscle in the corner of the left eye, like a secret wink—but the annoying thing was that it refused to disappear until an hour or so after the train or plane or whatever it was had been safely caught.

It was really extraordinary how in certain people a simple apprehension about a thing like catching a train can grow into a serious obsession. At least half an hour before it was time to leave the house for the station, Mrs. Foster would step out of the elevator all ready to go, with hat and coat and gloves, and then, being quite unable to sit down, she would flutter and fidget about from room to room until her husband, who must have been well aware of her state, finally emerged from his privacy and suggested in a cool dry voice that perhaps they had better get going now, had they not?

Mr. Foster may possibly have had a right to be irritated by this foolishness of his wife's, but he could have had no excuse for increasing her misery by keeping her waiting unnecessarily. Mind you, it is by no means certain that this is what he did, yet whenever they were to go somewhere, his timing was so accurate—just a minute or two late, you understand—and his manner so bland that it was hard to believe he wasn't purposely inflicting a nasty private little torture of his own on the unhappy lady. And one thing he must have known—that she would never dare to call out and tell him to hurry. He had disciplined her too well for that. He must also have known that if he was prepared to wait even beyond the last moment of safety, he could drive her nearly into hysterics. On one or two special occasions in the later years of their married life, it seemed almost as though he had *wanted* to miss the train simply in order to intensify the poor woman's suffering.

Assuming (though one cannot be sure) that the husband was guilty, what made his attitude doubly unreasonable was the fact that, with the exception of this one small irrepressible foible, Mrs. Foster was and always had been a good and loving wife. For over thirty years, she had served him loyally and well. There was no doubt about this. Even she, a very modest woman, was aware of it, and although she had for years refused to let herself believe that Mr. Foster would ever consciously torment her, there had been times recently when she had caught herself beginning to wonder.

Mr. Eugene Foster, who was nearly seventy years old, lived with his wife in a large six-storey house in New York City, on East Sixty-second Street, and they had four servants. It was a gloomy place, and few people came to visit them. But on this particular morning in January, the house had come alive and there was a great deal of bustling about. One maid was distributing bundles of dust sheets to every room, while another was draping them over the furniture. The butler was bringing down suitcases and putting them in the hall. The cook kept popping up from the kitchen to have a word with the butler, and Mrs. Foster herself, in an old-fashioned fur coat and with a black hat on the top of her head, was flying from room to room and pretending to supervise these operations. Actually, she was thinking of nothing at all except that she was going to miss her plane if her husband didn't come out of his study soon and get ready.

"What time is it, Walker?" she said to the butler as she passed him.

"It's ten minutes past nine, Madam."

"And has the car come?"

"Yes, Madam, it's waiting. I'm just going to put the luggage in now."

"It takes an hour to get to Idlewild," she said. "My plane leaves at eleven. I have to be there half an hour beforehand for the formalities. I shall be late, I just *know* I'm going to be late."

"I think you have plenty of time, Madam," the butler said kindly. "I warned Mr. Foster that you must leave at nine fifteen. There's still another five minutes."

"Yes, Walker, I know, I know. But get the luggage in quickly, will you please?"

She began walking up and down the hall, and whenever the butler came by, she asked him the time. This, she kept telling herself, was the *one* plane she must not miss. It had taken months to persuade her husband to allow her to go. If she missed it, he might easily decide that she should cancel the whole thing. And the trouble was that he insisted on coming to the airport to see her off.

"Dear God," she said aloud, "I'm going to miss it. I know, I know, I *know* I'm going to miss it." The little muscle beside the left eye was twitching madly now. The eyes themselves were very close to tears.

"What time is it, Walker?"

"It's eighteen minutes past, Madam."

"Now I really *will* miss it!" she cried. "Oh, I wish he would come!"

This was an important journey for Mrs. Foster. She was going all alone to Paris to visit her daughter, her only child, who was married to a Frenchman. Mrs. Foster didn't care much for the Frenchman, but she was fond of her daughter, and, more than that, she had developed a great yearning to set eyes on her three grandchildren. She knew them only from the many photographs that she had received and that she kept putting up all over the house. They were beautiful, these children. She doted on them, and each time a new picture arrived she would carry it away and sit with it for a long time, staring at it lovingly and searching the small faces for signs of that old satisfying blood likeness that meant so much. And now, lately, she had come more and more to feel that she did not really wish to live out her days in a place where she could not be near these children, and have them visit her, and take them for walks, and buy them presents, and watch them grow. She knew, of course, that it was wrong and in a way disloyal to have thoughts like these while her husband was still alive. She knew also that although he was no longer active in his many enterprises, he would never consent to leave New York and live in Paris. It was a miracle that he had ever agreed to let her fly over there alone for six weeks to visit them. But, oh, how she wished she could live there always, and be close to them!

"Walker, what time is it?"

"Twenty-two minutes past, Madam."

As he spoke, a door opened and Mr. Foster came into the hall. He stood for a moment, looking intently at his wife, and she looked back at him—at this diminutive but still quite dapper old man with the huge bearded face that bore such an astonishing resemblance to those old photographs of Andrew Carnegie.

"Well," he said, "I suppose perhaps we'd better get going fairly soon if you want to catch that plane."

"*Yes*, dear—*yes*! Everything's ready. The car's waiting."

"That's good," he said. With his head over to one side, he was watching her closely. He had a peculiar way of cocking the head and then moving it in a series of small, rapid jerks. Because of this and because he was clasping his hands up high in front of him, near the chest, he was somehow like a squirrel standing there—a quick clever old squirrel from the Park.

"Here's Walker with your coat, dear. Put it on."

"I'll be with you in a moment," he said. "I'm just going to wash my hands."

She waited for him, and the tall butler stood beside her, holding the coat and the hat.

"Walker, will I miss it?"

"No, Madam," the butler said. "I think you'll make it all right."

Then Mr. Foster appeared again, and the butler helped him on with his coat. Mrs. Foster hurried outside and got into the hired Cadillac. Her husband came after her, but he walked down the steps of the house slowly, pausing halfway to observe the sky and to sniff the cold morning air.

"It looks a bit foggy," he said as he sat down beside her in the car. "And it's always worse out there at the airport. I shouldn't be surprised if the flight's cancelled already."

"Don't say that, dear—*please*."

They didn't speak again until the car had crossed over the river to Long Island.

"I arranged everything with the servants," Mr. Foster said. "They're all going off today. I gave them half pay for six weeks and told Walker I'd send him a telegram when we wanted them back."

"Yes," she said. "He told me."

"I'll move into the club tonight. It'll be a nice change staying at the club."

"Yes, dear. I'll write to you."

"I'll call in at the house occasionally to see that everything's all right and to pick up the mail."

"But don't you really think Walker should stay there all the time to look after things?" she asked meekly.

"Nonsense. It's quite unnecessary. And anyway, I'd have to pay him full wages."

"Oh, yes," she said. "Of course."

"What's more, you never know what people get up to when they're left alone in a house," Mr. Foster announced, and with that he took out a cigar and, after snipping off the end with a silver cutter, lit it with a gold lighter.

She sat still in the car with her hands clasped together tight under the rug.

"Will you write to me?" she asked.

"I'll see," he said. "But I doubt it. You know I don't hold with letter-writing unless there's something specific to say."

"Yes, dear, I know. So don't you bother."

They drove on, along Queens Boulevard, and as they approached the flat marshland on which Idlewild is built, the fog began to thicken and the car had to slow down.

"Oh, dear!" cried Mrs. Foster. "I'm *sure* I'm going to miss it now! What time is it?"

"Stop fussing," the old man said. "It doesn't matter anyway. It's bound to be cancelled now. They never fly in this sort of weather. I don't know why you bothered to come out."

She couldn't be sure, but it seemed to her that there was suddenly a new note in his voice, and she turned to look at him. It was difficult to observe any change in his expression under all that hair. The mouth was what counted. She wished, as she had so often before, that she could see the mouth clearly. The eyes never showed anything except when he was in a rage.

"Of course," he went on, "if by any chance it *does* go, then I agree with you—you'll be certain to miss it now. Why don't you resign yourself to that?"

She turned away and peered through the window at the fog. It seemed to be getting thicker as they went along, and now she could only just make out the edge of the road and the margin of grassland beyond it. She knew that her husband was still looking at her. She glanced at him again, and this time she noticed with a kind of horror that he was staring intently at the little place in the corner of her left eye where she could feel the muscle twitching.

"Won't you?" he said.

"Won't I what?"

"Be sure to miss it now if it goes. We can't drive fast in this muck."

He didn't speak to her any more after that. The car crawled on and on. The driver had a yellow lamp directed on to the edge of the road, and this helped him to keep going. Other lights, some white and some yellow, kept coming out of the fog towards them, and there was an especially bright one that followed close behind them all the time.

Suddenly, the driver stopped the car.

"There!" Mr. Foster cried. "We're stuck. I knew it."

"No, sir," the driver said, turning round. "We made it. This is the airport."

Without a word, Mrs. Foster jumped out and hurried through the main entrance into the building. There was a mass of people inside, mostly disconsolate passengers standing around the ticket counters. She pushed her way through and spoke to the clerk.

"Yes," he said. "Your flight is temporarily postponed. But please don't go away. We're expecting this weather to clear any moment."

She went back to her husband who was still sitting in the car and told him the news. "But don't you wait, dear," she said. "There's no sense in that."

"I won't," he answered. "So long as the driver can get me back. Can you get me back, driver?"

"I think so," the man said.

"Is the luggage out?"

"Yes, sir."

"Good-bye, dear," Mrs. Foster said, leaning into the car and giving her husband a small kiss on the coarse grey fur of his cheek.

"Good-bye," he answered. "Have a good trip."

The car drove off, and Mrs. Foster was left alone.

The rest of the day was a sort of nightmare for her. She sat for hour after hour on a bench, as close to the airline counter as possible, and every thirty minutes or so she would get up and ask the clerk if the situation had changed. She always received the same reply—that she must continue to wait, because the fog might blow away at any moment. It wasn't until after six in the evening that the loudspeaker finally announced that the flight had been postponed until eleven o'clock the next morning.

Mrs. Foster didn't quite know what to do when she heard this news. She stayed sitting on her bench for at least another half-hour, wondering, in a tired, hazy sort of way, where she might go to spend the night. She hated to leave the airport. She didn't wish to see her husband. She was terrified that in one way or another he would eventually manage to prevent her from getting to France. She would have liked to remain just where she was, sitting on the bench the whole night through. That would be the safest. But she was already exhausted, and it didn't take her long to realise that this was a ridiculous thing for an elderly lady to do. So in the end she went to a phone and called the house.

Her husband, who was on the point of leaving for the club, answered it himself. She told him the news, and asked whether the servants were still there.

"They've all gone," he said.

"In that case, dear, I'll just get myself a room somewhere for the night. And don't you bother yourself about it at all."

"That would be foolish," he said. "You've got a large house here at your disposal. Use it."

"But, dear, it's *empty*."

"Then I'll stay with you myself."

"There's no food in the house. There's nothing."

"Then eat before you come in. Don't be so stupid, woman. Everything you do, you seem to want to make a fuss about it."

"Yes," she said. "I'm sorry. I'll get myself a sandwich here, and then I'll come on in."

Outside, the fog had cleared a little, but it was still a long, slow drive in the taxi, and she didn't arrive back at the house on Sixty-second Street until fairly late.

Her husband emerged from his study when he heard her coming in. "Well," he said, standing by the study door, "how was Paris?"

"We leave at eleven in the morning," she answered. "It's definite."

"You mean if the fog clears."

"It's clearing now. There's a wind coming up."

"You look tired," he said. "You must have had an anxious day."

"It wasn't very comfortable. I think I'll go straight to bed."

"I've ordered a car for the morning," he said. "Nine o'clock."

"Oh, thank you, dear. And I certainly hope you're not going to bother to come all the way out again to see me off."

"No," he said slowly. "I don't think I will. But there's no reason why you shouldn't drop me at the club on your way."

She looked at him, and at that moment he seemed to be

standing a long way off from her, beyond some borderline. He was suddenly so small and far away that she couldn't be sure what he was doing, or what he was thinking, or even what he was.

"The club is downtown," she said. "It isn't on the way to the airport."

"But you'll have plenty of time, my dear. Don't you want to drop me at the club?"

"Oh, yes—of course."

"That's good. Then I'll see you in the morning at nine."

She went up to her bedroom on the second floor, and she was so exhausted from her day that she fell asleep soon after she lay down.

Next morning, Mrs. Foster was up early, and by eight thirty she was downstairs and ready to leave.

Shortly after nine, her husband appeared. "Did you make any coffee?" he asked.

"No, dear. I thought you'd get a nice breakfast at the club. The car is here. It's been waiting. I'm all ready to go."

They were standing in the hall—they always seemed to be meeting in the hall nowadays—she with her hat and coat and purse, he in a curiously cut Edwardian jacket with high lapels.

"Your luggage?"

"It's at the airport."

"Ah yes," he said. "Of course. And if you're going to take me to the club first, I suppose we'd better get going fairly soon, hadn't we?"

"Yes!" she cried. "Oh, yes—*please!*"

"I'm just going to get a few cigars. I'll be right with you. You get in the car."

She turned and went out to where the chauffeur was standing, and he opened the car door for her as she approached.

"What time is it?" she asked him.

"About nine fifteen."

Mr. Foster came out five minutes later, and watching him as he walked slowly down the steps, she noticed that his legs were like goat's legs in those narrow stovepipe trousers that he wore. As on the day before, he paused halfway down to sniff the air and to examine the sky. The weather was still not quite clear, but there was a wisp of sun coming through the mist.

"Perhaps you'll be lucky this time," he said as he settled himself beside her in the car.

"Hurry, please," she said to the chauffeur. "Don't bother about the rug. I'll arrange the rug. Please get going. I'm late."

The man went back to his seat behind the wheel and started the engine.

"*Just* a moment!" Mr. Foster said suddenly. "Hold it a moment, chauffeur, will you?"

"What is it, dear?" She saw him searching the pockets of his overcoat.

"I had a little present I wanted you to take to Ellen," he said. "Now, where on earth is it? I'm sure I had it in my hand as I came down."

"I never saw you carrying anything. What sort of present?"

"A little box wrapped up in white paper. I forgot to give it to you yesterday. I don't want to forget it today."

"A little box!" Mrs. Foster cried. "I never saw any little box!" She began hunting frantically in the back of the car.

Her husband continued searching through the pockets of his coat. Then he unbuttoned the coat and felt around in his jacket. "Confound it," he said, "I must've left it in my bedroom. I won't be a moment."

"Oh, *please*!" she cried. "We haven't got time! *Please* leave it! You can mail it. It's only one of those silly combs anyway. You're always giving her combs."

"And what's wrong with combs, may I ask?" he said, furious that she should have forgotten herself for once.

"Nothing, dear I'm sure. But..."

"Stay here!" he commanded. "I'm going to get it."

"Be quick, dear! Oh, *please* be quick!"

She sat still, waiting and waiting.

"Chauffeur, what time is it?"

The man had a wristwatch, which he consulted. "I make it nearly nine-thirty."

"Can we get to the airport in an hour?"

"Just about."

At this point, Mrs. Foster suddenly spotted a corner of something white wedged down in the crack of the seat on the side where her husband had been sitting. She reached over and pulled out a small paper-wrapped box, and at the same time she couldn't help noticing that it was wedged down firm and deep, as though with the help of a pushing hand.

"Here it is!" she cried. "I've found it! Oh dear, and now he'll be up there for ever searching for it! Chauffeur, quickly— run in and call him down, will you please?"

The chauffeur, a man with a small rebellious Irish mouth, didn't care very much for any of this, but he climbed out of the car and went up the steps to the front door of the house. Then he turned and came back. "Door's locked," he announced. "You got a key?"

"Yes—wait a minute." She began hunting madly in her purse. The little face was screwed up tight with anxiety, the lips pushed outward like a spout.

"Here it is! No—I'll go myself. It'll be quicker. I know where he'll be."

She hurried out of the car and up the steps to the front door, holding the key in one hand. She slid the key into the keyhole and was about to turn it—and then she stopped. Her head came up, and she stood there absolutely motionless, her whole body arrested right in the middle of all this hurry to turn the key and get into the house, and she waited—five, six, seven, eight, nine, ten seconds, she waited. The way she was standing there, with her head in the air and the body so tense, it seemed as though she were listening for the repetition of some sound that she had heard a moment before from a place far away inside the house.

Yes—quite obviously she was listening. Her whole attitude was a *listening* one. She appeared actually to be moving one of her ears closer to the door. Now it was right up against the door, and for still another few seconds she remained in that position, head up, ear to door, hand on key, about to enter but not entering, trying instead, or so it seemed, to hear and to analyse these sounds that were coming faintly from this place deep within the house.

Then, all at once, she sprang to life again. She withdrew the key from the door and came running back down the steps.

"It's too late!" she cried to the chauffeur. "I can't wait for him, I simply can't. I'll miss the plane. Hurry now, driver, hurry! To the airport!"

The chauffeur, had he been watching her closely, might

have noticed that her face had turned absolutely white and that the whole expression had suddenly altered. There was no longer that rather soft and silly look. A peculiar hardness had settled itself upon the features. The little mouth, usually so flabby, was now tight and thin, the eyes were bright, and the voice, when she spoke, carried a new note of authority.

"Hurry, driver, hurry!"

"Isn't your husband travelling with you?" the man asked, astonished.

"Certainly not! I was only going to drop him at the club. It won't matter. He'll understand. He'll get a cab. Don't sit there talking, man. *Get going!* I've got a plane to catch for Paris!"

With Mrs. Foster urging him from the back seat, the man drove fast all the way, and she caught her plane with a few minutes to spare. Soon she was high up over the Atlantic, reclining comfortably in her aeroplane chair, listening to the hum of the motors, heading for Paris at last. The new mood was still with her. She felt remarkably strong and, in a queer sort of way, wonderful. She was a trifle breathless with it all, but this was more from pure astonishment at what she had done than anything else, and as the plane flew farther and farther away from New York and East Sixty-second Street, a great sense of calmness began to settle upon her. By the time she reached Paris, she was just as strong and cool and calm as she could wish.

She met her grandchildren, and they were even more beautiful in the flesh than in their photographs. They were like angels, she told herself, so beautiful they were. And every day she took them for walks, and fed them cakes, and bought them presents, and told them charming stories.

Once a week, on Tuesdays, she wrote a letter to her husband—a nice, chatty letter—full of news and gossip, which always ended with the words "Now be sure to take your meals regularly, dear, although this is something I'm afraid you may not be doing when I'm not with you."

When the six weeks were up, everybody was sad that she had to return to America, to her husband. Everybody, that is, except her. Surprisingly, she didn't seem to mind as much as one might have expected, and when she kissed them all good-bye, there was something in her manner and in the things she said that appeared to hint at the possibility of a return in the not too distant future.

However, like the faithful wife she was, she did not overstay her time. Exactly six weeks after she had arrived, she sent a cable to her husband and caught the plane back to New York.

Arriving at Idlewild, Mrs. Foster was interested to observe that there was no car to meet her. It is possible that she might even have been a little amused. But she was extremely calm and did not overtip the porter who helped her into a taxi with her baggage.

New York was colder than Paris, and there were lumps of dirty snow lying in the gutters of the streets. The taxi drew up before the house on Sixty-second Street, and Mrs. Foster persuaded the driver to carry her two large cases to the top of the steps. Then she paid him off and rang the bell. She waited, but there was no answer. Just to make sure, she rang again, and she could hear it tinkling shrilly far away in the pantry, at the back of the house. But still no one came.

So she took out her own key and opened the door herself.
The first thing she saw as she entered was a great pile of

mail lying on the floor where it had fallen after being slipped through the letter box. The place was dark and cold. A dust sheet was still draped over the grandfather clock. In spite of the cold, the atmosphere was peculiarly oppressive, and there was a faint and curious odour in the air that she had never smelled before.

She walked quickly across the hall and disappeared for a moment around the corner to the left, at the back. There was something deliberate and purposeful about this action; she had the air of a woman who is off to investigate a rumour or to confirm a suspicion. And when she returned a few seconds later, there was a little glimmer of satisfaction on her face.

She paused in the centre of the hall, as though wondering what to do next. Then, suddenly, she turned and went across into her husband's study. On the desk she found his address book, and after hunting through it for a while she picked up the phone and dialled a number.

"Hello," she said. "Listen—this is Nine East Sixty-second Street… Yes, that's right. Could you send someone round as soon as possible, do you think? Yes, it seems to be stuck between the second and third floors. At least, that's where the indicator's pointing… Right away? Oh, that's very kind of you. You see, my legs aren't any good for walking up a lot of stairs. Thank you so much. Good-bye."

She replaced the receiver and sat there at her husband's desk, patiently waiting for the man who would be coming soon to repair the lift.

1956

Lucky Escape
Berkely Mather

Berkely (sometimes misspelled as Berkeley) Mather was the pen-name of Gloucester-born John Evan Weston-Davies (1909–1996), whose family emigrated to Australia when he was young. There is some controversy about the accuracy of the biographical information widely associated with him, but it is at least clear that he left Australia and later joined the Indian Army; after India gained independence he served in the Royal Artillery until retiring in 1959 and lived until 1996. Having published short stories in the 1930s, after the Second World War, Mather turned to scriptwriting for radio and television with characteristic gusto—and considerable success; he created the detective series *Charlesworth* and wrote for the much better-remembered *Z Cars* and *The Avengers*. His contribution to TV drama was recognised in 1962 by a "Special Merit" award from the CWA, which he chaired for a year in the mid-sixties.

He published his first novel in 1959, and his second book won the admiration of such luminaries as Ian Fleming and

Erle Stanley Gardner. At Fleming's prompting he became involved as a writer for the film *Dr No*, although it is said that he made the mistake of opting for a flat fee rather than a share of the profits. He also worked on *From Russia with Love* and *Goldfinger*. Mather (whose nickname was "Jasper") once wrote an article titled "Don't Call Me a Swashbuckler," but "swash-buckling" really is an apt term for his approach to writing. This story, kindly brought to my attention by Jamie Sturgeon, first appeared in the *Evening Standard* on 3 April 1956.

———

IT WAS NOT UNTIL THE TRAIN ARRIVED AT Bryncochymawr that I realised the pair opposite were also bound for the Plas, although the rods, gaffs, and creels on the rack should have told me something. Father and daughter, I decided.

He jiggled the flaps and counters of a mechanical bridge player, absorbed in its combinations and permutations. She sat, hands loosely folded in her lap—palms upward—gazing out at the blue-grey landscape that so matched her eyes, even to the hint of soft impending rain.

He dropped his score-card, and the girl and I dived for it simultaneously, our heads almost colliding, retrieving it and returning it together. He acknowledged it with a grunt but thanked neither of us—less lack of courtesy, perhaps, than concentration, but none the more endearing for that.

But the ice was broken. By the time we arrived at Llandarw, we were thoroughly acquainted. He was Lieutenant-colonel Tudor Pryddach-Rhys (retired), late Maharashtar Lights

Cavalry ("—when they were horsed—and officered by sahibs"), and she was his only child, Dilys. They lived en pension in San Sebastian, returning to Wales yearly for a fortnight's salmon fishing.

"This is the last time, though," he said. "The Chancellor of the Exchequer has seen to that."

We shared the one station taxi up to the Plas, detouring to leave some letters and a bag of fertiliser at a farm—for which the Colonel promptly knocked four shillings off the agreed fare, leaving Idwal the Bus murderous but acquiescent. I felt the girl between us shrink back into the tattered upholstery. Poor little soul. But why in this era of full employment didn't she leave the cantankerous old devil?

Huw Price met us at the steps of the Plas. He knew the Colonel and Dilys well, and launched into an excited greeting in Welsh, to which they both replied. I stood outside this linguistic circle. Huw, however, quickly switched back to English and his duties as a host.

The fishing was unspectacular as yet, but promising. If there was light afterwards, he would show us our places— mine was across the river. And did the Colonel intend to use a coracle this year?

"Duw! You've never seen coracle fishing, sir," he told me, "until you've seen the Colonel and Miss Dilys in one together— a poem it is."

It was the third night before I had an opportunity of seeing just what sort of life she led. Fishing started soon after an early breakfast and continued while there was light. We usually retired early. This night, however, I lingered because the Colonel had got on to the subject of mahseer fishing in the Deccan—something we both knew.

Dilys, with a skill that fascinated me, was repairing her father's casting net the other side of the fire. Huw leant over the bar watching her closely. The Colonel sat back in an old rocker, one of the inn's long churchwardens curving in a white sickle from his thin lips to his third waistcoat button.

"A fighting fish, the mahseer. Fiercer than the best salmon, even if shorter-lived." He felt for his tobacco pouch, prodded into it with his forefinger and found it empty. "Dilys, that other half pound of tobacco—in the small leather trunk."

She put down the net and went quickly out of the room, Huw's eyes following her. The Colonel refused my offered pouch. "Only smoke my own," he grunted.

Dilys was back in a moment—without the tobacco. And the heavens fell.

"Damn it, girl," he roared. "I handed it to you myself and told you to pack it."

"Father, I'm sure you didn't," she began tremulously, "I thought—"

"Don't stand there making paltering excuses. Tomorrow get on to Jackson's by telephone and tell them to send some. And now go to bed."

I saw Huw's fingers curl on the dark oak bar. Dilys picked up the net without a word and left, her small beaten figure shrinking into itself. There was an uncomfortable silence, and shortly afterwards the Colonel left with a grunted goodnight which Huw chose to disregard.

The big blond Welshman came round the bar and sat in the Colonel's vacated seat, prodding at the smouldering logs in the grate viciously.

"Swine—swine—swine," he breathed. He turned to me. "How the hell I keep my hands off the old devil—"

"Not a very attractive character," I agreed, "but why the deuce does his daughter stand it?"

"What can she do?" asked Huw. "Living with a bully all one's life—"

"Get out. Get a job. Marry. She's not unattractive."

"Unattractive?" Huw's eyes took on a distant look. "She's the most beautiful thing that ever came out of these mountains." Which was, I thought, putting it a bit high.

"Well, there you are," I said. "Tell her so, and take her out of his clutches."

"No good. I have—many times. Duty, that's what it is, duty and a damned unfair, stupid will. Her mother had the money, a lot of it. She left it in trust to Miss Dilys to come to her on her father's death, provided she is still living with him, and is unmarried."

"Well, dammit," I said impatiently, "she can't have it both ways. She must weigh up the pros and cons for herself— whether the life of a doormat now is worth wealth in the future—when she'll probably be too old to enjoy it."

"You don't understand, Mr. Jefferies," Huw said sadly. "I'll be waiting for her—diawl, yes—even if he lives fifty years."

But Dilys didn't have to wait fifty years. In fact, she didn't have to wait more than eighteen hours.

Coracle fishing the following day, the Colonel got stuck into a twenty-seven-pounder. It fought for an hour and a half before he brought it alongside and slid the gaff under its gills. Dilys swung and twisted the crazy craft with consummate skill the whole time.

And then the unexpected happened.

Witnesses—four hundred yards up the opposite bank—saw the coracle tip, just on the edge of the Druid's Race, a seething maelstrom that cuts through the hills below the Plas and ends in a fifty-foot fall. The Colonel went overboard in a flurry of arms and legs, broke the surface for a moment, and clung to the side of the now-righted coracle.

Then, nobody quite saw how, he slipped back and disappeared.

They eventually fished his battered body out of the river a mile below. Dilys spun the flimsy boat into a mad whirl and made a last despairing effort to grab her father before she was swept into the willows, to which she was still clinging when they reached her.

Huw drove us down to the station, silent and suffering. In delicacy he had kept away from her since the tragedy, but now time was running out.

"Dilys, cariad," I heard him whisper at the booking office, "I must speak to you."

"Put my bags in a first-class non-smoker, Mr. Price," she directed him, then flashed a bright smile at me. "Thank you, Mr. Jefferies. You've been most kind." And she swept—yes swept—through the barrier.

I turned to the crushed, bewildered Huw. "Don't take it too badly," I told him. "On the whole a lucky escape."

"Yes, she's escaped. From hell," he muttered.

But I meant it for him. Because I had seen through my binoculars the short heavy salmon club—a "priest" they call it in those parts—that she had raised twice and brought down heavily.

I sighed—and wired Franklyn to meet us at Paddington with the Squad car. You can't get away from it—even on holiday.

1959

The Strong Room
Cledwyn Hughes

John Cledwyn Hughes (1920–1978) was the only child of John and Janet Hughes of Llansantffraid, Montgomeryshire. An avid reader of fiction as a child, he followed his parents' wishes to study pharmacy, taking a degree in chemistry in 1945 from the University of Liverpool. He worked in a dispensary at Wrexham before successes with short stories, often set in the Severn or Vyrnwy valleys and sometimes with a medical twist, prompted him to take up writing full-time. He produced novels, short stories, children's books, and books about his native country including *Royal Wales* and *Portrait of Snowdonia*. Perhaps his best-known work is the 1950 novel *The Civil Strangers*.

In 1947 Hughes met and married a fashion designer and artist, Alyna Tudor-Davies. They had two daughters, Janet and Rebecca, who have generously shared with me with a great deal of information about this interesting and currently unjustly neglected author. The majority of his life was spent in north Wales, and evocative writing about Snowdonia and the Welsh Marches is a recurrent element of his work. He died of a brain tumour in 1978, and an archive of his papers is now held at the National Library of Wales. This story was first published in *Suspense* magazine in 1959, and I am grateful to Jamie Sturgeon for drawing it to my attention.

———

AT FIRST I THOUGHT THAT THE NOISE WAS SOME TRICK of the cold winter wind sighing about the old block of houses in the university town where I was lodging. Or I thought that, perhaps, it was a record of beat music from a student's party in some nearby house. It was a curious, undefined sound and it bothered my senses by its strangeness and its irregularity. It was a sort of occasional throb, followed by the slight echo of ringing metal.

It was well after midnight, in the frosty months of the year, and I was doing post-graduate research. I had a bed-sitting room on a third floor, with a daytime view over spires and to distant meadows. It was always a rather lonely, remote room; I liked it that way.

Now the distant sound kept disturbing me, and after a while I went to the window and drew back the old-fashioned curtains. I looked down into the well of the back street, a street which hadn't altered much since Regency days. It was still lit by gas which wavered a little with every urgent wind.

The noise was coming from across the street, and I could suddenly sense its source. There, between an old pharmacy and an off-licence, was the small sub-branch of a famous bank. It was there I had my small account; there I paid in my scholarship grants, and from there I drew out my weekly cash to meet my needs.

The sound was coming from there, from those dark windows which concealed, perhaps, thirty thousand pounds in old and untraceable notes. It was a quiet branch, with solicitors' offices over the shops on either side and above it. An ideal branch to rob, and I knew suddenly that now there was some machinery at work within.

If I had a telephone I would have rung up the police, but there was no phone anywhere in the house. The nearest booth was down the road, beyond the soft shimmering light of one of the gas lamps. For a moment I thought of drawing the curtains again and returning to my studies. It would be easier that way. I was a struggling student; the banks were rich and great; they should make their own arrangements for security.

And yet in me, as in us all, there was the good citizen. We are all conditioned to the goodness of law and order, to the preservation of private property, to helping society's best friends, the police. I knew that I should not be able to work again tonight unless I did something.

I took down my old duffle-coat from behind the door and went downstairs. The rest of the inhabitants of the house were asleep. Some were students, others were people who worked in the factories which had come on the outskirts of the town and which constantly jarred with the traditions of its academic life.

I let myself out into the street and walked under the shadows of the houses towards the telephone box. The white sashes of the windows and fanlights were clear in the darkness. Somewhere in a basement a baby was crying; over in the heart of the city there was a sharp short burst of bell clanging, as if a man's hand had touched the button in the cab of an ambulance or fire engine.

I walked along the pavement and reached to open the door of the telephone box.

It was then that I heard a voice, from the direction of a dark shop doorway down the street. It was a low, well-accented voice, yet rather muffled.

"You, come back."

I turned, but could see only a faint shape standing on the pavement. I opened the door of the booth. The voice called now more swiftly and harshly: "Come back here, at once."

A man came forward towards the edge of the pool of gaslight near the telephone box, and I could see the scythe of shadow as he raised his arm and pointed a small black gun at me.

I am a man of peace, and I did not need to be a professor of ballistics to know that death is quite certain when the target stands in a strong light, and the gunman is in the shadows six feet away. I walked towards the man; in the dim light I could see that he had a silk-stocking mask over his face.

I said hurriedly, "Who are you? Is this a hold-up?"

The man shook his head and answered quietly, "No, I am just the lookout, the guard. I was in the doorway of the bank and saw you coming out and going to the phone."

"The bank?" I asked, with a sort of innocence. "The bank, did you say?"

"That's right. You heard a noise from the bank, didn't you? I saw you draw back your curtains and look down. Then I saw you come out and head for the phone. Come back with me, my friend."

I wasn't his friend, not at all, but I thought it better not to point this out to him. "Where to?"

"Into the bank, inside."

I wished with all my heart—law, justice, good citizenship, and everything notwithstanding—that I was back in my lonely room with my books. A student with a bad conscience, alive, was better than a good citizen dead.

We walked back along the street, the way I had come. The baby was still crying in the basement and a woman's soothing voice could be heard, reassuring and ordinary. A car passed at the end of the road, its lights bright and homely. The man with the mask drew me into a doorway, but after a slight halt we walked on until we reached the bank. The man opened the door with a thrust of his foot, and we went inside. The banking hall itself was dark and ordinary, with blotters and pens and stands neat with slips and papers on the wide polished counter.

The man with the silk-stocking mask took me through to a passageway at the side of the manager's private room. It was there, I knew, that the entrance to the strong room was; I had often noticed its inner grille and door when I was going into the manager's room to sign papers or talk over my small affairs.

This passage was now bright with light, but none of it could be seen from the outside. A window at the end of the passage had been carefully pasted over with adhesive plastic sheeting. The bottom of a door beyond had been covered with old sugar sacks carefully rolled and folded.

A man and a woman were at work on the door of the strong room. The man was tall, and wore a well-tailored suit. The girl was tall, too, a Nordic type of blonde with her hair done in a plaited coil across her head. She was wearing a smart black dress, and had a good fur coat hanging from a peg in the passageway. The tall man had a white silk cravat tied about his neck which he probably used as a mask outside, but which was now used to catch the sweat from his cheeks. The girl had no covering on her face, and she had the sweetest of expressions, full of tenderness and gentleness, with blue eyes and a brown mole on her cheek.

"What have you caught there, Jimmy?" she asked.

The man with the silk-stocking mask said casually, "This guy saw us, but I saw him first."

The girl with the fair hair smiled at me, and I wished that she was on my side of the law. I even wished that I was in her world; breaking into banks with such a creature would have been the best of recreations.

"You should have been in bed," the fair-haired girl said.

The tall man said impatiently, "Keep your mind on the job, Betty."

I saw then what they were doing. On the floor was an oxy-acetylene kit coupled up to a cutting head. There was also an electric arc, its power cable running directly to the meter in the passage, the current being taken from the main cables by two massive crocodile clips. There was also another cylinder of oxygen, coupled to give boost at the electric arc point. The tall man had hold of the oxy-acetylene cutter, the girl was using the electric welding arc. As I watched they both pulled down coloured goggles over their eyes and attacked the strong room door again.

"Sit down in the corner, friend," the man who had brought

me in said, "and don't move or she'll weld your knee-caps together, won't you, Betty?"

The blonde spoke above the noise of the equipment. "Not if he's a good boy."

After that they all worked fast. Sometimes Jimmy would go out to the front of the bank, and I would hear the street door opening, and then he would come back again. All the time Betty and the tall man were crouched over the door. I could see that they were working to a clever plan, using the electric arc boosted by oxygen, and the oxy-acetylene head, alternately. They were carving, for that is the only word to describe it, a long slit down the great strong room door at the side of the lock.

It was intense, exciting work, and I caught some of the infection of it. I watched Betty mostly as she stroked the blue-white light of the electric arc down on the door. Sometimes the taller man would strike the door handle with a crowbar. This was the noise which had attracted my attention.

After an hour or so, Betty turned to the tall man. "We're through, David. Fetch a bucket of water to cool down the job."

I realised then that Betty was the one who gave the orders; it was her job; she was the bright mind behind the break-in.

The tall man called David went down the passage to a toilet and brought back a bucket of water. Jimmy came back from the street and stood by my side.

"Mind yourself, my friend—the water will bring up some steam," he warned.

It was true. At first there was the sizzle of steam, but gradually the water cooled down the cut steel. Then the blonde girl put a long-fingered hand through the narrow slit and reached the inner handle of the safe door.

"Betty can feel the difference between right and wrong," said Jimmy to me, casually yet proudly.

The girl answered as she worked on the door: "This is a simple one, anyway."

She stood back then and beckoned to David. "Pull, and that'll only leave the grille and the inside door. We'll have to be careful on the inner job, too, so as not to heat the emergency locking trick. We only just missed it in this one."

Jimmy said to me, as if I were his friend, or as if I were an apprentice, "Safe-makers vary the position of the locking gear which comes into use if heat is used on a safe door. Betty knows most of the tricks, though."

The outer door swung back, they cut through the grille door easily, and they set to work on the inner door of the strong room.

Soon they were almost through that one; only once did Betty turn round and speak. "Chemical fuses in this one. Get me some peroxide from my handbag, Jimmy."

She poured some of the liquid into the aperture in the hot steel, waited a moment, and then carried on with the electric arc. After that David took a turn with the oxy-acetylene head.

It was left to Betty, the Nordic blonde, to open this door. That done, she calmly switched on the light inside and watched while David, the tall man, cut through the leads from the burglar alarm on the second grille-door. They severed the hinges of this grille and then David and Betty walked into the strong room. David played for a while with the lock of a safe standing against one wall and it opened easily. Inside were brown paper packages of notes, £1 and £5 written in crayon on the outside of the paper.

"Tempting," said David.

"Very," said Jimmy.

But Betty shrugged. "No, boys, not tonight. We're here for what I want, that's all."

She turned to the shelves of the strong room, on which were stored numbered deed and black security boxes. She seemed to be looking for a certain box, a certain number. She picked one up.

"Take this, David; this is what we've come for."

The tall man sighed, and pointed to the safe against the yellow wall of the strong room. "But all those—such a waste."

She answered sharply. "Not tonight, David. We've had enough in this past fortnight. And plenty more in the future, if you trust my little head."

"You're the genius," said David.

"Quite the brightest girl in town," went on Jimmy.

It was all too mysterious. I plucked up courage to speak. "But why are you robbing the bank and not taking any money, only that deed box?"

"Tell him, Jimmy," said Betty. "Tell him because he's been a quiet, gentle, good boy."

Jimmy answered through the stocking mask. "My friend, my quiet, gentle good friend, it's like this. Betty is our boss, and it's not for us to ask questions. She pays the wages and shares the golden cargoes. Tonight we're on this job because Betty wants that deed box. It belonged to her husband, who was a fine man, an officer in the Army who was killed in Cyprus when things were bad."

"God rest his soul," said David sincerely.

Betty was silent and I could see that all the memory of

an old and true love was within her. Jimmy went on quietly, "After he died, an Army pension being the pittance that it is, she turned to more remunerative adventures."

Betty turned round now, and I could see that she was in control of herself again for she said to me, with a sweet smile, "So don't you breathe a word about tonight or me to a living soul, or the boys will get you. Death would be sweeter than my revenge."

"Amen," said David. We all went into the dark of the banking hall. Then, with Jimmy carrying the black deed box, they opened the doorway to the darkened streets.

One thing puzzled me. "What's in the deed box?" I asked.

Betty said in a whisper, "What's in here could spoil my dead husband's memory. It will now be lost, this evidence, for ever."

Then they were gone and a few seconds later I heard the roar of a car, and I knew that they were leaving this town.

I stood in the dark banking hall and could sense the perfume that Betty, the beautiful girl who robbed banks, had used. And smelling its fragrance and its personification of femininity, I had a sudden longing to see her again, but I knew that that would never be. She and her two men were gone, passing adventurers in my drab and ordinary academic world.

Like all adventurers, she and her men had displayed a sense of character; a gesture of devil-may-care. Who, who indeed, except people of such mind, could have turned their backs on a fortune and been satisfied with the simple black box they had come to find?

A fortune indeed. I turned back then, and hastened into the corridor and through the broken, destroyed doors of the strong room to the safe. Using a great wire tray, I piled on to it brown paper bundles of old notes. Then, with this load staggering and swaying, I walked through the banking hall and to the threshold of the front door of the bank. The gas-lamp still shone at the end of the street, but the baby who had been awake had gone to sleep and all was still.

Boldly I walked across the road to the house where I lodged in a room at the top. I put the wire tray down on the top step while I used my latch-key, and after that I went in and closed the door. I walked calmly upstairs and stored away the packages of used notes in my tin travelling trunk under my bed.

I then went to sleep. It was daylight when I awoke and I could hear excitement in the street outside; talking, and the sounds of cars coming and going. Without going to the window I knew what it was all about. With my hands under my head, and lying on top of about fifteen thousand pounds in hard cash, I thought about the follies of mankind: greed, and all that. I thought, too, how remarkable a person was the girl, Betty. She had got what she wanted, and had made certain that I would keep the night's secret intact, for ever.

1962

Mamba

Jack Griffith

Jack Griffith is a thinly veiled pseudonym for probably the most obscure of the authors whose work appears in this anthology, and I am indebted to Jamie Sturgeon and John Herrington, as well as his daughter Siân Griffiths, for supplying me with information about him. His full name was Jack Edward Griffiths, and he was born in Blaenclydach in south Wales in 1902. He was a vicar, and it is intriguing to note that, over the years, a considerable number of members of the clergy have indulged in fictional crime. After studying as a mature student at Aberystwyth University, he was ordained in 1937, became a curate, and married a rector's daughter in 1939. He served in the Territorial Army as a Captain Chaplain and served on hospital ships and overseas during the Second World War. Later, his ministry took him from Leighton, near Welshpool, to South East Asia; he and his wife sailed to Malaya in 1952 with the apparent intention of staying there long-term, and he was Vicar of Penang from 1953–57. In 1960, the family returned to the Welsh Marches, and until retirement in 1975 he was responsible for the three Shropshire parishes of Easthope, Stanton Long, and Shipton, making his home in Easthope rectory, Much Wenlock. He died in nearby Bridgnorth in 1977.

Griffiths' literary specialism was the short story; although he wrote several novels over the years, none of them found a publisher. He was writing fiction for the *News Chronicle* at least as early as 1934, and after joining the Crime Writers' Association (for which he served as honorary chaplain), he became a regular contributor to the CWA's annual anthology, which in the 1960s and 1970s focused mainly on reprinting stories that had already appeared in books and magazines. His interest in crime was also reflected in a spell as a special constable. Several of his mysteries make use of his familiarity with South East Asia, including this one, which first appeared in *The New Strand Magazine* in 1962 and was reprinted in a CWA anthology edited by Herbert Harris, *John Creasey's Mystery Bedside Book 1974*.

———

HE WAS THINKING OF SNAKES AS HE DROVE HOME through the dark of a chill winter's night.

Before that he had been wondering what his wife would have for his supper. Whatever it was he would find something wrong with it; he always did.

He wondered why he had married her. She was the most unpleasant thing in his life.

Except snakes, of course; they were even worse.

He had hated snakes ever since he had almost grasped a black mamba which had been lying unnoticed along a pile of pipes in West Africa during the war. He had stooped to pick it up, mistaking it for the topmost pipe, when his Quartermaster Sergeant had shouted a warning.

"Look out, sir! Mamba!"

Despite the cry, and a swift leap backwards, he had not been able to get completely away. The snake, deadly and ever ready to attack and fight, had struck.

It had missed him, but only just, getting close enough to eject milky-white fluid over the rolled-up sleeve of his bush-shirt.

Everything had happened too quickly for him to be really frightened. He had been shocked, coldly and calmly shocked, that was all. Fright had come later.

When the incident was related by someone else in the Mess that evening, another officer had told how he had seen a green mamba—almost as deadly as the infamous black mamba—when he had gone to the lavatory, and had fled with his shorts down over his knees. This man had treated it as a joke now that he was out of danger. He himself could not understand how anyone could treat snakes as a joke.

Although it had taken this black mamba to make him hate snakes, he had always disliked them. He was unable to hold a worm in his hand, not only when he had been a child, but even now that he had become a man.

The only nightmare he remembered ever having was when he was ten years old. He had dreamt that a large snake was coiled upon his chest, weighing him down until he could scarcely breathe. He had awakened in terror—to discover that in his restless slumber a portion of the pillow had worked up on to his chest.

Unlike most dreams which melted like foam and were forgotten, this one remained as a permanent repellent memory. He could even recall what the snake looked like: vicious, twisting streak, patterned with large white diamonds surrounded by thick black lacing and bespattered by strange markings which might have been mystic symbols from some ancient temple...

Years after the scare of the black mamba he had been shown a tankful of sea-snakes in Malaya, poisonous and differing from land-snakes only by having tails like rudders instead of pointed. The sight had filled him with horror—and grey hate. He had loathed them!

Now he was back in England for good with no danger of seeing anything beyond a grass-snake in a field. At worst, an adder.

Unless...

Unless someone put a snake in the pocket of his car. He had once heard on a wireless programme that a racing driver had crashed to death because someone who knew of his fear of snakes had hidden one in the cubby-hole where he kept his cigarettes. The snake had not harmed him, but its presence had.

The same thing might happen to him!

He stopped the car and got out. It was drizzling and cold and bleak. He shivered. Leaning cautiously through the open doorway—ready to leap away instantly—he switched on the dashboard light. With a quick movement he snapped the lid of the pocket open.

There was nothing inside but cigarettes.

He swore. He should have known; he had smoked at least two of them on the way. But thinking of snakes did things like that to him.

He got into the car again and drove home. In low gear he swung through the front gates and along the short drive to the garage near the house.

Although ungraciously, he was glad to see that his wife had opened the doors ready for his return.

"I'm glad she had sense enough to do that, at least," he grunted. "Wonder what came over her."

He never realised that she opened the doors for him far oftener than he remembered to thank her.

Stopping the engine, he switched off the lights and got out.

Something slim and pliable slithered down from the darkness above his head and coiled itself loosely over his neck.

Shrieking, he clutched at it in terror. It was cold and silent and yielding. And clinging. He tried to toss it away, but had grasped the two ends, pulling it around his neck and helping it tighten, strangling him.

"Snake! Help!" he screamed, almost vomiting.

Struggling, stumbling on to his knees, breathing only with difficulty, choking and coughing, he was afraid to let go almost as much as he was afraid not to. Tighter he pulled, and tighter it became, tighter until he almost lost consciousness. Only then did his grip relax…

When he recovered, the light was on. Like the lights in most private garages, it was dim and inadequate, but bright enough for him to make out the anxious expression on his wife's face as she stooped over him.

"What happened?" she was saying. "Are you all right? You were such a long time coming into the house that I had to come and find out why. Tell me, what happened?"

"A snake!" he spluttered. "A snake fell on my neck! It was choking me! Where is it? *Where is it?*"

"It wasn't a snake, dear," she explained soothingly. "It was only a piece of hosepipe. It's been lying around the garage for months—ever since we came here."

"Hosepipe!" he shouted. "What stupid fool hung a hosepipe just over the car door? With my thrombosis it was enough to make me drop dead from shock. It couldn't have been better planned if someone had done it purposely to try to kill me. Who was it?"

His wife did not reply. His questions were always unanswerable. She was sick of his questions; she was sick of him and his selfishness and brutality.

But now she would have to contrive something else.

Next time, perhaps, she would be able to get a real mamba…

1966

The Chosen One

Rhys Davies

Vivian Rees Davies, known as Rhys Davies (1901–1978), was born in Blaenclydach, as was Jack Griffiths, so it is possible they knew each other in their youth, although life then took them in very different directions. After leaving school at fourteen, Davies moved to London and started writing short stories. Soon he was doing well enough to become a full-time author. He met D. H. Lawrence and his wife, Frieda, and over the years his eclectic group of close friends included the Scottish writer Fred Urquhart, with whom he lived for several years, and the novelist Anna Kavan, whose early life inspired his 1975 novel *The Honeysuckle Girl*.

Davies wrote in English, and mostly in England, but he made a significant contribution to Welsh literature. In all he published twenty novels, but arguably his literary forte was the short story. He was awarded an OBE in 1968, and in 1971 he was given the Welsh Arts Council's principal prize for his distinguished contribution to the literature of Wales, although he could not be persuaded to attend the reception in Cardiff. This mystery, which first appeared in *The New Yorker* on 27 May 1966, became the title story of a collection and earned Davies an Edgar Award from the Mystery Writers of America.

———

A LETTER, INSCRIBED "BY HAND," LAY INSIDE THE DOOR when he arrived home just before seven o'clock. The thick, expensive-looking envelope was black-edged and smelled of stale face powder. Hoarding old-fashioned mourning envelopes would be typical of Mrs. Vines, and the premonition of disaster Rufus felt now had nothing to do with death. He stared for some moments at the penny-sized blob of purple wax sealing the flap. Other communications he had received from Mrs. Vines over the last two years had not been sent in such a ceremonious envelope. The sheet of ruled paper inside, torn from a pad of the cheapest kind, was more familiar. He read it with strained concentration, his brows drawn into a pucker. The finely traced handwriting, in green ink, gave him no special difficulty, and his pausings over words such as "oral," "category," and "sentimental," while his full-fleshed lips shaped the syllables, came from uncertainty of their meaning.

Sir,

In reply to your oral request to me yesterday, concerning the property Brychan Cottage, I have decided not to grant you a renewal of the lease, due to expire on June 30th next. This is final.

*The cottage is unfit for human habitation, whether
you consider yourself as coming under that category
or not. It is an eyesore to me, and I intend razing it
to the ground later this year. That you wish to get
married and continue to live in the cottage with some
factory hussy from the town is no affair of mine, and
that my father, for sentimental reasons, granted your
grandfather a seventy-five-year lease for the paltry
sum of a hundred pounds is no affair of mine, either.
Your wretched family has always been a nuisance to
me on my estate, and I will not tolerate one of them
to infest it any longer than is legal, or any screeching,
jazz-dancing slut in trousers and bare feet to trespass
and contaminate my land. Although you got rid of the
pestiferous poultry after your mother died, the noise of
the motorcycle you then bought has annoyed me even
more than the cockerel crowing. Get out.*

Yours truly,
Audrey P. Vines

He saw her brown-speckled, jewel-ringed hand moving
from word to word with a certainty beyond any means of
retaliation from him. The abuse in the letter did not enrage
him immediately; it belonged too familiarly to Mrs. Vines's
character and reputation, though when he was a boy he had
known different behaviour from her. But awareness that she
had this devilish right to throw him, neck and crop, from the
home he had inherited began to register somewhere in his
mind at last. He had never believed she would do it.

Shock temporarily suspended full realisation of the catastrophe. He went into the kitchen to brew the tea he always made as soon as he arrived home on his motorbike from his factory job in the county town. While he waited for the kettle to boil on the oilstove, his eye kept straying warily to the table. The black-edged envelope was like something in a warning dream. He stared vaguely at the familiar objects around him. A peculiar silence seemed to have come to this kitchen that he had known all his life. There was a feel of withdrawal from him in the room, as though he was already an intruder in it.

He winced when he picked up the letter and put it in a pocket of his leather jacket. Then, as was his habit on fine evenings, he took a mug of tea out to a seat under a pear tree shading the ill-fitting front door of the cottage, a white-washed, sixteenth-century building in which he had been born. Golden light of May flooded the well-stocked garden. He began to reread the letter, stopped to fetch a tattered little dictionary from the living room, and sat consulting one or two words that still perplexed him. Then, his thick jaw thrust out in his effort at sustained concentration, he read the letter through again.

The sentence "This is final" pounded in his head. Three words had smashed his plans for the future. In his bewilderment, it did not occur to him that his inbred procrastination was of importance. Until the day before, he had kept postponing going to see the evil-tempered mistress of Plas Iolyn about the lease business, though his mother, who couldn't bear the sight of her, had reminded him of it several times in her last illness. He had just refused to believe that Mrs. Vines would turn him out when a date in a yellowed old document came round. His mother's forebears had occupied Brychan Cottage for hundreds of years, long before Mrs. Vines' family bought Plas Iolyn.

Slowly turning his head, as though in compulsion, he gazed to the left of where he sat. He could see, beyond the garden and the alders fringing a ditch, an extensive slope of rough turf on which, centrally in his vision, a great cypress spread branches to the ground. Higher, crowning the slope, a rectangular mansion of russet stone caught the full light of sunset. At this hour, he had sometimes seen Mrs. Vines walking down the slope with her bulldog. She always carried a bag, throwing bread from it to birds and to wild duck on the river below. The tapestry bag had been familiar to him since he was a boy, but it was not until last Sunday that he learned she kept binoculars in it.

She could not be seen anywhere this evening. He sat thinking of last Sunday's events, unable to understand that such a small mistake as his girl had made could have caused the nastiness in the letter. Gloria had only trespassed a few yards on Plas Iolyn land. And what was wrong with a girl wearing trousers or walking barefoot on clean grass? What harm was there if a girl he was courting screeched when he chased her onto the riverbank and if they tumbled to the ground? Nobody's clothes had come off.

He had thought Sunday was the champion day of his life. He had fetched Gloria from the town on his motorbike in the afternoon. It was her first visit to the cottage that he had boasted about so often in the factory, especially to her. Brought up in a poky terrace house without a garden, she had been pleased and excited with his pretty home on the Plas Iolyn estate, and in half an hour, while they sat under this pear tree, he had asked her to marry him, and she said she would. She had laughed and squealed a lot in the garden and by the river, kicking her shoes off, dancing on the grassy river-bank; she was only eighteen. Then, when he went indoors to put the kettle on for tea, she had jumped the narrow dividing ditch onto Mrs. Vines's land—and soon after came dashing into the cottage. Shaking with fright, she said that a terrible woman in a torn fur coat had come shouting from under a big tree on the slope, spyglasses in her hand and threatening her with a bulldog. It took quite a while to calm Gloria down. He told her of Mrs. Vines's funny ways and the tales he had heard from his mother. But neither on Sunday nor since did he mention anything about the lease of Brychan Cottage, though remembrance of it had crossed his mind when Gloria said she'd marry him.

On Sunday, too, he had kept telling himself that he ought to ride up to the mansion to explain about the stranger who had ignorantly crossed the ditch. But three days went by before he made the visit. He had bought a high-priced suede windcheater in the town, and got his hair trimmed during his dinner hour. He had even picked a bunch of polyanthus for Mrs. Vines when he arrived home from the factory—and then, bothered by wanting to postpone the visit still longer, forgot them when he forced himself at last to jump on the bike. It was her tongue he was frightened of, he had told himself. He could never cope with women's tantrums.

But she had not seemed to be in one of her famous tempers when he appeared at the kitchen door of Plas Iolyn, just after seven. "Well, young man, what do you require?" she asked, pointing to a carpenter's bench, alongside the dresser, on which he had often sat as a boy. First, he tried to tell her that the girl who strayed on her land was going to marry him. But Mrs. Vines talked to the five cats that, one after the other, bounded into the kitchen from upstairs a minute after he arrived. She said to them, "We won't have these loud-voiced factory girls trespassing on any part of my property, will we, my darlings?" Taking her time, she fed the cats with liver she lifted with her fingers from a pan on one of her three small oilstoves. Presently, he forced himself to say, "I've come about the lease of Brychan Cottage. My mother told me about it. I've got a paper with a date on it." But Mrs. Vines said to one of the cats, "Queenie, you'll have to swallow a pill tomorrow!" After another wait, he tried again, saying, "My young lady is liking Brychan Cottage very much." Mrs. Vines stared at him, not saying a word for about a minute, then said, "You can go now. I will write you tomorrow about the lease."

He had left the kitchen feeling a tightness beginning to throttle him, and he knew then that it had never been fear he felt toward her. But, as he tore at full speed down the drive, the thought came that it might have been a bad mistake to have stopped going to Plas Iolyn to ask if he could collect whinberries for her up on the slopes of Mynydd Baer, or find mushrooms in the Caer Tegid fields, as he used to do before he took a job in a factory in the town. Was that why, soon after his mother died, she had sent him a rude letter about the smell of poultry and the rooster crowing? He had found that letter comic and shown it to chaps in the factory. But something had told him to get rid of the poultry.

He got up from the seat under the pear tree. The strange quiet he had noticed in the kitchen was in the garden, too. Not a leaf or bird stirred. He could hear his heart thumping. He began to walk up and down the paths. He knew now the full meaning of her remark to those cats that no trespassers would be allowed on "my property." In about six months he himself would be a trespasser. He stopped to tear a branch of pear blossom from the tree, and looked at it abstractedly. The pear tree was *his*! His mother had told him it was planted on the day he was born. Some summers it used to fruit so well that they had sold the whole load to Harries in the town, and the money was always for him.

Pacing, he slapped the branch against his leg, scattering the blossom. The tumult in his heart did not diminish. Like the kitchen, the garden seemed already to be withdrawn from his keeping. *She* had walked there that day, tainting it. He hurled the branch in the direction of the Plas Iolyn slope. He did not want to go indoors. He went through a thicket of willows and lay on the riverbank staring into the clear, placidly flowing water. Her face flickered in the greenish depths. He flung a stone at it. Stress coiled tighter in him. He lay flat on his back, sweating, a hand clenched over his genitals.

The arc of serene evening sky and the whisper of gently lapping water calmed him for a while. A shred of common sense told him that the loss of Brychan Cottage was not a matter of life and death. But he could not forget Mrs. Vines. He tried to think how he could appease her with some act or service. He remembered that until he was about seventeen she would ask him to do odd jobs for her, such as clearing fallen branches, setting fire to wasp holes, and—she made him wear a bonnet and veil for this—collecting the combs from her beehives. But what could he do now? She had shut herself away from everybody for years.

He could not shake off thought of her. Half-forgotten memories of the past came back. When he was about twelve, how surprised his mother had been when he told her that he had been taken upstairs in Plas Iolyn and shown six kittens born that day! Soon after that, Mrs. Vines had come down to this bank, where he had sat fishing, and said she wanted him to drown three of the kittens. She had a tub of water ready outside her kitchen door, and she stood watching while he held a wriggling canvas sack under the water with a broom. The three were males, she said. He had to dig a hole close to the greenhouses for the sack.

She never gave him money for any job, only presents from the house—an old magic lantern, coloured slides, dominoes, a box of crayons, even a doll's house. Her big brown eyes would look at him without any sign of temper at all. Once, when she asked him, "Are you a dunce in school?" and he said, "Yes, bottom of the class," he heard her laugh aloud for the first time, and she looked very pleased with him. All that, he remembered, was when visitors had stopped going to Plas Iolyn, and there was not a servant left; his mother said they wouldn't put up with Mrs. Vines's bad ways any more. But people in the town who had worked for her said she was a very clever woman, with letters after her name, and it was likely she would always come out on top in disputes concerning her estate.

Other scraps of her history returned to his memory— things heard from old people who had known her before she shut herself away. Evan Matthews, who used to be her estate keeper and had been a friend of his father's, said that for a time she had lived among African savages, studying their ways with her first husband. Nobody knew how she had got rid of that husband, or the whole truth about her second one. She used to disappear from Plas Iolyn for months, but when her father died she never went away from her old home again. But it was when her second husband was no longer seen in Plas Iolyn that she shut herself up there, except that once a month she hired a Daimler from the county town and went to buy, so it was said, cases of wine at Drapple's, and stuff for her face at the chemist's. Then even those trips had stopped, and everything was delivered to Plas Iolyn by tradesmen's vans or post.

No clue came of a way to appease her. He rose from the riverbank. The sunset light was beginning to fade, but he could still see clearly the mansion façade, its twelve bare windows, and the crumbling entrance portico, which was never used now. In sudden compulsion, he strode down to the narrow, weed-filled ditch marking the boundary of Brychan Cottage land. But he drew up at its edge. If he went to see her, he thought, he must prepare what he had to say with a cooler head than he had now. Besides, to approach the mansion that way was forbidden. She might be watching him through binoculars from one of those windows.

An ambling sound roused him from this torment of inde-cision. Fifty yards beyond the river's opposite bank, the 7:40 slow train to the county town was approaching. Its passage over the rough stretches of meadowland brought back a reminder of his mother's bitter grudge against the family at Plas Iolyn.

The trickery that had been done before the railroad was laid had never meant much to him, though he had heard about it often enough from his mother. Late in the nineteenth century, her father, who couldn't read or write, had been persuaded by Mrs. Vines's father to sell to him, at a low price, not only decaying Brychan Cottage but, across the river, a great many acres of useless meadowland included in the cottage demesne. As a bait, a seventy-five-year retaining lease of the cottage and a piece of land to the riverbank were granted for a hundred pounds. So there had been some money to stave off further dilapidation of the cottage and to put by for hard times. But in less than two years after the transaction, a railroad loop to a developing port in the west had been laid over that long stretch of useless land across the river. Mrs. Vines's father had known of the project and, according to the never-forgotten grudge, cleared a big profit from rail rights. His explanation (alleged by Rufus's mother to be humbug) was that he had wanted to preserve the view from possible ruination by buildings such as gasworks; a few trains every day, including important expresses and freight traffic, did not matter.

Watching, with a belligerent scowl, the 7:40 vanishing into the sunset fume, Rufus remembered that his father used to say that it wasn't Mrs. Vines herself who had done the dirty trick. But was the daughter proving herself to be of the same robbing nature now? He could not believe that she intended razing Brychan Cottage to the ground. Did she want to trim it up and sell or rent at a price she knew he could never afford? But she had plenty of money already—everybody knew that. Was it only that she wanted him out of sight, the last member of his family, and the last man on the estate?

He strode back to the cottage with the quick step of a man reaching a decision. Yet when he entered the dusky, low-ceilinged living room the paralysis of will threatened him again. He stood gazing round at the age-darkened furniture, the steel and copper accoutrements of the cavernous fireplace, the ornaments, the dim engravings of mountains, castles, and waterfalls as though he viewed them for the first time. He could not light the oil lamp, could not prepare a meal, begin his evening routine. A superstitious dread assailed him. Another presence was in possession here.

He shook the spell off. In the crimson glow remaining at the deep window, he read the letter once more, searching for some hint of a loophole. There seemed none. But awareness of a challenge penetrated his mind. For the first time since the death of his parents an important event was his to deal with alone. He lit the lamp, found a seldom used stationery compendium, and sat down. He did not get beyond "Dear Maddam, Supprised to receive your letter..." Instinct told him he must wheedle Mrs. Vines. But in what way? After half an hour of defeat, he dashed upstairs, ran down naked to the kitchen to wash at the sink, and returned upstairs to rub scented oil into his tough black hair and dress in the new cotton trousers and elegant windcheater of green suède that had cost him more than a week's wages.

Audrey Vines put her binoculars into her tapestry bag when Rufus entered Brychan Cottage and, her uninterested old bulldog at her heels, stepped out to the slope from between a brace of low-sweeping cypress branches. After concealing herself under the massive tree minutes before the noise of

Rufus's motorcycle had come, as usual, a few minutes before seven, she had studied his face and followed his prowlings about the garden and riverbank for nearly an hour. The clear views of him this evening had been particularly satisfactory. She knew it was a dictionary he had consulted under the pear tree, where he often sat drinking from a large Victorian mug. The furious hurling of a branch in the direction of the cypress had pleased her; his stress when he paced the garden had been as rewarding as his stupefied reading of the deliberately perplexing phraseology of her letter.

"Come along, Mia. *Good* little darling! We are going in now."

Paused on the slope in musing, the corpulent bitch grunted, blinked, and followed with a faint trace of former briskness in her bandily aged waddle. Audrey Vines climbed without any breathlessness herself, her pertinacious gaze examining the distances to right and left. She came out every evening not only to feed birds but to scrutinise her estate before settling down for the night. There was also the passage of the 7:40 train to see; since her two watches and every clock in the house needed repairs, it gave verification of the exact time, though this, like the bird feeding, was not really of account to her.

It was her glimpses of Rufus that provided her long day with most interest. For some years she had regularly watched him through the powerful Zeiss binoculars from various concealed spots. He renewed an interest in studies begun during long-ago travels in countries far from Wales, and she often jotted her findings into a household-accounts book kept locked in an old portable escritoire. To her eye, the prognathous jaw, broad nose, and gypsy-black hair of this heavy-bodied but personable young man bore distinct atavistic elements. He possessed, too, a primitive bloom, which often lingered for years beyond adolescence with persons of tardy mental development. But this throwback descendant of an ancient race was also, up to a point, a triumph over decadence. Arriving miraculously late in his mother's life, after three others born much earlier to the illiterate woman had died in infancy, this last-moment child had flourished physically, if not in other respects.

Except for the occasions when, as a boy and youth, he used to come to Plas Iolyn to do odd jobs and run errands, her deductions had been formed entirely through the limited and intensifying medium of the binoculars. She had come to know all his outdoor habits and activities around the cottage. These were rewarding only occasionally. The days when she failed to see him seemed bleakly deficient of incident. While daylight lasted, he never bathed in the river without her knowledge, though sometimes, among the willows and reeds, he was as elusive as an otter. And winter, of course, kept him indoors a great deal.

"Come, darling. There'll be a visitor for us tonight."

Mia, her little question-mark tail unexpectedly quivering, glanced up with the vaguely deprecating look of her breed. Audrey Vines had reached the balustraded front terrace. She paused by a broken sundial for a final look round at the spread of tranquil uplands and dim woods afar, the silent river and deserted meadows below, and, lingeringly, at the ancient trees shading her estate. Mild and windless though the evening was, she wore a long, draggled coat of brown-dyed ermine and, pinned securely on skeins of vigorous hair unskilfully home-dyed to auburn tints, a winged hat of tobacco-gold velvet. These, with her thick bistre face powder and assertive eye pencilling, gave her the look of an uncompromisingly womanly woman in an old-style sepia photograph, a woman halted forever in the dead past. But there was no evidence of waning powers in either her demeanour or step as she continued to the side terrace. A woman of leisure ignoring time's urgencies, she only suggested an unruffled unity with the day's slow descent into twilight.

The outward calm was deceptive. A watchful gleam in her eyes was always there, and the binoculars were carried for a reason additional to her study of Rufus. She was ever on the lookout for trespassers and poachers or tramps on the estate, rare though such were. When, perhaps three or four times a year, she discovered a stray culprit, the mature repose would disappear in a flash, her step accelerate, her throaty voice lash out. Tradesmen arriving legitimately at her kitchen door avoided looking her straight in the eye, and C. W. Powell, her solicitor, knew exactly how far he could go in sociabilities during his quarterly conferences with her in the kitchen of Plas Iolyn. Deep within those dissociated eyes lay an adamantine refusal to acknowledge the existence of any friendly approach. Only her animals could soften that repudiation.

"Poor Mia! We won't stay out so long tomorrow, I promise! Come along." They had reached the un-balustraded side terrace. "A flower for us tonight, sweetheart, then we'll go in," she murmured.

She crossed the cobbled yard behind the mansion. Close to disused greenhouses, inside which overturned flower-pots and abandoned garden tools lay under tangles of grossly overgrown plants sprouting to the broken roofing, there was a single border of wallflowers, primulas, and several well-pruned rosebushes in generous bud. It was the only evidence in all the Plas Iolyn domain of her almost defunct passion for flower cultivation. One pure white rose, an early herald of summer plenty, had begun to unfold that mild day; she had noticed it when she came out. Raindrops from a morning shower sprinkled onto her wrist as she plucked this sprightly first bloom, and she smiled as she inhaled the secret odour within. Holding the flower aloft like a trophy, she proceeded to the kitchen entrance with the same composed gait. There was all the time in the world.

Dusk had come into the spacious kitchen. But there was sufficient light for her activities from the curtainless bay window overlooking the yard and the flower border in which, long ago, Mia's much-loved predecessor had been buried. Candles were not lit until it was strictly necessary. She fumbled among a jumble of oddments in one of the two gloomy little pantries lying off the kitchen, and came out with a cone-shaped silver vase.

Light pattering sounds came from beyond an open inner door, where an uncarpeted back staircase lay, and five cats came bounding down from the first-floor drawing room. Each a ginger tabby of almost identical aspect, they whisked, mewing, around their mistress, tails up.

"Yes, yes, my darlings," she said. "Your saucers in a moment." She crossed to a sink of blackened stone, humming to herself.

A monster Edwardian cooking range stood derelict in a chimneyed alcove, with three portable oilstoves before it holding a covered frying pan, an iron stewpan, and a tin kettle. Stately dinner crockery and a variety of canisters and tinned foodstuff packed the shelves of a huge dresser built into the back wall. A long table stretching down the centre of the kitchen was even more crowded. It held half a dozen bulging paper satchels, biscuit tins, piles of unwashed plates and saucers, two stacks of the *Geographical Magazine*, the skull of a sheep, heaped vegetable peelings, an old wooden coffee grinder, a leatherette hatbox, a Tunisian bird cage used for storing meat, several ribboned chocolate boxes crammed with letters, and a traveller's escritoire of rosewood. On the end near the oilstoves, under a three-branched candelabra of heavy Sheffield plate encrusted with carved vine leaves and grapes, a reasonably fresh cloth of fine lace was laid with silver cutlery, a condiment set of polished silver, a crystal wine goblet, and a neatly folded linen napkin. A boudoir chair of gilded wood stood before this end of the table.

When the cold-water tap was turned at the sink, a rattle sounded afar in the house and ended in a groaning cough—a companionable sound, which Mrs. Vines much liked. She continued to hum as she placed the rose in the vase, set it below the handsome candelabra, and stepped back to admire the effect. Pulling out a pair of long, jet-headed pins, she took off her opulent velvet hat.

"He's a stupid lout, isn't he, Queenie?" The eldest cat, her favourite, had leaped on the table. "Thinking he was going to bed that chit down here and breed like rabbits!"

She gave the cats their separate saucers of liver, chopped from cold slices taken from the frying pan. Queenie was served first. The bulldog waited for her dish of beef chunks from the stewpan, and, given them, stood morosely for a minute, as if counting the pieces. Finally, Audrey Vines took for herself a remaining portion of liver and a slice of bread from a loaf on the dresser, and fetched a half bottle of champagne from a capacious oak chest placed between the two pantries. She removed her fur coat before she settled on the frail boudoir chair and shook out her napkin.

Several of these meagre snacks were taken every day, the last just after the 11:15 night express rocked away to the port in the west. Now, her excellent teeth masticating with barely perceptible movements, she ate with fastidious care. The bluish light filtering through the grimy bay window soon thickened, but still she did not light the three candles. Her snack finished, and the last drop of champagne taken with a sweet biscuit, she continued to sit at the table, her oil-stained tea gown of beige chiffon ethereal in the dimness.

She became an unmoving shadow. A disciplined meditation or a religious exercise might have been engaging her. Mia, also an immobile smudge, lay fast asleep on a strip of coconut matting beside the gilt chair. The five cats, tails down, had returned upstairs immediately after their meal, going one after the other as though in strict etiquette, or like a file of replete orphans. Each had a mahogany cradle in the drawing room, constructed to their mistress's specifications by an aged craftsman who had once been employed at Plas Iolyn.

She stirred for a minute from the reverie, but her murmuring scarcely disturbed the silence. Turning her head in mechanical habit to where Mia lay, she asked, "Was it last January the river froze for a fortnight?… No, not last winter. But there were gales, weren't there? Floods of rain—Which winter did I burn the chairs to keep us warm? That idiotic oilman didn't come. Then the candles and matches gave out, and I used the electricity. One of Queenie's daughters died that winter. It was the year he went to work in a factory."

Time had long ago ceased to have calendar meaning in her life; a dozen years were as one. But lately she had begun to be obsessed by dread of another severe winter. Winters seemed to have become colder and longer. She dreaded the deeper hibernation they enforced. Springs were intolerably long in coming, postponing the time when her child of nature became constantly visible again, busy under his flowering trees and splashing in the river. His reliable appearances brought back flickers of interest in the world; in comparison, intruders on the estate, the arrival of tradesmen, or the visits of her solicitor were becoming of little consequence.

She lapsed back into silence. The kitchen was almost invisible when, swiftly alert, she turned her head toward the indigo blue of the bay window. A throbbing sound had come from far away. It mounted to a series of kicking spurts, roared, and became a loudly tearing rhythm. She rose from her chair and fumbled for a box of matches on the table. But the rhythmic sound began to dwindle, and her hand remained over the box. The sound floated away.

She sank back on the chair. "Not now, darling!" she told the drowsily shifting dog. "Later, later."

The headlamp beam flashed past the high entrance gates to Plas Iolyn, but Rufus did not even glance at them. They were wide open and, he knew, would remain open all night. He had long ceased to wonder about this. Some people said

Mrs. Vines wanted to trap strangers inside, so that she could enjoy frightening them when they were nabbed, but other townsfolk thought that the gates had been kept open for years because she was always expecting her second husband to come back.

At top speed, his Riley could reach the town in less than ten minutes. The fir-darkened road was deserted. No cottage or house bordered it for five miles. A roadside farmstead had become derelict, but in a long vale quietly ascending toward the mountain range some families still continued with reduced sheep farming. Rufus knew them all. His father had worked at one of the farms before the decline in agricultural prosperity set in. From the outskirts of the hilly town he could see an illuminated clock in the Assembly Hall tower. It was half past nine. He did not slow down. Avoiding the town centre, he tore past the pens of a disused cattle market, a recently built confectionery factory, a nineteenth-century Nonconformist chapel, which had become a furniture depository, then past a row of cottages remaining from days when the town profited from rich milk and tough flannel woven at riverside mills. Farther round the town's lower folds, he turned into an area of diminutive back-to-back dwellings, their fronts ranging direct along narrow pavements.

Nobody was visible in these gaslit streets. He stopped at one of the terraces, walked to a door, and, without knocking, turned its brass knob. The door opened into a living room, though a sort of entrance lobby was formed by a chenille curtain and an upturned painted drainpipe used for umbrellas. Voices came from beyond the curtain. But only Gloria's twelve-year-old brother sat in the darkened room, watching television from a plump easy chair. His spectacles flashed up at the interrupting visitor.

"Gone to the pictures with Mum." The boy's attention returned impatiently to the dramatic serial. "Won't be back till long after ten."

Rufus sat down behind the boy and gazed unseeingly at the screen. A feeling of relief came to him. He knew now that he didn't want to show the letter to Gloria tonight, or tell her anything about the lease of Brychan Cottage. Besides, she mustn't read those nasty insults about her in the letter. He asked himself why he had come there, so hastily. Why hadn't he gone to Plas Iolyn? Mrs. Vines might give way. Then he needn't mention anything at all to Gloria. If he told her about the letter tonight, it would make him look a shifty cheat. She would ask why he hadn't told her about the lease before.

He began to sweat. The close-packed little room was warm and airless. Gloria's two married sisters lived in poky terrace houses just like this one, and he became certain that it was sight of Brychan Cottage and its garden last Sunday that convinced her to marry him. Before Sunday, she had always been a bit offhand, pouting if he said too much about the future. Although she could giggle and squeal a lot, she could wrinkle up her nose, too, and flounce away if any chap tried any fancy stuff on her in the factory recreation room. He saw her little feet skipping and running fast as a deer's.

The torment was coming back. This room, instead of bringing Gloria closer to him, made her seem farther off. He kept seeing her on the run. She was screeching as she ran. That loud screech of hers! He had never really liked it. It made his blood go cold, though a chap in the factory said that screeches like that were only a sign that a girl was a virgin and that they disappeared afterward. Why was he hearing them now? Then he remembered that one of Mrs. Vines's insults was about the screeching.

His fingers trembled when he lit a cigarette. He sat a little while longer, telling himself he ought to have gone begging to Plas Iolyn and promised to do anything if he could keep the cottage. He would work on the estate evenings and weekends for no money; a lot of jobs needed doing there. He'd offer to pay a good rent for the cottage, too. But what he ought to get before going there, he thought further, was advice from someone who had known Mrs. Vines well. He peered at his watch and got up.

"Tell Gloria I thought she'd like to go for a ride on the bike. I won't come back tonight."

"You'll be seeing her in the factory tomorrow," the boy pointed out.

It was only a minute up to the town centre. After parking the bike behind the Assembly Hall, Rufus crossed the quiet market square to a timbered old inn at the corner of Einon's Dip. He had remembered that Evan Matthews often went in there on his way to his night job at the reservoir. Sometimes they'd had a quick drink together.

Thursdays were quiet nights in pubs; so far, there were only five customers in the cosily rambling main bar. Instead of his usual beer, he ordered a double whiskey, and asked Gwyneth, the elderly barmaid, if Evan Matthews had been in. She said that if he came in at all it would be about that time. Rufus took his glass over to a table beside the fireless inglenook. He didn't know the two fellows playing darts. An English-looking commercial traveller in a bowler sat at a table scribbling in a notebook. Councillor Llew Pryce stood talking in Welsh to Gwyneth at the counter, and, sitting at a table across the bar from himself, the woman called Joanie was reading the local newspaper.

Staring at his unwatered whiskey, he tried to decide whether to go to Evan's home in Mostyn Street. No, he'd wait a while here. He wanted more time to think. How could Evan help, after all? A couple of drinks—that's what he needed now. Empty glass in hand, he looked up. Joanie was laying her newspaper down. A blue flower decorated her white felt hat, and there was a bright cherry in her small wineglass.

He watched, in a fascination like relief, as she bit the cherry from its stick and chewed with easy enjoyment. She'd be about thirty-five, he judged. She was a Saturday-night regular, but he had seen her in the Drovers on other nights, and she didn't lack company as a rule. He knew of her only from tales and jokes by chaps in the factory. Someone had said she'd come from Bristol with a man supposed to be her husband, who had disappeared when they'd both worked in the slab-cake factory for a few months.

Joanie looked at him, and picked up her paper. He wondered if she was waiting for someone. If Evan didn't come in, could he talk to her about his trouble, ask her the best way to handle a bad-tempered old moneybags? She looked experienced and good-hearted, a woman with no lumps in her nature. He could show her the letter; being a newcomer to the town, she wouldn't know who Mrs. Vines was.

He rose to get another double whiskey but couldn't make

up his mind to stop at Joanie's table or venture a passing nod. He stayed at the counter finishing his second double, and he was still there when Evan came in. He bought Evan a pint of bitter, a single whiskey for himself, and, Joanie forgotten, led Evan to the inglenook table.

"Had a knockout when I got home this evening." He took the black-edged envelope from a pocket of his windcheater.

Evan Matthews read the letter. A sinewy and well-preserved man, he looked about fifty and was approaching sixty; when Mrs. Vines had hired him as estate keeper and herdsman, he had been under forty. He grinned as he handed the letter back, saying, "She's got you properly skewered, boyo! I warned your dad she'd do it when the lease was up."

"What's the reason for it? Brychan Cottage isn't unfit for living in, like she says—there's only a bit of dry in the floor boards. I've never done her any harm."

"No harm, except that you're a man now."

Uncomprehending, Rufus scowled. "She used to like me. Gave me presents. Is it more money she's after?"

"She isn't after money. Audrey P. Vines was open-fisted with cash—I'll say that for her. No, she just hates the lot of us."

"Men, you mean?"

"The whole bunch of us get her dander up." Recollection lit Evan's eyes. "She gave me cracks across the head with a riding crop that she always carried in those days. I'd been working hard at Plas Iolyn for five years when I got my lot from her."

"Cracks across the head?" Rufus said, sidetracked.

"She drew blood. I told your dad about it. He said I ought to prosecute her for assault. But when she did it I felt sorry for her, and she knew it. It made her boil the more."

"What you'd done?"

"We were in the cowshed. She used to keep a fine herd of Jerseys, and she blamed the death of a calving one on me—began raging that I was clumsy pulling the calf out, which I'd been obliged to do." Evan shook his head. "It wasn't *that* got her flaring. But she took advantage of it and gave me three or four lashes with the crop. I just stood looking at her. I could see she wanted me to hit back and have a proper set-to. Of course, I was much younger then, and so was she! But I only said, 'You and I must part, Mrs. Vines.' She lifted that top lip of hers, like a vixen done out of a fowl—I can see her now—and went from the shed without a word. I packed up that day. Same as her second husband had walked out on her a couple of years before—the one that played a violin."

"You mean…" Rufus blurted, after a pause of astonishment. "You mean, you'd *been* with her?"

Evan chuckled. "Now, I didn't say that!"

"What's the *matter* with the woman?" Rufus exclaimed. The mystery of Mrs. Vines's attack on himself was no clearer.

"There's women that turn themselves into royalty," Evan said. "They get it into their heads they rule the world. People who knew little Audrey's father used to say he spoiled her up to the hilt because her mother died young. He only had one child. They travelled a lot together when she was a girl, going into savage parts, and afterward she always had a taste for places where there's no baptised Christians. I heard that her first husband committed suicide in Nigeria, but nobody knows for certain what happened." He took up Rufus's empty whiskey glass, and pushed back his chair. "If he did something without her permission, he'd be for the crocodiles."

"I've had two doubles and a single, and I haven't had supper yet," Rufus protested. But Evan fetched him a single whiskey. When it was placed before him, Rufus stubbornly asked, "What's the best thing for me to do?"

"Go and see her." Evan's face had the tenderly amused relish of one who knows that the young male must get a portion of trouble at the hands of women. "That's what she wants. I know our Audrey." He glanced again at this slow-thinking son of an old friend. "Go tonight," he urged.

"It's late to go tonight," Rufus mumbled. Sunk in rumination, he added, "She stays up late. I've seen a light in her kitchen window when I drive back over the rise after I've been out with Gloria." He swallowed the whiskey at a gulp.

"If you want to keep Brychan Cottage, boyo, *act*. Night's better than day-time for seeing her. She'll have had a glass or two. Bottles still go there regularly from Jack Drapple's."

"You mean, soft-soap her?" Rufus asked with a grimace.

"No, not soft-soap. But give her what she wants." Evan thought for a moment, and added, a little more clearly, "When she starts laying into you—and she will, judging by that letter—you have a go at *her*. I wouldn't be surprised she'll respect you for it. Her and me in the cowshed was a different matter—I wasn't after anything from her. Get some clouts in on her, if you can."

Rufus shook his head slowly. "She said in the letter it was final," he said.

"Nothing is final with women, boyo. Especially what they put down in writing. They send letters like that to get a man springing up off his tail. They can't bear us to sit down quietly for long." Evan finished his beer. It was time to leave for his watchman's job at the new reservoir up at Mynydd Baer, the towering mountain from which showers thrashed down.

"Brychan Cottage belongs to me! Not to that damned old witch!" Rufus had banged the table with his fist. The dart players turned to look; Joanie lowered her paper; the commercial traveller glanced up from his notebook, took off his bowler, and laid it on the table. Gwyneth coughed and thumped a large Toby jug down warningly on the bar counter.

Evan said, "Try shouting at *her* like that—she won't mind language—but pipe down here. And don't take any more whiskey."

"I'll tell her I won't budge from Brychan Cottage!" Rufus announced. "Her father cheated my grandfather over the railway—made a lot of money. She won't try to force me out. She'd be disgraced in the town."

"Audrey Vines won't care a farthing about disgrace or gossip." Evan buttoned up his black mackintosh. "I heard she used to give her second husband shocking dressings-down in front of servants and the visitors that used to go to Plas Iolyn in those days. Mr. Oswald, he was called. A touch of African tarbrush in him, and had tried playing the violin for a living." A tone of sly pleasure was in his voice. "Younger than Audrey Vines. One afternoon in Plas Iolyn, she caught him with a skivvy in the girl's bedroom top of the house, and she locked them in there for twenty-four hours. She turned the electricity off at the main, and there the two stayed without food or water all that time." Evan took from his pocket a tasselled monkey cap of white wool, kept for his journey by motorbike into the mountains. "If you go to see her tonight, give her my love. Come to Mostyn Street tomorrow to tell me how you got on."

"What happened when the two were let out of the bedroom?"

"The skivvy had to go on her neck, of course. Mari, the housekeeper, told me that in a day or two Mrs. Vines was playing her piano to Mr. Oswald's fiddle as usual. Long duets they used to play most evenings, and visitors had to sit and listen. But it wasn't many weeks before Mr. Oswald bunked off, in the dead of night. The tale some tell that he is still shut away somewhere in Plas Iolyn is bull." He winked at Rufus.

"I've heard she keeps the gates open all the time to welcome him back," Rufus persisted, delaying Evan still longer. It was as though he dreaded to be left alone.

"After all these years? Some people like to believe women get love on the brain. But it's true they can go sour when a man they're set on does a skedaddle from them. And when they get like that, they can go round the bend without much pushing." He rose from the table. "But I'll say this for our Audrey. After Mr. Oswald skedaddled, she shut herself up in Plas Iolyn and wasn't too much of a nuisance to people outside. Far as I know, I was the only man who had his claret tapped with that riding crop!" He drained a last swallow from his glass. "Mind, I wouldn't deny she'd like Mr. Oswald to come back, even after all these years! She'd have ways and means of finishing him off." He patted Rufus's shoulder. "In the long run it might be best if you lost Brychan Cottage."

Rufus's jaw set in sudden obstinate sullenness. "I've told Gloria we're going to live there forever. I'm going to Plas Iolyn tonight."

When Rufus got up, a minute after Evan had left, it was with a clumsy spring; the table and glasses lurched. But his progress to the bar counter was undeviating. He drank another single whiskey, bought a half bottle, which he put inside his elastic-waisted windcheater, and strode from the bar with a newly found hauteur.

She came out of her bedroom above the kitchen rather later than her usual time for going down to prepare her last meal of the day. Carrying a candleholder of Venetian glass shaped like a water lily, she did not descend by the adjacent back staircase tonight but went along a corridor and turned into another, off which lay the front drawing room. Each of the doors she passed, like every other inside the house, was wide open; a bronze statuette of a mounted hussar kept her bedroom door secure against slamming on windy nights.

She had dressed and renewed her makeup by the light of the candle, which was now a dripping stub congealed in the pretty holder. Her wide-skirted evening gown of mauve poplin had not entirely lost a crisp rustle, and on the mottled flesh of her bosom a ruby pendant shone vivaciously. Rouge, lip salve, and mascara had been applied with a prodigal hand, like the expensive scent that left whiffs in her wake. She arrayed herself in this way now and again—sometimes if she planned to sit far into the night composing letters, and always for her solicitor's arrival on the evening of quarter day, when she would give him soup and tinned crab in the kitchen.

She never failed to look into the first-floor drawing room at about eleven o'clock, to bid a good night to the cats. The bulldog, aware of the custom, had preceded her mistress on this occasion and stood looking in turn at the occupants of five short-legged cradles ranged in a half circle before a gaunt and empty fireplace of grey stone. Pampered Queenie lay fast asleep on her eiderdown cushion; the other tabbies had heard the mistress approaching and sat up, stretching and giving themselves a contented lick. Blue starlight came from four tall windows, whose satin curtains were drawn back tightly into dirt-stiff folds, rigid as marble. In that quiet illumination of candle and starlight, the richly dressed woman moving from cradle to cradle stroking and cooing a word or two, had a look of feudally assured serenity. Mia watched in pedigreed detachment; even her squashed face achieved a debonair comeliness.

"Queenie, Queenie, won't you say good night to me? Bowen's are sending fish tomorrow! Friday fish! Soles, darling! *Fish, fish!*"

Queenie refused to stir from her fat sleep. Presently, her ceremony performed, Audrey Vines descended by the front staircase, candle in hand, Mia stepping with equal care behind her. At the rear of the panelled hall, she passed through an archway, above which hung a Bantu initiatory mask, its orange and purple stripes dimmed under grime. A baize door in the passage beyond was kept open with an earthenware jar full of potatoes and onions. In the kitchen, she lit the three-branched candelabra from her pink-and-white holder, and blew out the stub.

This was always the hour she liked best. The last snack would be prepared with even more leisure than the earlier four or five. Tonight, she opened a tin of sardines, sliced a tomato and a hardboiled egg, and brought from one of the dank little pantries a jar of olives, a bottle of mayonnaise, and a foil-wrapped triangle of processed cheese. While she buttered slices of bread, the distant rocking of the last train could be heard, its fading rhythm leaving behind all the unruffled calm of a windless night. She arranged half a dozen sponge fingers clockwise on a Chelsea plate, then took a half bottle of champagne from the chest, hesitated, and exchanged it for a full-sized one.

Mia had occupied herself with a prolonged examination and sniffing and scratching of her varicoloured strip of matting; she might have been viewing it for the first time. Noticing that her mistress was seated, she reclined her obdurate bulk on the strip. Presently, she would be given her usual two sponge fingers dipped in champagne. She took no notice when a throbbing sound came from outside, or when it grew louder.

"Our visitor, sweetheart. I told you he'd come."

Audrey Vines, postponing the treat of her favourite brand of sardines until later, dabbed mayonnaise on a slice of egg, ate, and wiped her lips. "Don't bark!" she commanded. "There's noise enough as it is." Becoming languidly alert to the accumulating roar, Mia had got onto her bandy legs. A light flashed across the bay window. The roar ceased abruptly. Audrey Vines took a slice of bread as footsteps approached outside, and Mia, her shred of a tail faintly active, trundled to the door. A bell hanging inside had tinkled.

"Open, open!" Mrs. Vines's shout from the table was throaty, but strong and even. "Open and come in!"

Rufus paused stiffly on the threshold, his face in profile, his eyes glancing obliquely at the candlelit woman sitting at the table's far end. "I saw your lighted window," he said. The dog returned to the matting after a sniff of his shoes and a brief upward look of approval.

"Thank God I shall not be hearing the noise of that cursed motorcycle on my land much longer. Shut the door, young man, and sit over there."

He shut the door and crossed to the seat Mrs. Vines had indicated. Placed against a wall between the dresser and the inner door, it was the same rough bench on which he used to sit during happier visits long ago. He sat down and forced himself to gaze slowly down the big kitchen, his eyes ranging over the long, crowded table to the woman in her evening gown, to the single, red jewel on her bare chest, and, at last, to her painted face.

Audrey Vines went on with her meal. The silence continued. A visitor might not have been present. Rufus watched her leisurely selection of a slice of tomato and an olive, the careful unwrapping of foil from cheese. Her two diamond rings sparkled in the candlelight. He had never seen her eating, and this evidence of a normal habit both mesmerised and eased him.

"I've come about the letter."

The words out, he sat up, taut in justification of complaint. But Mrs. Vines seemed not to have heard. She sprinkled pepper and salt on the cheese, cut it into small pieces, and looked consideringly at the untouched sardines in their tin, while the disregarded visitor relapsed into silent watching. Three or four minutes passed before she spoke.

"Are you aware that I could institute a police charge against you for bathing completely naked in the river on my estate?"

It stirred him anew to a bolt-upright posture. "There's nobody to see."

She turned a speculative, heavy-lidded eye in his direction. "Then how do I know about it? Do you consider me nobody?" Yet there was no trace of malevolence as she continued. "You are almost as hairy as an ape. Perhaps you consider that is sufficient covering?" Sedate as a judge in court, she added, "But your organs are exceptionally pronounced."

"Other people don't go about with spying glasses." Anger gave his words a stinging ring.

Turning to the dog, she remarked, "An impudent defence from the hairy bather!" Mia, waiting patiently for the sponge fingers, blinked, and Audrey Vines, reaching for the tin of sardines, said, "People in the trains can see."

"I know the times of the trains."

"You have bathed like that all the summer. You walk to the river from Brychan Cottage unclothed. You did not do this when your parents were alive."

"You never sent me a letter about it."

"I delivered a letter at Brychan Cottage today. *That* covers everything."

There was another silence. Needing time to reassemble his thoughts, he watched as she carefully manipulated a sardine out of the tin with her pointed fingernails. The fish did not break. She held it aloft by its tail end to let oil drip into the tin, and regally tilted her head back and slowly lowered it whole into her mouth. The coral-red lips softly clamped about the disappearing body, drawing it in with appreciation. She chewed with fastidiously dawdling movements. Lifting another fish, she repeated the performance, her face wholly absorbed in her pleasure.

She was selecting a third sardine before Rufus spoke. "I

want to go on living in Brychan Cottage," he said, slurring the words. The sardine had disappeared when he continued. "My family always lived in Brychan Cottage. It belonged to us hundreds of years before your family came to Plas Iolyn."

"You've been drinking," Audrey Vines said, looking ruminatively over the half-empty plates before her. She did not sound disapproving, but almost amiable. Rufus made no reply. After she had eaten a whole slice of bread, ridding her mouth of sardine taste, she reached for the bottle of champagne. A long time was spent untwisting wire from the cork. Her manipulating hands were gentle in the soft yellow candle light, and in the quiet of deep country night filling the room she seemed just then an ordinary woman sitting in peace over an ordinary meal, a flower from her garden on the table, a faithful dog lying near her chair.

Making a further effort, he repeated. "My family always lived in Brychan Cottage."

"Your disagreeable mother," Audrey Vines responded, "allowed a man to take a photograph of Brychan Cottage. I had sent the creature packing when he called here. The photograph appeared in a ridiculous guidebook. Your mother knew I would *not* approve of attracting such flashy attention to my estate. My solicitor showed me the book."

Unable to deal with this accusation, he fell into headlong pleading. "I've taken care of the cottage. It's not dirty. I could put new floor boards in downstairs and change the front door. I can cook and do cleaning. The garden is tidy. I'm planning to border the paths with more fruit trees, and—"

"Why did your parents name you Rufus?" she interrupted. "You are dark as night, though your complexion is pale...and pitted like the moon's surface." The wire was off the cork. "I wonder were you born hairy-bodied?"

He subsided, baffled. As she eased the cork out, there was the same disregard of him. He jerked when the cork shot in his direction. She seemed to smile as the foam spurted and settled delicately in her crystal glass. She took a sip, and another, and spoke to the saliva-dropping dog.

"Your bikkies in a second. Aren't you a nice quiet little Mia! A pity *he* isn't as quiet, darling."

"Got a bottle of whiskey with me. Can I take a swig?" The request came in a sudden desperate burst.

"You may."

She watched in turn while he brought the flat, half-sized bottle from inside his windcheater, unscrewed its stopper, and tilted the neck into his mouth. She took further sips of her wine. Absorbed in his own need, Rufus paused for only a moment before returning the neck to his mouth. About half the whiskey had been taken when, holding the bottle at the ready between his knees, his eyes met hers across the room's length. She looked away, her lids stiffening. But confidence increased in Rufus.

He repeated, "I want to live in Brychan Cottage all my life."

"You wish to live in Brychan Cottage. I wish to raze it to the ground." A second glass of wine was poured. "So there we are, young man!" She wetted a sponge finger in her wine and handed it to Mia.

"My mother said the cottage and land belonged to us for-ever at one time. Your father cheated us out of…" He stopped, realising his foolishness, and scowled.

"Mia, darling, how you love your drop of champagne!"

She dipped another sponge finger; in her obliviousness, she might have been courteously overlooking his slip. "Not good for your rheumatism, though! Oh, you dribbler!"

He took another swig of whiskey—a smaller one. He was sitting in Plas Iolyn and must not forget himself so far as to get drunk. Settling back against the wall, he stared in wonder at objects on the long table and ventured to ask, "What...what have you got that skull for? It's a sheep's, isn't it?"

"That? I keep it because it shows pure breeding in its lines and therefore is beautiful. Such sheep are not degenerate, as are so many of their so-called masters. No compulsory education, state welfare services, and social coddling for a sheep!" Rufus's face displayed the blank respect of a modest person hearing academic information beyond his comprehension, and she appended, "The ewe that lived inside that skull was eaten alive by blowfly maggots. I found her under a hedge below Mynydd Baer." She finished her second glass, and poured a third.

As though in sociable alliance, he allowed himself another mouthful of whiskey. Awareness of his gaffe about her cheating father kept him from returning to the subject of the cottage at once. He was prepared to remain on the bench for hours; she seemed not to mind his visit. His eyes did not stray from her any more; every trivial move she made held his attention now. She reached for a fancy biscuit tin and closely studied the white roses painted on its shiny blue sides. He waited. The silence became acceptable. It belonged to the late hour and this house and the mystery of Mrs. Vines's ways.

Audrey Vines laid the biscuit tin down unopened, and slowly ran a finger along the lace tablecloth, like a woman preoccupied with arriving at a resolve. "If you are dissatisfied with the leasehold deeds of Brychan Cottage," she began, "I advise you to consult a solicitor. Daniel Lewis welcomes such small business, I believe. You will find his office behind the Assembly Hall. You have been remarkably lackadaisical in this matter... No, *not* remarkably, since he is as he is! He should live in a tree." She had turned to Mia.

"I don't want to go to a solicitor." After a pause, he mumbled, half sulkily, "Can't...can't we settle it between us?"

She looked up. Their eyes met again. The bright ruby on her chest flashed as she purposelessly moved a dish on the table. But the roused expectancy in Rufus's glistening eyes did not fade. After a moment, he tilted the bottle high into his mouth, and withdrew it with a look of extreme surprise. It was empty.

Audrey Vines drank more wine. Then, rapping the words out, she demanded, "How much rent are you prepared to pay me for the cottage?"

Rufus gaped in wonder. Had Evan Matthews been right, then, in saying that nothing was final with women? He put the whiskey bottle down on the bench and offered the first sum in his mind. "A pound a week?"

Audrey Vines laughed. It was a hoarse sound, cramped and discordant in her throat. She straightened a leaning candle and spoke with the incisiveness of a nimble businesswoman addressing a foolish client. "Evidently you know nothing of property values, young man. My estate is one of the most attractive in this part of Wales. A Londoner needing weekend seclusion would pay ten pounds a week for my cottage, with fishing rights."

It had become "my cottage." Rufus pushed a hand into his sweat-damp black hair, and mumbled, "Best to have a man you know nearby you on the estate."

"For a pound? I fail to see the advantage I reap."

"Thirty shillings, then? I'm only drawing a clear nine pounds a week in Nelson's factory." Without guile, he sped on, "Haven't got enough training yet to be put on the machines, you see! They've kept me in the packing room with the learners."

"That I can well believe. Nevertheless, you can afford to buy a motorcycle and flasks of whiskey." She clattered a plate onto another. "My cottage would be rent-free to the right man. Would you like a couple of sardines with your whiskey?"

The abrupt invitation quenched him once more. He lowered his head, scowling, his thighs wide apart. His hands gripped his knees. There was a silence. When he looked up, she was straining her pencilled eyes toward him, as though their sight had become blurred. But now he could not look at her in return. His gaze focussed on the three candle flames to the left of her head.

"Well, sardines or not?"

"No," he answered, almost inaudibly.

"Grind me some coffee, then," she rapped, pointing to the handle-topped wooden box on the table. "There are beans in it. Put a little water in the kettle on one of those oilstoves. Matches are here. Coffeepot on the dresser." She dabbed her lips with her napkin, looked at the stain they left, and refilled her glass.

He could no longer respond in any way to these changes of mood. He neither moved nor spoke. Reality had faded, the kitchen itself became less factual, objects on the table insubstantially remote. Only the woman's face drew and held his eyes. But Audrey Vines seemed not to notice this semi-paralysis; she was allowing a slow-thinking man time to obey her command. She spoke a few words to Mia. She leaned forward to reach for a lacquered box, and took from it a pink cigarette. As she rose to light the gold-tipped cigarette at a candle, he said, "Brychan Cottage always belonged to my family."

"He keeps saying that!" she said to Mia, sighing and sitting back. Reflective while she smoked, she had an air of waiting for coffee to be served, a woman retreated into the securities of the distant past, when everybody ran to her bidding.

"What do you want, then?" His voice came from deep in his chest, the words flat and earnest in his need to know.

The mistress of Plas Iolyn did not reply for a minute. Her gaze was fixed on the closely woven flower in its silver vase. And a strange transformation came to her lulled face. The lineaments of a girl eased its contours, bringing a smooth texture to the skin, clothing the stark bones with a pastel-like delicacy of fine young flesh. An apparition, perhaps an inhabitant of her reverie, was fugitively in possession.

"I want peace and quiet," she whispered.

His head had come forward. He saw the extraordinary transformation. Like the dissolving reality of the room, it had the nature of a hallucination. His brows puckering in his effort to concentrate, to find exactness, he slowly sat back, and asked, "You want me to stay single? Then I can keep Brychan Cottage?"

In a sudden, total extinction of control, her face became

contorted into an angry shape of wrinkled flesh. Her eyes blazed almost sightlessly. She threw the cigarette on the floor and screamed, "Did you think I was going to allow that slut to live there? Braying and squealing on my estate like a prostitute!" Her loud breathing was that of someone about to vomit.

With the same flat simplicity, he said, "Gloria is not a prostitute."

"Gloria! Good God, *Gloria!* How in idiocy can they go? Why not Cleopatra? I don't care a hair of your stupid head what happens to you and that wretched creature. You are *not* going to get the cottage. I'll burn it to the ground rather than have you and that born prostitute in it!" Her hands began to grasp at plates and cutlery on the table, in a blind semblance of the act of clearing them. "Stupid lout, coming here! By the autumn there won't be a stone of that cottage left. Not a stone, you hear!"

Her demented goading held such pure hatred that it seemed devoid of connection with him. She had arrived at the fringe of sane consciousness; her gaze fixed on nothing, she was aware only of a dim figure hovering down the room, beyond the throw of candlelight. "The thirtieth of June, you hear? Or the police will be called to turn you out!"

He had paused for a second at the far end of the table, near the door. His head was averted. Four or five paces away from him lay release into the night. But he proceeded in her direction, advancing as though in deferential shyness, his head still half turned away, a hand sliding along the table. He paused again, took up the coffee grinder, looked at it vaguely, and lowered it to the table. It crashed on the stone floor.

She became aware of the accosting figure. The screaming did not diminish. "Pick that thing up! You've broken it, clumsy fool. Pick it up!"

He looked round uncertainly, not at her but at the uncurtained bay window giving onto the spaces of night. He did not stoop for the grinder.

"*Pick it up!*" The mounting howl swept away the last hesitation in him. He went toward her unwaveringly.

She sat without a movement until he was close to her. He stopped, and looked down at her. Something like a compelled obedience was in the crouch of his shoulders. Her right hand moved, grasping the tablecloth fringe into a tight fistful. She made no attempt to speak, but an articulation came into the exposed face that was lifted to him. From the glaze of her eyes, from deep in unfathomable misery, came entreaty. He was the chosen one. He alone held the power of deliverance. He saw it, and in that instant of mutual recognition his hand grasped the heavy candelabra and lifted it high. Its three flames blew out in the swiftness of the plunge. There was a din of object crashing to the floor from the tugged tablecloth. When he rose from beside the fallen chair and put the candelabra down, the whimpering dog followed him in the darkness to the door, as though pleading with this welcome visitor not to go.

He left the motorbike outside the back garden gate of Brychan Cottage, walked along a wicker fence, and, near the river, jumped across the ditch onto Plas Iolyn land. Presently, he reached a spot where, long before he was born, the river had been widened and deepened to form an ornamental pool. A rotting summerhouse, impenetrable under wild creeper, overlooked it, and a pair of stone urns marked a short flight of weed-hidden steps. The soft water, which in daytime was as blue as the distant mountain range where lay its source, flowed through in lingering eddies. He had sometimes bathed in this prohibited pool late at night; below Brychan Cottage the river was much less comfortable for swimming.

He undressed without haste, and jumped into the pool with a quick and acrobatically high leap. He swam underwater, rose, and went under again, in complete ablution. When he stood up beside the opposite bank, where the glimmering water reached to his chest, he relaxed his arms along the grassy verge and remained for moments looking at the enormous expanse of starry sky, away from the mansion dimly outlined above the pool.

He was part of the anonymous liberty of the night. This bathe was the completion of an act of mastery. The river was his; returning to its depths, he was assimilated into it. He flowed downstream a little way and, where the water became shallow, sat up. His left hand spread on pebbles below, leaned negligently there, like a deity of pools and streams risen in search of possibilities in the night. He sat unmoving for several minutes. The supple water running over his loins began to feel much colder. It seemed to clear his mind of tumult. Slowly, he turned his head toward the mansion.

He saw her face in the last flare of the candles, and now he knew why she had tormented him. She had been waiting long for his arrival. The knowledge lodged, certain and tenacious, in his mind. Beyond his wonder at her choice, it brought, too, some easing of the terror threatening him. Further his mind would not go; he retreated from thinking of the woman lying alone in the darkness of that mansion up there. He knew she was dead. Suddenly, he rose, waded to the bank, and strode to where his clothes lay.

His movements took on the neatness and dispatch of a man acting entirely on a residue of memory. He went into Brychan Cottage only to dry and dress himself in the kitchen. When he got to the town, all lamps had been extinguished in the deserted streets. The bike tore into the private hush of an ancient orderliness. He did not turn into the route he had taken earlier that night but drove on at top speed through the market place. Behind the medieval Assembly Hall, down a street of municipal offices and timbered old houses in which legal business was done, a blue lamp shone alight. It jutted clearly from the porch of a stone building, and the solid door below yielded to his push.

Inside, a bald-headed officer sitting at a desk glanced up in mild surprise at this visitor out of the peaceful night, and, since the young man kept silent, asked, "Well, what can we do for you?"

1974

No More A-Maying
Christianna Brand

The books of Christianna Brand (1907–88) include an excellent novel of suspense set in Wales, *Cat and Mouse*. The biographical note which appeared on the first edition said she "was born and brought up in Malaya. She came home to England to be educated at a convent…and at the age of seventeen, her father having lost all his money, was turned out into the world to earn her own living. She became in turn a nursery governess, a dress packer, night club receptionist, secretary, professional dancer, and a model in Bond Street dress shops. She later ran a girls' club in the slums, demonstrated gadgets at Olympia, did some unsuccessful market gardening and house decorating; she was 'always broke and often cold and hungry.'" But she established herself as a detective novelist of distinction, those early jobs furnishing background material for her fiction. Her husband, the surgeon Roland Lewis, was born in Ystalyfera, in the Swansea Valley, and played rugby for London Welsh.

Twisty, skilful plotting was Brand's supreme strength as a writer. *Green for Danger, Death of Jezebel,* and *Suddenly at*

His Residence have been published as British Library Crime Classics, as has Anthony Berkeley's *The Poisoned Chocolates Case*, for which she wrote a seventh solution. This story first appeared in *Buffet for Unwelcome Guests* in 1974.

———

THE ROLLING SUMMIT OF THE BARE WELSH MOUNTAIN was patched with gorse, standing like sparse tufts of hair on a bald man's head. "Come in by the bushes, Gwennie," said Boyo. He had been nerving himself for this for a long time. When they were safe from observation, he blurted it out at last. "Gwennie! Show me?"

"Show you what?" said Gwennie. There's dense, for a girl of nearly six.

He went very red, having to say it outright, but he summoned up all his temerity. "Show me your chest."

Gwennie seemed not unduly offended. But… "How can I show you up by here?" She peered out from the frail shelter of the prickly patch. "Someone might see us." And indeed from where they crouched they could see across the valley to her farm, Penbryn. Mam and Da had gone over to Llangwyn for the mart. Ianto would be out in the woods with Llewellyn the Post and Blodwen off somewhere with Nancy James; but their big brother Idris had been left to work in the yard, cleaning out the silo pit, shifting the hay, ready for the new crop. "Not up here, Boyo. Come down to the cave."

"If we go to the cave—will you show me?"

In the yard outside the hay-barn, her swing hung idle. "If I show you, Boyo, will you push me on the swing?"

"Yes, all right," said Boyo.

"A hundred times?"

"All right, all right," said Boyo. But a hundred times!

They tumbled down the hillside to the trees that edged the little river; crept across the rough path to the green glade that lay at the opening of the cave. It was not a cave, really, but a sort of rock tunnel that opened out again where the low bank dropped, grass over crumbling earth, to the water's edge. But when, hidden within the cave's mouth, she had, with much struggling, hauled up her thin cotton dress—nothing! Just a plain old flat chest like his own, two tiny pale pink seed pearls on a flat white front. "That's not a girl's chest," said Boyo, disgusted. "You're not a girl. You're a boy."

"I'm not," said Gwennie, indignant.

"Oh well! Let's go in by the river, then," suggested Boyo craftily, "and make boats out of leaves and launch them down the running water." Better than a hundred times pushing her on her old swing. And all for nothing.

But someone was there already. A girl was lying drinking out of the river as they themselves often stooped to drink, lying with her shoulders hunched and her head right down to the water, one arm still on the bank, lying at an uncomfortable angle, turned at the elbow, palm upward. Huge-eyed, they clapped their hands to their mouths and backed silently away. "Boyo—it was your Megan!"

"If she'd seen us!"

"If she knew I'd shown you my chest!"

"She wouldn't tell," said Boyo, gaining confidence with distance from danger.

"Well, perhaps not. She's funny, that old Megan of yours."

"Lost her 'ealth," said Boyo, laconically, in the language of the grown-ups. If you'd lost your health, that was an act of God and no more to be done about it. And Megan had never exactly had her health, not really. Not in her head, anyway. Nevertheless… "Never tell, Gwennie! Never tell that we went to the cave. If *she* didn't think, other people might. If they guessed that you'd shown me your chest!"

They started back to the farm but for a moment had to shrink back into the bushes bordering the path. One of the Hippies came running down into the glade and looked about and called out a name: a funny name, not one that either of them knew—and at last, looking as if he didn't like doing it, hunched his thin shoulders and went into the cave, still calling. They hared away back to the farm as though devils were after them.

The Hippies had bought up a derelict, small holding with tumble-down farm cottage of stone held together by crumbling clay, its chimneys nested by jackdaws, its slate roof caving in. They had restored it, painstakingly, patiently; cleared and tilled the rough ground, planted a garden there, kept chickens and ducks and a goat and an elderly Jersey cow. Emlyn Lewis had cheated them over the cow; but, fair play, Hippies deserved nothing better—an ignorant, thriftless, carefree lot with their beards and long hair and the girls in long untidy dresses and hair hanging all about their shoulders. And immoral! Walking about pregnant for all to see! The men drove around in a shabby van with goat cheese and "natural yoghourt" and produce from the garden. Who bought enough to make this worth while, remained a mystery. The farmers' wives simply said roughly, "No!" and turned their stout backs, criss-crossed with the straps of speckled overalls, till, unoffended, the intruders drove away. Summer visitors, perhaps, with their too-bright tents and caravans and lines of washing hung out to dry?—but they were very, very few and far between.

They were toiling in the garden when Christo came back from the cave. They called him that because he was so beautiful with his long face and scrappy golden beard like the face of the Christ imprinted on the sacred veil. He was married to Primula. They were in fact all married; it seemed rather pointless to resist what, after all, comforted their parents and made life so much simpler, especially when it came to the babies. There were three babies, one to each couple—Christo and Primula, Rohan and Melisande, Abel and Evaine. They all lived well enough on the produce of their land; and Rohan and Melisande sold their pottery to the local shops. They had beautiful names because they had rechristened themselves when they came to settle in Wales. They loved everything around them to be beautiful, and if they were sometimes a little intense about it, would also often fall into laughter at their own pomposity. But it was true that their whole intention in forming their tiny community, had been to be beautiful in all ways, all through their lives.

Christo did not look beautiful now. His white face, whose skin never tanned, was all patched and streaked with pink. He gasped out: "It's Corinna! She's drowned herself!" and sat down on the bench outside the cottage door and put his face in his hands and burst into tears.

"Christ!"

"I was late," said Christo. "She must have thought I wasn't coming."

They stood round him, stricken, the gardening tools still in their hands, stupidly staring—as the foolish wild mountain sheep do, faced, starving, with an artificial feed. "Oh, Christo, love!—don't blame yourself."

"She wasn't—accountable," said Rohan, comforting.

The girl was Megan Thomas, daughter of the farmer, who also carried the post; but they called her Corinna, out of Herrick, because she would wander along the hedges picking sprays of the white May blossom, holding it in a sort of ecstasy to her face, feeling the soft brush of the stamens, the caressing roughness of the hidden thorns; snuffing up the strange, musky scent. "Corinna's going a-Maying…" She was the only one of the farming people who would come near the wicked Hippies. Her Mam told her not to and her Da said he would beat her, but she came, nevertheless, and hung about the cottage. Seeing his beautiful face, hearing his name, she had in her hazy, dazy mind come to fancy that here was an incarnation of Iesu Grist, come again; and now, deeply in a trouble she did not fully understand, had turned to him for help—for comfort, for absolution—who could tell? If he would meet her, down in the glade? They would not go into the cave—Christo suffered violently from claustrophobia, could not endure an enclosed space—the very doors of the house were kept open if he were alone in there. But they must go somewhere secret; if her Da knew, he would beat her. And if he knew—if he knew… "My Da would kill me! My Da would *kill* me!"

They had supposed her to be having a baby and advised

him that he must at least meet her and try to comfort and advise. If people had faith in one... After all, to love and be kind was the whole foundation of their lives. But now... "Was she in the river?"

"On the bank. Hanging—hanging over." He could not bear to re-live the horror of it, to re-visualise it. He had called to her, but she hadn't been in the glade; had thought he heard a rustling of leaves, seen nothing around him, forced himself to creep through the tunnel to the bank. "Her head was in the water, and one arm—one arm was trailing in the water and her hair all like—like seaweed..."

"Did you lift her out?" said Abel. Abel was the able one, they used to say, laughing; the alert one, the do-er. Christo—well, really, he was like a child in some ways, such a dreamer, so much at the mercy of emotions too delicate for a man.

"She was dead. I couldn't bear to—"

"You're certain she was dead?"

"Oh, yes, yes," said Christo. "I touched her arm, the other arm. It was—sort of doubled up behind her. It was—cold." He shuddered. "Her face under the water was all... I couldn't bear to touch her again, I couldn't bear the—the oppression of that horrible cave behind me. So I came to tell you." But he stumbled to his feet. "Just to leave her there!—I shouldn't just have left her there. I should have lifted her out." He looked at them, sick and guilty. "I ought to go back."

"We'll go," said Abel. "Rohan and I can go."

"They'll say he did it," said Melisande, suddenly. "They'll say he made her pregnant and then he killed her. They'll say it was Christo."

They turned upon one another terrified eyes, the whitening

of their faces turning the outward tan to an ugly grey. "Oh, God, Christo—they'll say it was you."

If Corinna had been "simple," Christo also was simple; though only perhaps in the sense of an absolute simplicity— those who loved him would have said of an absolute goodness. Now, the thought that he might have injured, let alone slaughtered, any creature in the world, turned him almost faint with horror and disbelief. "Us so-called Hippies," said Rohan. "They'd believe anything of us. They knew she hung around Christo. Her parents had warned her not to."

Abel said: "Rohan—do you think she did kill herself?"

"An accident? Leaning over too far and then—? Oh, my God," said Rohan, "you don't mean—?"

"If she was pregnant," said Abel, "or only if she'd been seduced—because with a girl like that, that's what it would have been—someone else was involved. She said that if her father knew, he would kill her. But what would he do to that other one?"

"Christo," said Primula, imploring, "do you think it could have been an accident?"

He considered it, forcing himself to gather-in his flying wits, to concentrate upon recollection. "Leaning over the bank like that—you could get back if you wanted to. You could lift up your head if you wanted to."

"Could a person just force themselves to keep their head under water and drown, Abel, if by just lifting it up—?"

"No," said Abel, sharply resolute.

"Wait!" said Primmy suddenly. She ran into the house. The movement, the translation into action, relaxed them, they found themselves standing rigidly holding rakes and hoes:

threw the tools aside, rested, sitting or half kneeling, still in their ring, gazing into the sick white face with its fringe of ragged gold. "Either way, they'll still think Christo seduced her. Her father—"

"We can deal with fathers," said Abel. "If it's murder— that's the Law."

"There was someone else involved. They'd be bound to investigate—"

"Where else would they do their investigating?" said Abel simply. "When they've got us."

Primmy came back. The front of her long cotton dress had dribbles of wetness down it and she held in her hand a sodden paper. She said: "She did kill herself."

She had printed in straggling capitals, in a rough estimate of Megan's probable spelling: I AM TO UNHAPY. I WILL DROUN MYSELF. "I've made it all wet, as though she dropped it in the water or something; no one could say it was her writing or anyone's writing. I haven't said anything about being wicked or pregnant or anything. It needn't have been that; and we don't want to put the idea into people's heads."

"Primmy—if she was murdered!"

"Anything's better," said Primula, "than Christo being put in."

And the words had been spoken at last: they faced it at last. Christo raised his head. "In prison? Dear God, if they put me in prison—!" A sort of darkness closed in upon him at the bare thought of it. The closeness and the suffocation. "I couldn't. I couldn't."

"I'll take it there," said Primmy; and before they could stop her had darted away across the little paved yard and was gone.

Abel and Rohan started after her, but the girls held them back, clinging to their arms. "If she's seen, no one will blame *her* for anything. Besides she knows the way."

"Besides," said Evaine, "she loves him. She wants to be the one to go."

It was five o'clock. The sun was high and bright so that the shadows made dark troughs between the tall bean rows and the air was hot with the scents and smells of a farming countryside. Melisande went into the cottage and made a great can of coffee, carrying it out to them carefully on the wooden tray with two rather wobbling stacks of pottery mugs. They crouched on the dry ground about the bench and when the children toddled up to claim love and petting from them, gently sent them back to play. There was perhaps no love to spare from their passionate protection of one who so deeply, deeply needed it.

On the mountain behind them, two small boys hung about aimlessly, kicking out with stout scuffed shoes at the curled fronds of the bracken. "Say we've been here the whole time, Llew. If anyone asks you, say we was up here on the mountain. Never went near the woods above Cwm-esgair, never went near the kites…" A dozen pairs of kites or less, in the British Isles, and their nests guarded jealously, with penalties for disturbing, let alone robbing them. But a man in Llangwyn was offering two pounds for an egg. "Playing cops and robbers up here on the mountain," assented Llewellyn, comfortably. Given a little to the histrionics, Llew; you could always rely on him to embroider things…

And Nancy and Blodwen, creeping back down the side

of the mountain, along the sheep track, the short cut to Llangwyn. Been to the cinema—there's sinful! A dirty old picture—Blod's big brother Idris had told her about it, warned her not to tell Mam. But once there, they hadn't dared to go into the picture house after all. Blod had seen Mam and Da talking to a man—it was mart day—and suppose they'd glanced up and seen her, and Nancy in that bright red dress! "Well, all right, say there's lots of red dresses like that," said Blodwen impatiently. "We was never in Llangwyn, we was sitting over there in the fields below Cwm-esgair, reading our books." They had at least contrived some somewhat highly coloured magazines. "Come on now, get to the fields!" Nancy was silly, really; and fancy coming to the Llangwyn at all in such a bright dress! "One day, Nancy James, I won't be best friends with you any more."

Primmy had returned from her errand. Her lovely face was very grey and strained, but she was triumphant. "I had a better idea, I put the note on a bush near the entrance to the cave. Anyone passing down the path would see it. Otherwise, if no one went into the cave—and they mightn't for ages—"

"Did you—see her, Primmy?"

"Well, I…I just went into the middle of the cave, where you can begin to see the river. She's still there. I could—I could see her legs." Plump, sun-burned legs, like a child's legs, toes turned down and digging into the grass. She confessed: "I couldn't bear any more."

"There was no point," said Melisande in her own kind, comforting way. "You couldn't do her any good, if she was dead."

Christo struggled to his feet again. "If no one goes to the cave—she'll be lying there. She might lie there all night. We can't leave her, we couldn't."

"Christo, love, she's dead."

If Christo found a dead creature in the woods, he made a grave and buried it: not with little crosses and sentimentalities—he just said it wasn't decent, it was too pitiful. Even to animals, he showed respect. And now… "Just lying there—with her head hanging down into the water…" He said miserably: "It was bad enough to run away and leave her: even for a little while. If it hadn't been for the cave—but it seemed to be pressing down, lowering down, just there behind me. We can't leave her there all night."

"If someone sees the note—"

"Who'll be using that path?" said Melisande, reluctantly.

"It gets more and more awful," said Christo, "to think I just left her there." He took a huge and frightening resolve. "I must go and tell the police."

They were terrified. "Wait, Christo, wait! There must be another way out."

"If it was children that found her!" said Evaine; there were two small children always playing about at Penbryn, across the valley.

"We could pretend we were all going along the path," said Primmy, "and saw the note and went into the cave and found her."

"Who'll believe us?" insisted Abel.

Christo was coming out of his state of shock, out of the claustrophobic horrors that had driven him from the cave. "I can't leave her there, and that's the end of it. All night and perhaps the next and the next… I'll go to the police. I'll simply say that she'd asked me to meet her and I found her there."

"At least, at least, say that you saw the note?"

"Well, all right, I'll say that I saw the note. Actually, I thought I heard someone moving and as she wasn't in the glade, I went through to the river."

"Christo! It could have been the murderer!"

"Well, then I'll tell them—No, I can't if I'm going to say the note was there." He looked shocked and horrified, nevertheless.

"We'll all go down now," said Abel. "We'll—we'll get her out of the water. We'll go to the police and tell them about it, say that you rushed back and told us. Only you've got to swear that you'll say you saw the note."

Evaine stayed with the babies. The rest went down to the woods, hurrying, lest anyone should observe them, as though on an anxious errand. Through the fields, skirting the growing crops, over a gate tied as usual intricately with string which a farmer must each day patiently unknot: why not a simple noose or even a metal catch they never could understand— but that was farming in dear Welsh Wales. Into the cool of the woods and so, crossing the path, to the green glade, the late sunshine thrusting its bright slanting rays down through the branches, like the golden rays from old pictures of God the Father in heaven.

No one had passed that way. The dampened paper still hung, pierced through by a thorn, blue-grey against the whiteness of the starry blossom. Christo picked a sprig of it, wrenching it off from the tough parent bough, and carried it with him, creeping after them, tense again with the suffocating horror of the dark cave, close about him. "Is she still there?"

She was still there: still in both senses, a lump, a thing, lying on the low bank, two humped shoulders where the head disappeared hanging down into the water; one arm trailing, the other bent behind her. Christo, half fainting, turned aside as they lifted her out and laid her on the bank. Her face was terrible, turned up to the afternoon sunshine, lank hair spread across it like dark weed. He knelt down beside her and looked with juddering self-control into the blank blue eyes; and placed in the drowned hand his little sprig of May. "Someone must stay with her," he said. "We can't leave her alone again."

"I'll stay," said Rohan at once. "Mellie and I will stay. You three go down to the village and tell the police."

They toiled along the narrow path to the tiny police station; saw, unastonished, the freezing of the constable's face as they filed wretchedly in. They had done no harm, never been brought to his attention, but—the Hippies! Christo said steadily: "We came to tell you that we've found a girl dead, down by the river. She's been drowned."

"It's Megan the Post," said Melisande, in the Welsh idiom.

"Megan Thomas? Drowned? Duw, duw!" said the man. He looked at them for a moment suspiciously but accepted the obvious way out. "Drowned herself, is it? Lost her health, poor thing, everyone knew it. Not too surprising after all."

"She left a note," said Abel. He handed it over. "It seems to have got wet."

The constable peered down at it: looked up sharply, suspicious again. "Funny she wouldn't write it in Welsh?"

Primmy went ashen. Stupid, stupid mistake—of course a girl like that would write in her familiar tongue! But Abel said coolly: "We think it was meant for—him—so that's why it would be in English." He told the little story, quietly, reassuringly. The man accepted it readily enough. To his somewhat simple mind, the likelihood of a mad girl's drowning herself seemed pretty logical. "Duw, duw! Well, well—poor girl!" And when they brought him to the Corot-green evening gloom of the bank by the water, he knelt over her and, seeing how they had laid her out, reverently, with the sprig of blossom in her hand, said again: "Poor girl—there's pitiful!"

But he wore a very different look when next afternoon he came with the sergeant from Llangwyn, to the cottage. He had known the dead girl from her childhood and now was black with anger. He summoned them all into the single big room which they had constructed from all the little downstairs parlours and larders and kitchen, now thrown into one; and said to the three men, viciously, not waiting for his superior: "Well—which one of you, then?"

"She was pregnant," said the sergeant. "And murdered. Held down by her shoulders with her head in the stream. You heard what the constable said. Which one of you?"

"We found her there, dead."

"*He* found her," said the constable, hand fisted, lifted as though he could hardly restrain himself from hitting Christo in the face. "Or so he says. But she wasn't dead, was she—not yet?"

They stood with the big, scrubbed wooden table between them—six, bunched close together, quivering with fear; and

The Law. "She told me she was in great trouble," said Christo, "and asked me to come there."

"And you're the one who got her into great trouble."

"No, I never touched her." He did not know that he straightened up his thin shoulders and spoke out boldly a truth about himself. "I wouldn't harm anyone so helpless and innocent."

"So someone else got her pregnant," said the sergeant, "but it's you she turns to." Tell me another one, his voice insinuated.

"She thought he was terribly good," said Rohan. "She thought he was a sort of saint."

"She thought he was Jesus Christ," said Primmy.

"For Christ's sake—Jesus Christ!"

"Because of his face and his beard," said Melisande. "And because of himself. It's true; he would never hurt anything or anyone. She could understand that, she could recognise it. So she turned to him."

"And he turned *her*—over on her face with her head in the water."

"You've got the note," said Rohan.

"A bit of old printing, all wet. How do we know he didn't write it himself?"

The girl had been dead some hours, the doctor had said, by the time he saw her. She had left her home at about half past two. If this young man's story were true, she might well have waited down by the cave for quite a long time before he came along; and after all, these were not the only young men in the valley. They had eliminated most of them, but... Facts stirred uncomfortably in the constable's mind. Idris Jones, Dai Jones Penbryn's boy—his name stank not at all sweetly in the nostrils of the local farmers. A man from Llangwyn had gone the rounds last night with brief, routine questions: Idris had said simply that he'd been in the yard all the afternoon, never saw nothing, never moved from the farm. Nothing to confirm that. On the other hand... A bit awkward it was for Constable Evans: Dai Penbryn was a good friend of his and a deacon of the chapel. A better way, he thought, than starting a lot of special enquiries, might be to bring Idris into it as though as an outsider and just keep an eye on his reactions. He suggested: "The children from Penbryn—they're always all over the place, up the mountain, down by the river. They could have seen something: people coming and going." He suggested to the sergeant, all innocence: "Why not take this lot over there and ask them?"

"Good idea," said the sergeant; not innocent at all of the tortuous methods of conducting police enquiries in isolated communities.

So they all went over to Penbryn and stood in the farmyard like children at a game in the school playground, divided into two vague clumps, confronting one another. Beneath their feet, the cobbles were clean and swept by Idris's labours yesterday; running down to the stony garden of rough grass, patched with bare earth, ridged where the children's feet had kicked or drifted along the ground, starting or stopping the swing. Mr. and Mrs. Jones, Jones glancing dark and uneasy at the sullen face of his son, Idris, Mrs. Jones darting looks of angry unreason at the Hippies with their beards and long hair, the girls carrying each a small child, in the Welsh fashion, almost weightless, in the folds of a shawl, formed into a sort of sling at the left shoulder, brought round under the right arm and tucked in at the waist. Idris shuffled a little, head bent, scuffing back grit with his feet, like a hen sorting grain; Ianto and his friend Llewellyn stood side by side, serge coat-sleeves touching, twitching hands signalling danger; Blodwen faced uncertainty thankful that chicken-hearted Nancy was not here to give secrets away; Gwennie and the inevitable Boyo Thomas the Post, gazing up with large, scared eyes. The heat hung like a haze, heavy with the scent of the hay, the sour tang of the empty silo pit. The sergeant laid the situation before them briefly. "All we want to know is—did any of your family see anything—anything at all, never mind what—yesterday afternoon?"

Everyone waited for everyone else to speak. He prompted: "You young ones, for example?"

"We was playing on the swing," said Gwennie with the easy untruth of small-childhood.

"What, the whole afternoon?"

"True it is, sergeant, they'll play on that swing all day."

"All right, Mrs. Jones, I understand that. But you might have gone down to the trees a bit, Gwennie, when it got too hot? Nothing wrong with that?" he suggested, an eye turned to the mother. She shrugged and shook her head. Nothing to tell fibs about in that.

But, "No, sir, never, sir," insisted Gwennie, small fat hands now beginning to tremble. (If they'd known she'd been down to the cave to show Boyo her chest!)

"Not by the river? There's cool on a hot day, the river! Down by that old cave, perhaps?" suggested the constable, temptingly.

Mad Megan, Boyo's sister Megan, lying on her front out beyond the cave by the river's edge. Drinking they'd thought she was but now it seemed that she'd been dead, been drowned. And the Hippy had come, running and calling, and gone at last into the cave where she was lying, and they'd scampered away. "No, sir, we was on the swing," insisted Gwennie, growing a little tearful.

Idris spoke for the first time; idly, casually but looking up shiftily from under his eyebrows. "That's right. I was working in the yard. They was playing on the swing."

"All afternoon?" said the sergeant, sharply: this was an alibi that might too conveniently break both ways.

"From dinner time," said Idris, hardly able now to keep the insolent challenge from his voice.

The little ones had turned upon him large round eyes of astonished gratitude. Had Idris guessed? Was he protecting them? Idris himself was "dirty"—dirty old pictures he kept hidden in the barn, Blod had told Ianto so, and Gwennie had heard. He wouldn't give them away. And this must be it—for after all, they *hadn't* been in the yard. First they'd been quite a long time up on the mountain; and then by the river.

The sergeant turned slowly. Beside him, the constable said: "Idris—Mr. Jones' eldest son."

"You had nothing to do with this business, Idris?"

"Me? I told you, I told the man last night. I was here, working in the yard."

"You have a bit of a name round here, I believe?"

The constable looked wretchedly, anywhere but at Mr. and Mrs. Jones. Got to do your duty, there you are!—but these were his friends. The sergeant observed his expression and interpreted it. "Everyone knows it," he said.

"I never touched the girl," said Idris. "Not in the way of—of killing her, or any other way." He added in a voice of contemptuous dismissal: "She was mental."

"That would make her easy," said the sergeant. "Easy to kill—and easy 'any other way.'"

"I was in the yard," repeated Idris, sullenly. "From dinner time on."

Here was some capital to be made for Ianto and Llewellyn. If Idris said that he and the little ones had been in the yard at Penbryn all the time—then it would be safe to have seen them there; and if they had not been in the woods after kites' eggs. Ianto gave the touching hand a warning twitch. "*We* could see them in the yard, Sergeant. We was up on the mountain across the valley."

"Could you see the Hippies' place?"

"Not from there, Sergeant. Only Penbryn. We could see Penbryn all the time, sir," said Llewellyn, officiously, "and the little ones swinging."

"And Idris?"

"Yes, sir, Idris doing the silage and then the hay and then clearing up the yard…"

"Nancy and me could see them too, Sergeant," said Blodwen. In the fields we was, reading our books, but we could see Penbryn, and Gwennie and Boyo Thomas on the swing."

"And Idris?"

"Yes, sir, Idris starting with the silage." When Idris had started on the silage, Blodwen and Nancy had been in Llangwyn. "But we never saw no Hippies, sir: only over to Penbryn."

"All right," said the sergeant. He had been keeping Idris Jones in reserve, but here were three separate alibis which seemed to have no reason behind them but simple fact. "All the other boys round here have been eliminated," he said to Christo—and surely the man must be guilty, just standing there, dumbly. The sergeant averted his gaze from the horrible shaking of the thin hands. "Now this one, too. So what about it, then?"

Christo stood utterly immobile but for the terrible trembling; paralysed with a black, an animal fear. If they should arrest him! Shut him up in a cell! I should go mad, he thought: and knew that, literally, it was true. I should go mad. Shut up there, closed in, helpless, in the dark, alone... He would go mad, and he knew that he must pray for nothing less: that madness would be best for him then.

They watched him, terrified: watched Idris, watched the shifty lout with his cocky face, safe in the circle of his convenient alibis, a pack of kids under his thumb. "You!" said Abel, breaking out at him, violently. "Everyone knows the sort you are! You got her into trouble; and—knowing she was meeting him, perhaps—you got to the cave first and murdered her."

The sergeant stood with a light hand on Christo's wrist. He said coolly: "So why did she leave a suicide note?"

"A note?" said Idris, in a curious voice. "She left a note?"

The note!—which they themselves had written and placed there. "Perhaps... Perhaps," suggested Abel, "she intended to kill herself so she wrote the note. But she couldn't do it and he found her there and held her head down in the water."

"The same could go for him," said Idris with a jerk of the chin towards Christo; and now he spoke confidently, subtly jeering.

"Or the murderer wrote the note himself?" suggested the sergeant, smoothly. That reaction of Idris's hadn't escaped his notice.

"He'd have had to," said Idris, triumphantly. "She couldn't write."

Couldn't write? She couldn't *write*? Rohan hung on to his swinging senses. "All the more reason to say that you did it. You killed her, you wrote the note—" But his voice trailed away in despair.

"What, me? Knowing that everyone would know she couldn't write?" said Idris; and the sergeant unconsciously tightened his grip on Christo's arm. Throughout all the valley, the Hippies must have been the only people unaware that Mad Megan couldn't read or write.

So... The girl, pretty and alluring enough, ignorant and foolish... Conceives a passion for one of these free-living young men and conceives indeed. Terrified of her father's vengeance if she gives away her lover's name, he takes her down to the cave and there pushes her head under water; fastens up the false note and—with or without the collusion of his friends—arranges to "find" her and duly informs the police. "We'll go along to the station," said the sergeant to the constable over Christo's bent head; and added civilly: "You'll come with us?"

"He'll come," said the constable, not civilly at all.

Christo made no answer: went with them, dumb.

And dumbly, helplessly, they watched him. The big farm gate swung-to, its post dragging through the dry earth, kicking up a little cloud of dust. Outside, the small, dark police car waited. That alone would be torment, the closed windows and doors.

Along the way, the hedges were milky white; but Corinna would go no more a-Maying down the country lanes. He sat in the rear seat, the sergeant's hand now light again, on his wrist. He said: "Will you have to lock me up?"

"And do it with pleasure," said the constable, not waiting for his sergeant to reply.

"Now? When we get there? And all through the night?" He struggled to explain. "I get claustrophobia. I can't bear to be closed in."

"You didn't mind being closed in, in that cave, did you?" said the constable, only half his attention on the dangerous windings of the narrow country road. "You didn't mind being in there, holding her down, drowning her? You were closed in there; and you'll be closed in now. Now and for the rest of your life. And God damn you!"

"Now, now," said the sergeant. "That'll be enough!"

"*You* didn't know the girl," said the constable, savagely. "I knew her from a child. Helpless, she was..."

"Well, well—he isn't convicted yet."

Christo did not hear them: already was beyond hearing. Now, tonight, for the rest of his life. But the rest of his life need not matter. He would know little about it by the end of this one coming night, this endless night.

Endless night... Endless night... "What's that you're mumbling now?" said the constable, forgetting the road altogether, to turn and look back over his shoulder. "What's that about drowning?"

From Herrick. From "Corinna." He mumbled it a little louder. "All love, all liking, all delight, Lies drowned with us in endless night." And he repeated it, "Endless night!" and put his white face into his hands and abandoned himself to the engulfing dark: to his only defence against it—to witlessness.

Gwennie and Boyo had dashed across the field to catch the last possible glimpse of the car. It was their Hippy, the one they'd seen calling to Megan when she was already dead, lying there by the river, dead and drownded.

Duw, duw—what an escape! If anyone had guessed that they'd gone down to the cave so that Gwennie could show Boyo her chest!

Y Mynyddoed Sanctiaidd

Michael Gilbert

Michael Gilbert (1912–2006) was a very high achiever. As well as being a solicitor who enjoyed a long and successful career in the law, he was one of the finest British crime writers of his time. He received the CWA Diamond Dagger and Grand Master awards from the Mystery Writers of America and the Swedish Academy of Detection. He published thirty novels and one hundred eighty-five stories and wrote for radio, television, and the stage. Three of his books were filmed. He edited an anthology of essays about crime writing and also a series of Classics of Detection and Adventure for Hodder, which ran to thirteen titles and exerted a significant influence on my own tastes as a teenager—and provided a model for introduction-writing that I continue to keep in mind!

However, all writers experience setbacks. In the mid-1980s, Gilbert wrote this story for a competition, submitting it under the pen-name "Justus." As he told John Cooper in correspondence, the story not only did not win, it did not earn a mention. So he put it aside, hoping that perhaps one day a Welsh-themed anthology might give him the opportunity to place it. That day has finally come, but the story's first appearance in print was in one of Cooper's admirable collections of Gilbert's writings, *The Murder of Diana Devon and Other Mysteries* (2009).

————

DAI MORGAN WAS THE IDEAL WALKING COMPANION. HE was twenty years older than me, but much fitter, and he was not only a good walker, he was a good talker. He had crammed a lot of experience into sixty-five years of living.

When he'd finished his service in the Royal Navy as a C.P.O. he'd joined the Liverpool Docks Police. After that he had been Chief Security Officer for Carfrae, the Shippers, and could, no doubt, have retired on his pension at sixty. However, he had decided that life had more to offer and had become a probation officer. He was neither sentimental nor cynical about the job. I sometimes thought that if we had a few more probation officers like Dai there would be less juvenile crime.

On this occasion we started at Porthmadog and set off north easterly across the Cambrian Mountains and the Clwydian Range. We covered twenty-five miles on the first day, and nearly thirty on the second, finishing at a cottage at Llangwypan, a village at the end of a road that led to nowhere. There was no difficulty about lodging. Dai had worked for most of the courts along the North coast of Wales, from Bangor to Flint. Old Mrs. Philpott, who owned the cottage, knew him well. As we sat in her parlour, happily relaxed after our exertions, I could sniff the supper she was cooking for us.

The sun was going down behind the odd-shaped mountains, hump-backed like a line of camels. Dai said, "You're looking at Y Mynyddoed Sanctiaidd."

"Meaning what?"

"Come on, boyo. You've lived five years in Swansea. Haven't you got your tongue round our beautiful language?"

"I can order a pint of beer, and I can shout 'Put the boot in Llanelli.'"

"Shame on you, Y Mynyddoed Sanctiaidd are the Holy Mountains."

"What's holy about them?" I said. They looked much like the other hills we had trudged over that day.

"I've no idea. Probably some holy man lived and died up there."

I had a feeling that there was more to it than that, so I waited. In the end Dai said, "They're holy to me for a particular reason." There was another pause. I could hear the clatter of pans in the kitchen. If our meal had come in then, I should never have heard about Carwyn.

"It was one of my first jobs," said Dai. "My Superintendent was a nice man called Hubble. Known to everyone in the service as Hubble-bubble. Not a fool, by any means. He said, 'This lad Carwyn. He's on remand until Monday. I want you to pick him up and take him to Court. I've had a word with the magistrate, and he's agreed to commit him to the Probation Hostel at Prestatyn. You can take him there by rail.'

"'If he's on remand I imagine he's already at the Police Station, or did they send him home?'

"'Neither. He's at my house. He's been there for the last week.'

"This surprised me. It is not normally part of the duties of a probation officer to house delinquent children.

"'It's an odd case altogether,' said Hubble. 'He was offered the chance of going home, but he refused. He said he'd rather stay in prison. That's when I offered to look after him.'

"'Might he have been scared of his parents?'

"'He's got no parents. He's been looked after by his aunt since his mother died five years ago. She was in Court at the first hearing. She didn't look to me like the sort of woman a child would be afraid of. It might have been her husband. He's said to be a hard case. I haven't been able to find out much about him yet.'

"The Liverpool magistrate's Court is in the Town Hall by the Royal Liver Building. The Clerk was an old friend. He said, 'It seems the boy's uncle got him a job with Curleys, the Estate Agents, in Chester Street. It was only an office boy job, but you have to start somewhere, and they liked the look of him. Then, on his first Friday there, he helped himself to a couple of pound notes out of the petty cash, and did it so clumsily that one of the girls saw him, and reported him. He didn't even trouble to deny it. Of course, they had to run him in.'

"It sounded odd to the magistrate, too. He gave us the promised probation order. So far Carwyn hadn't opened his mouth, and I hadn't tried to talk to him, because that usually shuts them up worse than before. He was a silent child. I suppose his age must have been given as sixteen or he wouldn't have got a job, but he didn't look much more than twelve. His face was whitish for a boy who had spent the last five years on a farm in the country, but the overall impression I got was of sadness. He really was the saddest looking boy I had ever seen. I don't mean that he was crying or complaining. But he had those dark inward-looking eyes that Welsh children sometimes have, and he seemed to be spending most of his time thinking about life and finding it hollow.

"It's a ninety-minutes run from Liverpool to Prestatyn. We had the carriage to ourselves, and I was relieved, if a mite surprised, when he opened the conversation. He said, 'Have you ever known a lion eat straw?'

"I said, 'I don't know a lot about lions. I saw one or two in Africa. When I was in the Navy.'

"'Do you think they'd eat straw?'

"'More usually they ate other animals.'

"'That's what I thought.'

"He sat for a moment looking out of the window. I feared that our conversation might be at an end. No. He was assembling his ideas.

"'Have you ever seen a leopard?'

"'Only in the zoo.'

"'Would one lie down with kids?'

"'Certainly. Even the fiercest animals are friendly with their own children.'

"He thought about this, but decided to pass it up. He said, 'Do you know what a cockatrice is?'

"I had an idea where we were going now. I said, 'I always thought of it as something like a scorpion.'

"'I guessed it might be something like that. Do you think a wolf and a lamb could lie down together?'

"Thanks to a strict Chapel upbringing I was on grid by this time.

"I said, 'Book of Isaiah. Right?'

"'I heard it in Church on Sunday. Mr. Hubble took me. It seemed funny when I heard it, but I've been thinking about it. Lots of animals who are supposed to be enemies aren't really. We had a dog and a cat would curl up together on the rug by the fire. So I suppose a wolf and a lamb might hit it off.'

"'I think it would depend on how hungry the wolf was.'

"He didn't like this. He said reproachfully, 'The Bible didn't say it would work any old place. Just when they were in the Holy Mountains. It's what they call the mountains where I live, see?'

"I remembered then that his address had been given as Waen. Incidentally, you can see them from that window."

I got up to have a look. The sun was on its way down. I was beginning to be interested in Carwyn. "Did he say anything else?"

"Nothing until we were getting near Prestatyn. Then he said, 'I could believe the animals lying down together. It was the lion eating straw that worried me. It seemed funny somehow.' And he smiled, just that once.

"When I handed him over to the Superintendent of the Hostel I said, 'I don't think you'll have much trouble with this number.'

"The Superintendent, who seemed to have taken to him at sight, said, 'Fine. We'll put him in the gardening squad.'

"When I got back to Liverpool I walked round to Chester Street. It's a sad place because it was one of the business centres of Liverpool, but it was dying. The only buildings in use were a big office block on the corner, then Curley's office, then a derelict and boarded-up structure. Then the Bank and a few shops. I knew Bill Armitage, the Senior Partner in Curleys, quite well from my time with the Shipping Company.

"He said, 'It's the oddest case I've ever met. The boy came here on the Monday. His aunt brought him. A bit down in the mouth, I thought, but natural if it was his first job away from home. Then, on Friday, he helps himself out of the petty cash, as cool as you please. You could almost have said he wanted to be found out.'

"'Might he have been protecting himself?'

"'What from?'

"'I don't know. But he refused to go home between the two hearings.'

"'His aunt didn't look like a dragon. I got the impression they were very fond of each other. Maybe it's the uncle.'

"'He seems to be the mystery man in the case,' I agreed. Then I had to get on with half a dozen other jobs that Hubble had ready for me. It was on the Thursday of that week that he said, 'I've just heard Carwyn's decamped. Can you find out what's happened, and cope with it?'

"Those were the sort of instructions you get in the probation service. I telephoned the Superintendent. He sounded upset. He said, 'I haven't got the whole story yet. You know how these boys clam up. But what I understand happened was that two men drove up in a car, forced their way through the hedge at the bottom of the garden, and Carwyn went off with them.'

"'Willingly?'

"'That's just what I don't know.'

"I said, 'If he's gone anywhere, it'll be his aunt's house. I'd better get out there quick.'

"I'd found out the name of the aunt by now. It was Thomas. Like a million other people in Wales. Rebecca Thomas lived on this steading outside Waen. It was a modest place, with a run of chicken houses, well protected against the foxes, and a few cows in the field. The sort of place a woman could just manage, particularly if she had a boy to help her.

"She was in her working clothes, not the smart gear she'd worn to Court. She seemed to be expecting me, but there was something in her attitude, something I couldn't, at that moment, unriddle. It was when she led the way into the parlour that the shock hit me.

"There was a photograph on the side board. It was a good photograph, and I could see it very clearly. Two men, head and shoulders. I recognised them at once. You don't forget a face when you have seen it behind a sawn-off shot gun, and had plenty of opportunity to study it later in Court.

"The Procter brothers, Malvyn and Tam, had broken into the bonded warehouse of the Carfrae Shipping firm. We got a last-minute tip off and I arrived with the police at the moment they were making off. They had tried to shoot it out, but had been outgunned. One of the policemen was badly wounded. One of them slightly. The Procters got ten years. I did some rapid arithmetic. With full remission, they could both have been out, but only for a month or so.

"Mrs. Thomas must have seen me looking at the photograph. She said, without a trace of feeling in her voice,

"'Mal is my husband. I changed my name when he went inside.'

"I took a deep breath and said, 'Tell me, Mrs. Thomas, what have they done with Carwyn?'

"As I said that she crumpled up. There is no other word to describe it. Then she started to cry, quite gently. It went on for a long time, whilst I sat looking at her. Then she dried her eyes and started to talk.

"As soon as I got back to Liverpool, I had a word with Jack Solomon. He was head of the Liverpool Special Crimes Squad.

"I said, 'I've reason to believe that the Procter brothers and two of their friends are underneath the branch of the Home Counties Bank in Chester Street at this moment waiting for it to close on Friday evening, so that they can get busy on the inner wall of the strong room.'

"'You don't often talk nonsense,' said Jack. 'Tell me how they'd get there. And don't suggest they broke into the derelict house next door. It's guarded as strongly as the Bank.'

"'They didn't bother. They put this kid Carwyn into Curley's office to scout the way to the cellar and get copies of the keys. They let themselves in there on Wednesday night, and were under the empty house by Thursday morning with everything cleared up behind them.'

"'And just how do you know this?'

"'Mal miscalculated. He didn't realise how fond a lonely woman could get of a lonely boy.'

"Jack thought about this. He said, 'I take it, then, that what Carwyn did was to protect himself.'

"'That's right. He wanted to put himself in baulk. I doubt if he intended to split, but they couldn't take a chance on it. That was their second mistake.'"

The story seemed to be at an end. I said, "Go on. What happened?"

"Oh, they laid for them at the Bank. The Procters tried to use their guns. This time the police weren't pulling any punches. Mal was killed. Thomas died that night in hospital. The other two didn't resist. They got five years."

The way he said it didn't make it sound important. I knew he was thinking about Carwyn.

I said, "Did they find the boy?"

Dai was staring out of the window. There was a glow in the sky. A colour you sometimes get in hilly country, difficult to describe, more green than pink. There were still a few small cushion-shaped clouds hanging stationary over the tops, and the sun, as it went down, was starting to throw long shadows into the corries.

"He's up there somewhere," said Dai softly. "I'd guess he's happy now, with the tigers and the kids and the wolves and lambs all playing together on the holy mountains. Maybe he's found out by now whether lions do eat straw when they're hungry."

The lady of the house came in with a loaded tray. She said, "What's that you're talking about Mr. Morgan, some nonsense. Lions, is it?"

"Just a bit of nonsense, Mrs. Philpott. What's under that dish? It smells good."

If you've enjoyed
Crimes of Cymru: Classic Mystery Tales of Wales
you won't want to miss

the most recent BRITISH LIBRARY CRIME CLASSIC
published by Poisoned Pen Press,
an imprint of Sourcebooks.

Praise for the
British Library Crime Classics

"Carr is at the top of his game in this taut whodunit... The British Library Crime Classics series has unearthed another worthy golden age puzzle."

—*Publishers Weekly*, STARRED Review,
for *The Lost Gallows*

"A wonderful rediscovery."

—*Booklist*, STARRED Review, for *The Sussex Downs Murder*

"First-rate mystery and an engrossing view into a vanished world."

—*Booklist*, STARRED Review, for *Death of an Airman*

"A cunningly concocted locked-room mystery, a staple of Golden Age detective fiction."

—*Booklist*, STARRED Review, for *Murder of a Lady*

"The book is both utterly of its time and utterly ahead of it."

—*New York Times Book Review* for *The Notting Hill Mystery*

"As with the best of such compilations, readers of classic mysteries will relish discovering unfamiliar authors, along with old favorites such as Arthur Conan Doyle and G.K. Chesterton."

—*Publishers Weekly*, STARRED Review, for *Continental Crimes*

"In this imaginative anthology, Edwards—president of Britain's Detection Club—has gathered together overlooked criminous gems."

—*Washington Post* for *Crimson Snow*

"The degree of suspense Crofts achieves by showing the growing obsession and planning is worthy of Hitchcock. Another first-rate reissue from the British Library Crime Classics series."

—*Booklist,* STARRED Review, for *The 12.30 from Croydon*

"Not only is this a first-rate puzzler, but Crofts's outrage over the financial firm's betrayal of the public trust should resonate with today's readers."

—*Booklist,* STARRED Review, for *Mystery in the Channel*

"This reissue exemplifies the mission of the British Library Crime Classics series in making an outstanding and original mystery accessible to a modern audience."

—*Publishers Weekly,* STARRED Review, for *Excellent Intentions*

"A book to delight every puzzle-suspense enthusiast."

—*New York Times* for *The Colour of Murder*

"Edwards's outstanding third winter-themed anthology showcases 11 uniformly clever and entertaining stories, mostly from lesser known authors, providing further evidence of the editor's expertise...This entry in the British Library Crime Classics series will be a welcome holiday gift for fans of the golden age of detection."

—*Publishers Weekly,* STARRED Review, for
The Christmas Card Crime and Other Stories

Poisoned Pen
PRESS

poisonedpenpress.com